WINDSTORM

A. L. HAWKE

PHANTOM HEART, LLC

ISBN:978-1-953919-26-7 (hardback)

ISBN: 978-1-7329563-9-1 (ebook)

ISBN: 978-1-7329563–8-4 (paperback)

Library of Congress Control Number: 2020914012

This is a work of fiction. It comes directly from the author's imagination. Witchcraft is included to infuse a sense of realism to the novel, but in no way is it supposed to represent actual practicing witchcraft, witches or the religion of Wicca. The book also includes fictitious names, characters, places, and incidents. Any public names are used solely for creative purposes. Any resemblance to actual people, living or dead, or to companies, institutions, or locales is entirely coincidental or accidental.

Line edited by Stephanie Ward

Proofread by Eliza Dee of Clio Editing Services

Cover Design © 2020 by Regina Wamba of MaeIDesign.com

Published by Phantom Heart, LLC

27702 Crown Valley Pkwy, STE D4 #201

Ladera Ranch, CA 92694

Printed and bound in the United States of America

First printing September, 2020

Learn more about A.L. Hawke at www.alhawke.com

Correspondence: contact@alhawke.com

❀ Created with Vellum

1

DARKNESS

Some people are afraid of the dark; others can't seem to turn away. It's so weird at Hawthorne University that my friends and I are actually having a back-to-school party just to watch it. And Maddie can't stop laughing. She keeps tapping my shoulder as we meander from a dirt parking lot, across the lawn, onto a lovely dirt path in Alondra's front garden. She taps me on my arm again. By the time we reach the white-columned deck at the entrance to Alondra's house, I finally turn. Maddie thinks it's soooo funny that she's wearing these cheap cardboard sunglasses I gave her. We're also wearing damp T-shirts and shorts—I say *damp* because it's hella hot outside.

Normally my friends and I meet at Alondra's house to gather around a witch bonfire on Friday Sabbath, but we're here Wednesday the week before the fall semester because this afternoon is very special. It's special for everyone in Hawthorne.

"Will you loosen up, Cadence?" Maddie says, still laughing.

"Take those off. You look dumb."

"Yeah, well, you don't look dumb. Because you're not having any fun."

"I'm just a little nervous, that's all," I say with a shrug.

"I know, babe." Maddie loses her smile and takes off the stupid cardboard things. "You'll be fine. Everybody wants to see you again."

Do they? I haven't spoken to most of my witch friends since the night I lost control. I haven't even had a chance to apologize. I feel so terrible about what happened.

The view at Alondra's place is to die for. Every time I come here, I feel like it takes me back to the nineteenth century. It's perched on a hilltop, surrounded by the forest and the flowing sound of a nearby brook. The perfectly manicured lawn is bordered by lilies and red and yellow roses, recently planted. In the center of it all is Alondra's white antebellum house. The place is quintessentially *antebellum* (I know what the word *antebellum* means, by the way, because I'm a history major at Hawthorne U). Only Alondra knows the right way to mix Neoclassical with chic, like her swanky dark gray Jaguar parked behind an antique red carriage in the driveway.

"I invited Rock, Katie," Maddie says. We're walking up the concrete steps onto Alondra's lovely outside deck.

"Why'd you do that?"

"Because he's cute." She cocks her head with a big smile. I laugh. Then Maddie raps on the door with this really big antique brass knocker. As we wait, she winks at me.

Wouldn't you know it but Alondra herself answers. She doesn't look at all like I expected. I was half expecting her in a dark witch cloak, but she's dressed in a loose saffron blouse over white shorts and sandals. She greets us with her familiar grin.

Alondra smiles a lot. She's always trying to be happy and nice. Sometimes it's really fake. Right now her expression gives me the feeling she's not dwelling on how I nearly killed her and her husband the last time I visited.

"Hey, Maddie. Cadence. Come in."

Her house is just as stunning inside as it is outside. I'm standing under a huge to-die-for diamond chandelier. Down the hall, I see her elegant dining room. This is my favorite room, with a window lining the wall looking out into the forest. It's next to her kitchen, with travertine floors, Viking stoves and a Sub-Zero refrigerator.

"Did you girls have a nice summer?" Alondra asks, pleasant as always.

"I had so much fun with Kate," Maddie says.

"Yes, you and Cadence stayed at your Aunt Jane's house, right?"

"Aha. How about you, Alondra?" asks Maddie. "Were you here in Hawthorne?"

Alondra is full of mysteries. I saw her practically every day last year, and I still feel like I don't know her.

"You girls excited?" Alondra says, avoiding Maddie's question.

"Yeah," I say.

"Did you bring protective shades? I don't think I have enough."

"You're talking about Katie, Alondra," Maddie replies. "My BFF has never failed to prepare for anything."

"How are you feeling, Alondra?" I ask solemnly.

Alondra has terminal cancer. You wouldn't think it, watching her agile step and cheerful demeanor, but I see bags under her eyes and a new habit of taking deep breaths. I'm guessing she's in pain. She told us the terrible news during our last ceremony. That's one of the reasons I lost control of myself. It drove me crazy that she'd been hiding that from me for so long, along with all the other horrible stuff last year. Then she made me their High Priestess, the leader of our coven. That's the thing about Alondra. See, even now, as she's walking with a quick step, she's being phony. I know she's unhappy. It's like my circle of witches. I love them so much, but I hate their secretiveness. And their deceptions. I mean, I love them all, but I hate them. Do you understand? ...If you do, please explain it to me.

"I hope everybody makes it on time." Alondra takes her cell phone from her pocket. She doesn't answer my question either.

We walk by her living room and Tammy, a cute bald black girl in our coven, is on her knees sorting through grocery bags on the coffee table. This room is just as I remembered, with the white leather sofa, fluffy white carpet, and elegant, modern stone fireplace and chimney. Through the sliding glass door is Alondra's backyard, where my coven held weekly Sabbaths last year.

Tammy jumps up and runs into Maddie's arms.

"Hey, girl!" Maddie says.

"Hey, guys!" says Tammy. She looks at me. "It's so good to see you! I missed you so much!" She hugs me.

Alondra's trying to pry open the glass door with all her weight. It's been stuck ever since I first stepped foot in her house. I walk over, lean against the bottom of the door, and pull it. It unlatches and opens. It's a trick Mira taught me last year.

"Oh, thank you, Cadence."

The door opens into her backyard. The yard is really the wilderness. It's the opposite of the front yard—no manicured lawn, tended flowers, or raked leaves—only wild grass surrounded by the dense forests of Hawthorne. In the center is a pile of logs. That's where we light our bonfires. But today Alondra has set up two picnic tables with yellow-and-red tablecloths. The tables are surrounded by the white plastic chairs we use during séances and rituals worshipping Selene, but now I see watermelons, a stack of soy patties, a few plastic bags of burger buns, red plastic cups, and a couple of glass pitchers of what looks like lemonade on one of the tables. I love lemonade. There's a Weber grill out too and a burly guy named Rocky, Maddie's boyfriend. Rocky is holding tongs, watching the soy burgers cook. Maddie runs into his arms.

"Katie," Maddie says after giving him a long embrace. "Look who's here. Can you believe it?"

He gives me a warm smile. "Hi, Cadence." I stick a palm up and wave.

"Babe," Rocky says to Maddie with a chuckle, "let me work."

"I love this guy," Maddie says.

Someone taps me on my back. I hear a quiet "hi" in a thick Brazilian accent. It's Frida. Frida is one of the shyest witches in our coven, shyer than I am. She's a petite, skinny girl with dark golden skin. Her family immigrated from Brazil fifteen years ago. She and I have always gotten along so well. As we hug, I spot Alondra walking back into her house. She just leaves us without a word.

"You stayed with Maddie in Hawthorne, right?" asks Frida. "I went home. It was hot and sweaty in New York." Frida lives in Jersey. "Awful," she says with a laugh. I'm swatting flies from my face. It's not cool in Georgia either. "Is Bryce here?"

I really wish he was.

"At least your man will be here in school," Frida adds after seeing my expression. "I'll be FaceTiming Greg every night."

We talk a little more, and Frida leaves, saying she's going to help Tammy and Mandy in the kitchen.

It's not too long before our whole coven is in Alondra's backyard. There are eleven of us (not counting my warlock boyfriend, who's still not here). Actually, twelve today as Gilda is visiting. Gilda graduated last semester.

I clam up. Large crowds turn me into a wallflower. So I sit near one of the tables in the yard, fold my arms over my lap, and do nothing. But I face the trees. The forest. I love the woods.

A butterfly lands on my finger. I'm not kidding, an actual butterfly just lands right on the back of my finger. I love that. I watch it slowly open and close its yellow-and-black wings.

Then a shadow hovers over me. As I look up, I feel the butterfly fly off. The only witch actually wearing our black hooded cloak —in the hot humidity—is my overweight goth friend, Mira. The sun shines along the red-and-black devil tattoos on her neck and glistens on her nose ring. Her face is coated in thick makeup. Her black lips curl in nasty smugness.

"Are you ready, Cadence?"

"Hi, Mira."

"I can't wait to see it." She smiles, looking around.

"Yeah."

"I'm sure your magic will come up too." I think she's the only one weird enough to actually want my magic to appear. "You know, Cadence, I did a lot of spell casting this summer. Learned a lot about tarot reading from Falconsong." Falconsong is Alondra's witch name. "The cards predict some interesting things on your horizon."

"We're going to eat burgers?"

"Falconsong is running the session. She said you wouldn't mind. You don't, right? We're gonna just talk."

As long as talking doesn't involve a two-story conflagration, ghosts, and possession. Or dancing around a pyre naked. Or taking drugs.

She surprises me by leaning over and gathering me in her arms. "I missed you, Cadence." And she means it.

"I missed you too, Mira."

"They're separated, you know," Mira says.

"Who?"

"Bill and Alondra. After your magic, Alondra kicked him out."

"I heard."

"And he's not a part of the coven anymore. I'd think that would make you happy."

"It does."

She sits down in a chair beside me. "You know..." Mira puts her hand on my leg. Then she runs her fingers over my bare knee. "I was in town two weeks ago. I texted you but you didn't answer."

The annoying thing about Mira is she knows why I didn't text her, and she's smirking about it. Yet she's not hurt, and she doesn't even look like she cares.

"I didn't get the text," I fib, biting my lip.

"Oh," Mira says with another wink. She touches my leg again. "I think it's gonna be a good year. Now that you're our leader. I can't wait for our first meeting. I'd love to try a summoning. I dealt the Magician card last night. That means great concentration and psychic powers are in our midst. There's a presence in Hawthorne and it's growing. But I also dealt the Devil card and the Death card. There's also black magic afoot." She looks around us as if searching for it. "I feel that too. Especially today. Left-sided magic."

What can I say to that? So I look at the trees again. From the corner of my eye, I see that Mira is also looking out into the forest, because she loves the trees too. She's a nature-loving witch like me.

"I also dealt the Lovers card," she continues, practically talking to herself. "But it was reversed. That means trouble in paradise. After meditating on it, I don't think it was for me." She chuckles. "I mean, I'm not much into lovers, you know. I much prefer raw sex. I think the card was for you. It came right after the High Priestess card. It was probably something about Bryce and you fucking."

"Mira!" I snap.

"What?" she asks innocently, laughing again. "I know you miss him. Is he gonna be here soon?"

She had to ask me that. But Maddie rescues me, handing paper plates with soy burgers to me and Mira. Then she gives Mira a hug.

"Hey, bitch," Maddie says to Mira. "You want to join me and Rock, Katesie?"

Yeah. But then Mira says, "I'll come too."

At Maddie's table, things go smoother. She has me talking with everyone. That's the kind of friend she is. She brings me out of my shell.

When everyone has had their fill of lemonade and soy burgers, Maddie starts clearing the plates. Mira and Gilda collect large wooden logs and throw them on the woodpile at the center of the yard. Other girls gather the plastic chairs from the tables and arrange them in a circle around the fire. Then Gilda takes a bag full of white chalk and carefully pours it around the perimeter of the chairs.

Maddie says goodbye to Rocky. She really doesn't want to, especially before the upcoming event, but she says our "club" has to meet in private.

Soon we're all sitting around a shallow fire, leaving a few chairs empty. Maddie sits on my right and Frida on my left. There's not much ceremony. It's more like a cozy campfire. But I prefer this. The only weird thing is it's the middle of the day. The sky is clear, and it's around three thirty in the afternoon. Our meetings are always at night.

Mira jumps up pointing when Alondra comes out of the house. It's like she's been waiting for her to appear all after-noon. Alondra is wearing our black cloak—the same one Mira's wearing—holding a fiery torch. Her face is covered by thick goth makeup like Mira's. By her side is another witch in a black cloak. I don't recognize this one. And following them are two other ladies in similar garb.

As the stranger walking beside Alondra pushes her hood back, I am struck by how beautiful she is. She looks like a model, with penetrating blue eyes, a perfectly tanned face, and long dark hair like mine. The stranger's skin is darker than Alondra's, like mine. She looks maybe five or six years older than I am. The two witches walking behind them are expressionless under their cloaks.

Alondra leans her torch into the fire. Then she says to us all with a big smile, "*Lux alba.*"

"*Lux tenebris,*" the stranger says.

"*Lux alba,*" we all echo almost in a chant.

Then, still standing, Alondra stretches her arms out wide with a big smile and says, "Blessed be the day that the circle is brought together again. Blessed be the coven under the gods Gaia, Selene, and Astraeus."

Her words and the chanting of the circle make my stomach turn. I'm haunted by the consequences of my magic at the last meeting. I might be a witch, but I don't like magic. Maybe it's the ghosts and throwing my friends into the fire thing.

"Atman," says Mira.

"Atman," the rest of us say.

Alondra sits down near Mira, across from me. The stranger sits on her other side with her two friends. Alondra looks at me. "The High Wizard couldn't come, Windstorm? I can't believe it." She's referring to my boyfriend, Bryce. As the only male in our coven, Bryce is the High Wizard.

"I hope he'll be here soon," I say.

"He will be," the stranger says to Alondra. "I've assigned him the job of being the apothecary for your illness, Falconsong. He'll be coming back after he collects the herbs."

How the hell does she know where my Bryce is?

"That's quite a sacrifice," Alondra says. "He should be here this afternoon. Especially this afternoon. Our circle is incomplete, Cadence." As if I want it to be incomplete. Believe me, the last thing I want right now is for Bryce not to be here.

"I don't think you realize how much your sisters care for you, Falconsong," the stranger says.

"So be it," Alondra says with a nod and a sigh. Then she turns and addresses all of us. "Allow me to introduce you all to

Enora." She gestures to the witch sitting beside her. "Enora's mystic coven name is Panthera. Panthera is a guest from her coven in Albany, Georgia. Tonight, she is our sister and we welcome her. And she has brought Beatrix and Cordelia, witches from her coven. In Panthera's circle, their mystic names are Manthis and Adder. Please welcome our guests, sisters."

Beatrix looks so much younger than me. She's short and thin. Really puny. In fact, the girl seems to be high school age. Her youth seems indecent in our circle, but she's so serious and focused, like an adult. Cordelia looks wicked. Black tattoos cover her face, and she scowls at everything. Actually, both of them look like shifty, evil witches. Even Beatrix's expression isn't innocent, although she looks like a little girl. Not like the witches of my coven. My coven is full of students studying at Hawthorne University and casting witchery on the side. These two strangers literally look like they spend evenings drinking the blood of babies and eating little children. I don't like them.

"Yatu, Panthera," says Gilda. "Yatu, Manthis, Adder."

"Yatu," says Mandy.

"Yatu," says Mira.

We all greet them.

"And you visit us as well, Red Fox?" Alondra says to Gilda. Gilda's sitting near Frida, to my left. "Welcome to our circle again."

Everyone erupts, welcoming Gilda.

"Enora is the leader of her coven and a very good friend of mine," says Alondra. Then Alondra points to me across the shallow flames with an outstretched hand. "Cadence is our High Priestess, the leader of our coven, Enora. Her mystical name is Windstorm."

"Yatu, Windstorm," Enora says with a nod and a sly smile. Then she squints and glares at me. Even as Alondra introduces her to the rest of the circle, her bright blue eyes study mine. I don't like that.

Alondra looks up to the clear sky. She smiles again.

"Ah, it approaches. We have only a short time left, witches." Alondra looks to me. "High Priestess, what say you before I officiate?"

Me? Great. I'm supposed to talk now?

I never wanted to be their leader. I joined the coven because my best friend and boyfriend were part of the group last year. Alondra appointed me High Priestess after she announced she was dying. And then, like I told you, all hell broke loose. I'm a little surprised that they still want me to be their leader. I never even formally accepted the title.

"Well...I'm just happy we're together again," I say stupidly. My words fall flat. I turn quiet. Everyone looks disappointed, expecting me to say more. I clear my throat and add, "You're all my closest friends. It's so great to see you and I...I...think we should all go around and tell each other what we did this summer."

There's complete silence. I guess nobody wants to.

Beatrix whispers something in Cordelia's ear. It's so quiet I can almost hear the bad things she's saying about me. I'm sure it's bad because they glare derisively at me.

When it's obvious that no one intends on sharing, I decide to take the opportunity to bring up something that's been on my mind since summer break. "I...haven't seen a lot of you since that last meeting. It was terrible what happened, and I've been wanting to apologize. To all of you. I love you all so much, and I'm sorry if I scared you. It scared me. I'm so sorry for what happened. I've felt so bad about it."

There. I said it. I've been wanting to apologize for months. But I don't feel any better after seeing the reactions of my coven. They all look down or avert their eyes. The two witches from the other coven even laugh, but Enora puts her hand up and they quickly stop.

"That's sweet, Windstorm, but no one got hurt during the

transfer of Selene last year," Alondra says. But she's not smiling anymore. She doesn't seem to like my mentioning it either.

"I frightened you. All my closest friends. I'm so sorry."

"You don't need to apologize," Alondra says. And there's an edge to her voice.

"What happened?" Enora asks.

How does she not know? That upsets me. I find it hard to believe that Alondra wouldn't have told her or one of the other witches. And she knew where Bryce was and I didn't. How? I really don't like her. I turn and look at Maddie. Maddie nods. Maddie and I are so close that we can read each other's minds. I know Maddie doesn't like her either.

"Windstorm had a little hissy fit after Falconsong announced that she's dying, Panthera," Mira says with a big grin. "Then Windstorm used her powers to manifest the ghosts of her ancient ancestors Maverick and Escoba to drag Professor William Reardon into our fire. She wanted to kill Bill for having sex with her best friend. She nearly threw Falconsong, me, and the rest of us in the fire too."

"Thank you, Mira, for being blunt as always." Alondra shakes her head. Mira laughs but Alondra remains very solemn. "It's difficult, Enora—very traumatic." Then she looks at me. "You did frighten us, Cadence. But of course we forgive you. You'll learn to control your powers."

There's silence. Like really uncomfortable loud nothingness, and everyone has her head down or is looking in any direction she can to avoid me. Boy was that a stupid thing for me to do. I so wish my Bryce was here.

"You guys know what I did last summer?" Tammy asks sweetly, trying to change the subject. "I met a boy."

"Ahh, do tell," says Maddie with a laugh.

"Yeah. My family and I traveled to California. I met him at Pier 39 watching the seals." She wrinkles her nose. "It stinks, but the seals are cute. And I forgot all about the stench when he came over to talk to me." She laughs and some of the other witches laugh too. "Before I knew it, he was taking me to the Golden Gate Bridge. It was so much fun. You know, you're so high up on that bridge. It's actually kinda scary walking the sidewalk and looking down. It's like you're on top of a high rise."

"What's the boy's name?" asks Helen.

"Davey."

"Is he cute?" asks Mira. A lot of the other girls giggle.

Alondra closes her eyes tightly and casts a stray glance at me. I think she's in pain. I don't think anyone else notices. Not even the new bitch, Enora. Enora is looking at Tammy, for the first time someone besides me. Alondra looks at me again and forces a smile, but she's not fooling me. She's hurting. And that hurts me. It makes me feel sorry for her.

"He's gorge," says Tammy. "An Asian guy, strong, like he can carry me with one hand. I probably weigh a third of what he weighs."

"Like Rocky," Maddie interjects.

Tammy laughs with a nod. "When we went to San Fran, I had gone with my folks. But after meeting Davey, the two of us left on our own and saw Alcatraz and that zigzaggy narrow street together. I can't recall the name of the street. And shopping. And walking in the parks near the Golden Gate... It was just so much fun."

"How were his lips?" Maddie asks.

She just laughs.

"How 'bout his bed?" asks Mira.

"Really, Mira," says Alondra, rolling her eyes.

"Just asking."

"What about you, Gilda?" asks Alondra. "You returned home to Savannah and got married, right?"

Gilda nods.

"Congratulations. The circle congratulates you and wishes you two well under Juno's blessing."

"It was a blending of Christianity and our handfasting," Gilda explains. "He was willing to incorporate both traditions."

"I wish I could have officiated," says Alondra. Then she looks at me. "Or Windstorm could have."

Gilda tells everyone about her new husband and their ceremony. The whole time the girls are talking about their summer, Enora is watching me again. It's creepy.

And I'm still squirming over mentioning our last meeting. I should never have said anything.

"You and Maddie stayed in town, right, Katie?" Marilyn asks me.

"What?" I ask.

"You were at her Aunt Jane's house?"

"Oh yeah."

"You guys just stayed near campus?" asks Tammy.

"We went to New Orleans." Maddie smiles and hugs me. "It was amazing. Bourbon Street. Gumbo. Crawfish. I love the food. There's so much history in New Orleans, you know. We took the carriage together, like Alondra's outside, only this one worked. We toured the French Quarter. I met a hot guy there too." The girls laugh. "Of course Cadence didn't. She kept talking about Bryce." We all laugh again. "We were there for a whole week. It wasn't long enough."

"Are you working here at school, Enora?" asks Gilda.

Enora tears her eyes from me and shakes her head. "I have an art studio in Albany. I'm a painter."

"Is your coven large?"

"Thirteen," she says with a nod. "Like yours." Then she looks right at me as if challenging me. About what? Why can't she look somewhere else?

"When I created the Hawthorne coven," Alondra says,

"Enora was a part of our first circle. It was when we were just starting out. I had met her at Beltane."

"Too bad we missed Beltane last year because of Firestarter over there." Mira points at me.

"Mira, put a lid on it," warns Maddie.

"Windstorm brought it up," Mira says with a shrug.

"She apologized," Enora snaps. I'm surprised. It seems this stranger is defending me. "If your High Priestess lost control, you all have to respect her intentions. I can tell she loves all of you so much from her words. It was touching. I sense a great deal of energy from this witch." *Is that why you're staring at me?* "She has powerful chakras. Her anahata binds the circle, Falconsong."

"No doubt," Mira quips. "Well, I was impressed."

"So says the guest to our coven," Alondra says, smiling at me again. "Take heed of Panthera's wisdom, girls. She is very wise." Then Alondra looks up at the sky and her smile grows. "Blessed be the day. It is nearly time. Look up, girls. Everyone, put your cloaks on and grab your glasses."

The cloaks have been taken off the hooks in the outside patio and stacked in a pile not far from the bonfire. We all get up and grab a cloak. No one owns one; we just grab whichever one is available. They're all matching black druid-like cloaks with hoods.

"Do you have shades, Katie?" asks Hope. "I forgot mine."

"No, I don't, but if you want we can share."

"Don't be so nice," Mira says near me. Then she hands Hope a pair of plastic lenses. "I brought a few spare."

We all return to the circle and Alondra, who is once again across from me, raises her arms as high as she can toward the clear sky. She is ecstatic, almost as if in a trance, as she seems to speak to the sky itself.

"Today is a special day of magic, witches! Today we see a glimmer of Astraeus fighting Apollo and, for a moment, conquering the heavens. But do not forget that it is only due to the blessing of our revered Selene that such darkness manifests itself. It is like Yule, where the rain and snow manifest tenebris. Powerful Ceres and her daughter, Proserpina, who took the pomegranate, cycle every year from light to darkness and then to light again. Natural mysteries manifest themselves today. A blessed day. *Lux alba*."

"*Lux alba*," everyone repeats.

"Don your glasses," Alondra says. "Let us walk together, holding hands with love, facing the fire. But do not look at the fire today. Today, at this magic moment, look up to the stars and heavens. Walk now and wait for Selene to travel across the sky, causing day to turn to night. Nyx shall reign, witches."

And we walk.

As we walk, everything seems to slow. Just as Mira said, there is magic afoot. I can feel it. And I feel a trance coming on. I don't always look up. Occasionally, I look at my sisters. But they are seemingly in rapture, staring up at the sky through their dark plastic glasses. I see shade forming over the sun above as it darkens before my eyes.

I feel a squeeze to my right arm and turn. It's Maddie. She looks funny with her shades, and she's smiling so widely, loving this.

Soon the sun is covered halfway, and Alondra's backyard and the surrounding woods have become darker. I don't feel my hands touching Frida and Maddie by my sides, but I know they're still there. And it seems we're walking more and more slowly around the fire.

A black bird with a streak of rainbow light soars off in the horizon. And oddly, there's color on the horizon, above the trees, like the red-orange of a sunrise. Rationally, I know that such a thing cannot be, for I see the eclipse above me; it's there. It's as if it is twilight or dawn out there while, up above, the moon is covering the sun.

When I look down, my heart skips. Alondra's face is changing. Her nose is stretching into a beak, and her cloak and outstretched arms have become large wings with dark feathers. Her fingers are turning into talons. Her bird eyes are still covered by the black shades. My right hand is holding a wing. My best friend has transformed as well—Blackbird is Maddie's mystic name. And Frida, known as Robin, looks like a bird with red splashed over her chest. My arm looks shiny, almost scaly. It's frightening what is happening, for we haven't partaken in any hallucinogens. In the past, I've taken mandrake with similar effects. But this is pure magic. It must be the effect of the eclipse on my coven.

The fire changes. Instead of a low flame, I see a pile of black snakes writhing on top of one another. It startles me and I jump. Maddie turns. Her face is still misshapen, with sunglasses. I point at the fire. She shakes her head. She must not see the snakes. I hate snakes. Then I hear a shriek and, instead of the joy of being part of our circle, I feel dread. I turn and there's a couple, only a few feet from the circle, lying naked in the grass in each other's arms.

"*Lux tenebris!*" Alondra shouts in ecstasy.

My dread is lifted. Alondra, though altered, is so joyous under the eclipse. It makes me feel good too.

All becomes dark. Completely dark. And still. I smell something rotting, like sulfur. Looking up, I can see the stars as clearly as in a night sky. That would normally fill me with joy, but instead I begin to feel cold. Only a minute ago, it was hot.

I feel something touching my feet. I look down and see a trail of black snakes slithering on the ground as I continue walking around the pyre of snakes. My fear is enough for me to want to break from the circle, but I feel locked in step with my friends.

"Nyx!" cries Alondra. "Holy of holies, bring your darkness

on our coven! Shroud us in your protection under your loving arms!"

I force my eyes to look away from all the writhing snakes and gaze upon the couple on the wild grass, now covered by a purple fog. This must be an illusion.

The fog thins around the couple, and I watch them fornicating on the wild grass. A naked man with short dark hair uses his strong arms to support his naked body over his lover. Black snakes are slithering over their naked bodies too. The lovers' eyes are locked. The girl's tits are pressed against the man's body, and his butt squeezes tightly as he presses into her.

The circle stops. I feel like it's been dark for an hour. The conscious part of my mind, still dim, tells me this is impossible. I've never witnessed a complete solar eclipse, but I've read that they only last a moment. It seems like a moment passed long ago. And we're not circling; we're just standing. Even Alondra, who is ecstatic, is looking up to the stars, immobile, like a bird statue.

The purple mist beside the couple turns red as they continue to have sex. My friends don't even seem to notice. They're frozen, staring up at the sky like Alondra.

The woman on the grass is beautiful. Her breasts are perfect. Her long hair flows along the ground. She's pinned under the man, and I see her digging her black fingernails deep into his back. Her nails, along with the serpents, move under the thick red fog.

I feel sleepy. Drugged. But there was no nightshade or mandrake. This is real magic.

Then I hear laughter. The woman under the man turns and faces me. My heart jumps. Her eyes are piercing blue. I recognize her as the stranger I just met: Enora. She is Enora. In fact, Enora has left the circle. And then, in horror, I recognize the boy on top. When he recognizes me, his eyes open wide and he quickly averts them. He is my boyfriend, Bryce.

There's a scream.

The light grows, and I feel like we're moving around in a circle again, ever faster, swirling as if on a spinning ride in an amusement park. The terrible vision fades and I feel dizzy.

I sink. I feel like my whole body is weighing me down like a lead weight. Maddie tugs on me hard, still trying to circle the pyre. I feel like I don't have the strength to move anymore. But the snakes are gone. And the slowly crackling fire burns once more. Then the sun shines brilliantly forth, turning night to day. It's a bright, hot afternoon again. And Enora is standing with us in the circle without my boyfriend.

"Glory be the day!" Alondra drops her hands and takes a deep breath. "Ah, glory be the day for our circle. What a gift to see this vision, even if only once in one's lifetime. *Lux alba.*"

"*Lux alba!*" everyone cries joyously.

I don't. I've lost my will to move.

"Everyone sit," Alondra says, smiling joyfully as ever. She's taken off her shades. We all sit in the chairs behind us and face the fire. "Any of you, if you saw a vision, please share it with our circle."

Enora turns and looks at me with a wide grin.

2

––––––––––

CLASS

I awaken to Maddie hitting my shoulder, pulling my arm, touching my cheeks, and pulling at my feet. She's doing all kinds of things to get me out of bed. She could have just touched my shoulder, but I hate mornings. I can't function until, like, noon. And since our alarm didn't sound, I guess I'm skipping breakfast. Like I care. I've been moping around for days, since that vision during the eclipse. I hardly slept last night, not falling asleep until five in the morning. The last thing I want is to get up or get food. She's got that covered too. She's pushing a lightly toasted bagel toward my nose.

"Let's go! Come on! You're gonna miss class."

"It's not class," I mutter. "It's a study group."

And it's not our first day. It's Tuesday. Monday we had lecture, which, of course, Maddie didn't go to. And Bryce still hasn't gotten back yet.

"Up, up," she says, pulling me again. The bagel falls on the floor, and that ticks her off more. "Come on!"

I sit upright, stretch out my arms, and take a deep breath. She throws clothes on my lap.

"Just go without me."

"It's time for school. Now get up, Cadence!"

I lie back down.

"Get up!"

"Why? Why do you care?"

"Because you do. And we're both in the same class, so we can go together."

I force my eyes open, reach down, and pick up the bagel from the ugly red-and-brown carpet. I pull off my nightgown. Then I toss a white T-shirt over my bra, pull on some jeans, and reach for my backpack. She yanks me out the door before I can grab it.

There are a lot of students walking to and fro, among the brick buildings, to their classes. We rush off the cement path, across the quad of buildings, into a small room that reminds me of high school. I recognize it. It's the same classroom where my boyfriend taught my metaphysical history class last year. You know, the boyfriend who's not back yet and who I watched having sex with Enora during the solar eclipse. Well, there's no TA at the front of the classroom now. I suppose we're not that late.

The classroom's full and there are only three empty seats at the front. Both of us forgot our computers in the shuffle, but I did remember to grab my art textbook. It's the only class Maddie and I are taking together: art history.

"Why'd you have to rush me?" I ask as we sit down.

"Just eat your bagel." She turns and smiles at me.

"So," I say, "what's with you and Rocky?"

"What do you mean? We just met."

"Didn't seem like that at the party. You couldn't keep your hands off him."

She just smiles.

Our teacher walks in. I almost drop my bagel.

"See?" says Maddie, gesturing to the door. "I was hoping you guys could talk, dope. Why would *I* rush to class?"

I can't believe my eyes. It's my boyfriend. My to-die-for unshaven, broad-shouldered Adonis, wearing a gray polo shirt and black slacks. His short hair is perfectly trimmed. His eyes are gazing firmly at me, and he's smiling. At me. I have an urge to get up and throw my arms around him, but I resist. I'm not the only one staring at him. Bryce has most of the girls eyeing him. But as he lugs his leather bag onto the front desk and takes out a laptop, he flashes another smile right at me. Me.

"Did you know he was teaching this class?" I whisper.

"That's why I wanted to get here before class, dope! You ruined it." She's whispering—or trying to.

"Why didn't you tell me?"

"It was a surprise."

"You could have just told me."

"This is more fun."

"I can't believe you didn't tell me."

"Shush."

"Please, everyone..." Bryce looks right at us with a big grin. "Quiet."

But isn't this wrong? Am I going to have another class with him as my teacher?

"Everyone, please take a look at our lesson plan. You can access it on our website." He writes the web address on the whiteboard with a green marker. "You can follow along if you'd like. You all should have read about Leonardo da Vinci?" He presses a button on his computer, and *Virgin of the Rocks*, the one in the Louvre, shows up on a screen on the wall. I know it's in the Louvre because, yesterday after the lecture, I studied like I was supposed to, unlike Madison.

I'm munching on my bagel. I'm not sure if I'm allowed to, so I kinda eat it slowly and close to the desk.

"This is *Virgin of the Rocks*. There were two paintings. One is currently in the National Gallery of London, and the other is in the Louvre in France. For Dr. Riker's class, you're going to have to know that the first was painted in 1483, the second in 1509. There's some debate over whether Leonardo touched the second or if it was created by his assistants. It's not certain, but it's likely that Leonardo worked on both. Of course, the one in the Louvre is better. So if you're planning a trip to Europe to see Leonardo, you'll want to go to Paris, not London."

Some of the girls snicker. Especially a snooty Kappa Alpha Kappa. She's wearing school colors, a red sweater with gold Greek letters, and staring at *my* boyfriend.

I could light her hair on fire. I'm a witch, you know. I touch my black fingernails together, but before I can do anything naughty...

"What do you think, Cadence?"

Huh? I stopped listening. "What?"

Somebody laughs. It's probably the sorority snoot.

"Can you tell us what one-point perspective is?" Bryce asks.

Yes. I read it in the textbook last night, and I recall Dr. Riker discussing it in the lecture Maddie didn't go to yesterday.

"Uh, one-point perspective is how Renaissance artists created the sense of depth in their paintings."

"Exactly," Bryce says. "It's why I love Renaissance art."

You love Renaissance art? You never told me that.

"Dr. Riker is not only a great history prof," says my tall-dark-and-handsome TA, "he's a lover of art. What he wants to instill in you guys is the sophistication that comes out in this period. Leonardo da Vinci was a genius. He created a robotic lion that walks, he drew sketches of helicopters, and he sketched anatomical drawings based on actual human cadavers that he dissected." Grisly. That's something Alondra would have focused on last year in her metaphysical history class. "Do you know which painting of his really excelled in using the one-point perspective? It's a perfect example."

He's still looking at me, which is annoying. Last year I told him not to call on me. I don't like attention. Just because we're going out doesn't mean I want to be made an example of—especially 'cause we're going out.

After I don't say anything, he says, "The one-point perspective was key to *The Last Supper*. It placed Jesus Christ at the center of the painting and at the center of his disciples. Know this for your exam."

I daydream through the rest of the class. I'm less excited about seeing him, and I'm starting to get mad because Bryce didn't tell me he was in town today. So I stop taking notes and focus on finishing the half-eaten bagel on my desk.

I'm surprised when class ends.

Maddie drags me up to the front by my arm, and we wait in line while a couple of girls come up with "questions." I think they just want to talk to him. They're so stupid and giggly. But who can blame them? He's hot.

When it's finally our turn to talk to Bryce, Maddie says, "You have a knack for making her sound stupid."

I ignore her and jump into his arms, kissing him on the lips. Bryce laughs.

"Katie," he says, stroking my hair. Then he sees a couple of students still walking out of class, staring at us, and quickly pulls away.

"Why didn't you tell me you were back?" I snap. It's this weird mix of ecstasy and anger.

Bryce laughs. "I got in from Atlanta at four in the morning." He turns and stuffs his laptop back in his bag.

"I would have come by," I say.

"You need sleep."

"Don't tell me what I need. I told you to tell me when you arrive."

"I don't get it," Maddie says. "Are you guys fighting or happy to see each other?"

I embrace him again.

"Please, Cadence, we're still in class."

"I've got to run to sociology," Maddie says with a laugh. "And it looks like you two have some catching up to do. But, Bryce, I told you not to use my best friend as an example in class. 'Kay?"

We're not listening to her. We're looking into each other's eyes like stupid lovestruck schoolchildren.

"Toodles," Maddie says.

Bryce and I walk outside. He's holding my hand, rubbing my fingers. God, I missed him.

We head down the main drag of campus. There are so many students rushing back and forth now. It will thin out in another week when the school year isn't new anymore.

"You didn't pick Riker's class so you could teach me, I hope?" I ask.

"Of course not," Bryce says, still rubbing my fingers. "It was assigned to me yesterday."

"Well, it's not proper. How are you going to grade my exams?"

"I thought of that, but then I realized almost all his tests are based on multiple-choice questions. It's only extra credit when you show up to my study group. Actually, I was thrilled when Dr. Riker assigned me."

"Because I'm in the class?" I ask stupidly.

"No. He's the best teacher next to Alondra. I only wish Alondra were teaching this year."

We head over to a parking lot not far from Yorkshire Dorms, where Maddie and I are roommates again this year. I see his old gray BMW. He stops and turns to me. He runs his hand through my long black hair again, and I feel tingles down my spine.

"I think it'll be fine, Kate. If Riker assigns anything for me to grade, I can always tell him our situation and ask him to grade it."

I barely hear a word he says. You've got to understand it's

been over a month since we've seen each other. We've been FaceTiming, but it's not the same. We hug each other again. For a long time. Tight.

"I missed you so much," he says.

I nod with my head still leaning on his chest, just listening to his breathing and feeling his heartbeat. He's breathing slowly, but his heart is thumping fast.

"I'm off to unpack," he says finally.

"Can I come?" I look up at him.

"Don't you have class?"

"Not till midafternoon."

3

———

UNPACKING

BRYCE HAS A STUDIO APARTMENT RIGHT OFF THE NORTH SIDE OF campus, with a combined living room and kitchen separated from the bedroom by a wall. I practically lived there toward the end of last year. Then he had to go to his folks' farm in Missouri for the summer. Right now, I'm sitting on his bed, watching him unpack his shirts and jeans.

"I can help."

"That's okay, Katie. How's Alondra?"

"Fine."

He reaches down to his suitcase for more clothes, and I hand him a stack of socks. "Thanks," he says. As he stuffs more clothes into his cabinet, made of dark wood, he says, "What about Maddie? Is she okay?"

"You know Maddie. When isn't she?"

He laughs. "Her mom?"

"Everybody's fine, Bryce. Why don't you tell me about Enora?"

He closes a drawer and furrows his brow. "Whaddaya mean?"

"You know her?"

"I've known her for years. She's a powerful witch in her coven. She came to help Alondra. I told you that's why I was away."

"I know, but...how well do you know her? Like, were you two ever extra close?"

I don't like his expression. He averts his gaze. "She used to be a part of our coven. I think Alondra thought she was going to take over one day before she learned about you. Enora doesn't have your ancestry, but she has an innate understanding of witchcraft that's very rare. She picked up incantations and spells faster than anyone I've ever met. She even caught Bill's attention, and he shared things with her that he never shared with anyone else."

"That's not exactly what I meant."

"What did you mean?" He raises his eyebrows, leans against his dresser, and puts his hands in his pockets.

"Did you two have a romantic relationship?"

"Huh?"

"Did you have sex?" *God, do I have to spell it out for him?*

I figure he's being evasive. That upsets me more. Somehow, I think he had a very romantic relationship with her. No, I know he did... I don't know, maybe it's having seen him lying naked and having sex with her by our bonfire that makes me think that.

His eyes blink and he runs his hand through his short dark hair. He always does this when he's flustered. He also does it when he's trying to keep things from me. "It was a long time ago, Cadence." Yeah, they had sex.

I finally look away and say rather morosely, "It wasn't so long ago for me."

"What do you mean?"

He walks over. I look up into his mesmerizing eyes and

smile in spite of myself. "During the eclipse, I saw you and her naked together."

He cocks his head and seems to ponder this. I'm not pondering it. I'm pissed.

"Really?" he asks. "During the eclipse?"

"Yeah. I saw snakes and other weird shit too."

"Then it was a vision. Cadence..." He takes my hand. Why is he doing that while talking about having sex with another woman? "It was a long time ago. I haven't dated her in years. I certainly haven't been close with her in a long time."

"I know. I figured that. And now, I suppose, I get why I saw it. I must have been seeing the past. But it bothers me."

He cups my chin with his hand and kisses me on the lips. His lips are so soft. And his breath smells like spearmint. That's so Bryce. This guy's always dressing right and smelling good.

"I missed you," he says quietly. And we kiss some more. But... *Hey...wait a minute, mister...*

"Enora told the circle that she sent you to some...somewhere to get something. Like you were her gofer. I was shocked that she knew where you were, because I thought you were still back in Missouri with your parents. That's what you told me. Why didn't you say you were in town? What were you doing, and what were you doing with Enora? Why did she know your whereabouts before I did?" I must be pouting. He smiles widely, which upsets me more. "Really, Bryce. Cut it out! Why?"

"Don't be jealous," he says, shaking his head. He sits beside me on the mattress. "I did it for Alondra. Alondra contacted Enora. Enora called me and asked if I could gather some things. I told you, I hadn't spoken to Enora in years."

"But why *you*?"

"Bill was cast out. Now I'm the High Wizard of our coven. The High Wizard is expected to get these things."

Hmm.

"You told me you'd be with your parents watching the eclipse," I persist.

He sighs. Then he takes my hand again. "Katie, it was for Alondra. When Enora told me she was here with Alondra, to make amends and help her with her cancer, I put our past aside and offered to do anything I could. For Alondra. I know Enora's magic is nearly as powerful as Alondra's. Enora gave me a list of herbs, many very rare and only found in the city. I gladly went to get them. The fact that it would mean I'd miss the eclipse with our coven was a huge sacrifice, and Enora said that would make the potion that much stronger for Alondra. But there's nothing between Enora and me anymore. I swear it."

"So you didn't get to see the eclipse?"

"I watched what I could in the city."

"It was pretty cool." I shake my hair back and take a deep breath. Then I look deeply into his eyes. "At least you didn't see what I saw."

"Oh, come on, babe." He holds my cheek and leans his forehead on mine. Then we kiss again. "There's nothing between Enora and me anymore."

"I know," I say. But I sound hurt. I reprimand myself for sounding stupid. I saw a vision, but I'm acting like I caught him cheating on me.

"I miss your perfume." He backs away and takes a deep breath.

"I just can't get over what I saw."

"Panthera is a tigress, Katie. Literally. The word *panthera* means wildcat. A tiger. She's the last person I'd want to be with, trust me. Her magic is more powerful than Alondra's because she uses black magic. Alondra doesn't. You know Alondra uses white, right-handed, good magic. Black magic was taught to Enora by Bill. Enora still worships Satan with her coven. She's a devil worshipper. So much so that Alondra cast her out years ago." Now he takes another deep breath and turns to the window. Through a crack between the unopened drapes, he looks at the parking lot for a moment. "I think she heard what you did. I don't think she came only at Alondra's invitation. Stories about your power probably spread all over the state. Maybe the whole country. Now I wonder if she had something to do with your seeing us together..." Then he emphasizes, "*In the past*, Katie."

"She looked like a real arrogant bitch," I say. "Shifty. She reminded me of Bill Reardon. Now I know why."

"Bill trained her. Personally. And there's more." But he clams up all of a sudden. He just sits there, looking down, shaking his head. "I shouldn't say."

"Hey," I say, "no *secrets*, remember?"

"Alondra should tell you, not me."

This time, I take his chin in my hands. I'm not going to let him off so easily.

"You weren't the first one to cause a rift in Alondra and Reardon's marriage, Katie," he says with a nod. "About four years ago, Reardon took Enora as a mistress."

"That dick," I say, dropping his chin. "Why did you ever have anything to do with him?"

"Back then, I was a student of Alondra's like you, and I didn't know Professor Reardon that well. But I knew Alondra. Alondra introduced me to the Hawthorne coven. I watched Alondra suffer more from her marriage with Bill than she's suffering now from her cancer. You know, she used to be a lot cheerier, like your friend Maddie. The affair really brought her down. I think she separated from him, not in marriage, but emotionally and, well, she distanced herself from everyone after that."

"I didn't even know Alondra was married until late last year."

"Bill did that. She drifted apart from everyone. And here's the weirdest part—Bill sort of made up with Alondra. They became the couple you know. A shell of a husband and wife. Alondra never forgave him, but Bill made peace with her. He did that, I think, in order to ask for protection from Enora... Reardon was terrified that Enora would conjure something horrible against him. So Reardon had Alondra cast shield spells to protect him from her."

"Reardon asked Alondra to protect him from the girl he'd been having an affair with? You're kidding."

"Yes. That's Alondra. And she's such a bright white light that she helped him. She shut off Enora's magic, like you do with fire. But her shield cost her. Who knows, maybe Enora made Alondra fall ill with cancer."

"Then why the hell did you help her?"

Bryce takes a deep breath, seeming impatient. "I told you, Cadence. For Alondra. Alondra needs any possible help she can get. And I've learned enough about potions over the years that I'd have a hunch if Enora were tricking me. She wasn't. The stuff she asked for made sense."

"But why would Alondra invite her?"

"I really don't know," he replies, shaking his head. "Maybe she's desperate. Maybe for the same reason I'm helping her. For her health."

He grabs my hand. "How's the rest of the gang? Mira?"

"Creepy. You know Mira."

"Mira cares about Alondra more than any of us. And she likes you. She likes you more since your magic show last semester. She respects you now."

"She doesn't act like it."

"She's Mira," Bryce says with a chuckle. "And Gilda? She got married, right?"

"Aha."

"How's—"

I surprise him by pushing him onto his bed and running

my hand along the short stubble on his cheek. I can't resist anymore. We lock lips again, kissing passionately.

"Frida?" he asks between kisses. "I hear her brother is studying to be a priest. How's—"

"Aha," I mutter and press my lips on his. I don't want to talk. I want to kiss. So I do. Again. And he laughs as we press our lips together harder. I enter his mouth with my tongue, and he tastes delicious. "Umm," I say. "You don't know how much I missed you. How dare you not tell me you were back!"

"Sorry." He closes his eyes tightly and nods. "But you might have stopped me from going."

"I wouldn't have stopped you from helping Alondra."

"Okay."

"I wouldn't have. You have to trust me."

"I do. I love your long hair, Katie. Your smell."

"I smell nice?"

"I'm addicted to your smell."

"It's a very expensive perfume." I throw my legs over him and straddle him. He laughs more.

"And your humor."

"Shh," I say. Our lips touch again. At first it's soft, but then I press hard.

"Your youthfulness..."

I press my lips hard against his again so he can't talk. But he manages. "Your innocence. But, behind it"—I start lifting up his gray shirt—"there's an inferno."

"An inferno, huh?" I laugh, pulling off his shirt.

"A windstorm."

I stroke the bristles of hair along his cheek again and then move down to his short chest hairs. He's so muscular and hard. I touch his pecs and can feel his heart racing. Mine is racing too.

"You should have let me come with you," I whisper near his ear. "Don't you dare ever do that again."

I pull off my T-shirt, leaving just my black bra while I gyrate a little up and down his waist.

"Cadence," he says, pulling back again. "Maybe we shouldn't..." He looks at the window. "It's the middle of the day."

"It's really hot in here," I say with a chuckle. "Isn't it? I think I should take this off."

I reach back while still straddling him and unclasp my black bra. Then I throw it to the side. He's staring at my naked chest. He's running his hands along my naked skin, the curves of my breasts, and my nipples. I'm so aroused.

We're committed now. And I want him. I want to fuck him. I've missed him sooo much.

"I saw how all the other girls were looking at you in class."

He answers by cupping his mouth over one of my hard nipples. He starts sucking. It sends tingles down my back and legs. I pull him toward me, with my hips pressed against the bulge in his pants, and lock my lips on his again.

"I love you, Cadence," he says. "I love you so much." He's breathing heavily now. And so am I.

"Show me," I say.

I jump off and put up a single finger with a sly smile. Then I yank off my jean shorts and panties. I'm naked. I had already removed my sandals by his door. To be honest, I knew what I wanted when I entered his apartment; I just wanted the right moment. I kneel down, unzip his pants, and yank down his black slacks and underwear. He's holding a condom in his hand, and I wait as he rolls it down his long shaft.

I sit on him again and grind slowly. He moans again. Then he finally does what I've wanted since I saw him in the classroom this morning. He enters me. It's electrifying.

"Oh God, Bryce. Make love to me."

I'm rocking slowly, forward and backward, sliding slowly up and down on him while he massages my boobs. His fingers press deep along my soft skin, sliding down like drips of water from the curves of my breasts, down my sides, until settling on my butt. There his hands remain, supporting me as I move up and down on him slowly.

"And I missed this too," I say with a chuckle.

"Oh, Cadence."

I reach down and our lips touch again. I enter with my tongue and taste his while continuing to move up and down on him. Our lips become wet from sucking and tasting each other. I run my fingers along the stubble on his cheeks once more and then over his short hair. Then I sit up and straighten my back, allowing my tits to protrude, as I feel him press even deeper inside me.

"Oh, God, Cadence."

The sex is better than I remembered. I think it's because we've been away from each other for so long. I've missed him so much.

Now I love the warmth of his skin. I love his bright blue eyes. I even love it when he closes them, enjoying me. Loving me.

It gets heavy. It feels so good. I lean down and run my hand along his chest and down to the ripples of his abs. He's so fit. The passion becomes hotter, and I start to move faster and faster. I bounce hard up and down on him while moaning loudly. There's a clapping sound as my pelvis rides up and down on him. I don't want it to stop, but I think I'm bouncing so hard that he's about to be spent. I'm groaning so loudly that it's almost a shout.

"Shh," he says, putting a finger over my lips.

But I can't. I kiss and lick his fingers and just moan louder. Over and over I land on him until I finally feel him collapse under me. I haven't climaxed yet, so my man, being Bryce, so nice, stays inside me until I come. After a few more thrusts, I climax too.

"Oh God, Bryce!" I kiss him hard on the lips, falling on top of him. "That was sooo good."

"I love you, Cadence," he says, out of breath, staring into my eyes again. Those baby blues are looking into my eyes so innocently, so sweet and kind. "I love you so much."

I lean over him in an embrace. We lie naked in each other's arms for the longest time. I don't think I could ever be happier.

4

———

PANTHERA

I'm holding my lover's hand as we walk under leaves and thin branches that darken the clear, starry night in patches. We tread over pine-needle paths, smelling the clean woodsy air, passing dirt trails, streams, and brooks, up into the hills that overlook our campus. It's so lovely out that I convinced Bryce to walk with me from his apartment. It's Friday night, and we're heading to Alondra's.

Somehow Bryce convinced me to go with him to our second Sabbath of the year. We're going to try a healing spell, he told me. But the closer I get to the house, the heavier my feet feel. Maddie's told me we're planning a summoning. That means it's not going to just be a meet-and-greet; it's going to be a full-fledged witch show. I don't know if I'm ready for that.

Bryce raps Alondra's large antique brass knocker. He turns to me because my hand is shaking.

"Relax, babe," he says.

"Why did I say yes?"

"Because I didn't want to go alone." He leans down and kisses me on the cheek. "And because you care about Alondra as much as I do."

"I guess."

The door creaks open, and Madison opens the door wearing a black hooded cloak, looking like an ancient druid, with her hood down and her black hair flowing behind her. She's got a gaping grin.

"We're out in the back, High Priestess," Maddie says with a tight hug. Then she puts her hands on my shoulders in the foyer. She knows I'm nervous. "You ready?"

"No."

"Mira's chanting," she says.

I roll my eyes. Mira does this thing where she makes up words and dances around the fire like a fool.

"It'll be fine," Maddie adds.

"Just don't call me High Priestess," I say, shrugging her hands off.

A gray cat scurries by my legs and I jump in fright. "Shit!"

"That's Pete," Bryce says.

"Come on, girlfriend," Maddie says, "everybody's waiting for you."

Everybody's waiting for me. Great.

We make our way down the hallway to the living room. The sliding glass door is wide open. I hear chanting from the yard. It sounds like gibberish. I lurch back at the sight of a tall bonfire; it's about the height of a person. I don't want to go out there. This isn't the campfire we had last week. It's a witch's bonfire, like the one I once stoked with my magic. But Bryce takes my hand, and my feet somehow carry me.

Large white rocks, instead of chalk, circle the white plastic chairs around the fire. The smell of smoke and fire permeates the backyard. I can see the witches, my friends, walking slowly around the bonfire in their black druid coats. At the front of the group is Mira, dancing like a fool, with my witches walking in single file behind her.

"*Yelee alterban exeet solimader infotado*," cries Mira. Whatever that means.

"Does she have to do that?" I ask Bryce as we walk forward.

"She's got passion," he says, "you've gotta give her that."

"Yatu!" Mira shouts spotting me. "Yatu!" She stops dancing and everyone stops.

They all turn as we approach. I realize Alondra isn't here. And what's worse, Enora is standing beside her henchwomen, Beatrix and Cordelia. Cordelia scowls at me. Enora narrows her eyes. I wonder how she feels about me holding Bryce's hand?

Mira walks over and crouches on one knee as the other girls remain beside the fire. It feels ridiculous, like I'm some sort of queen or something. The flames are raging over Mira's head behind her welcoming grin. "Yatu, High Priestess, Windstorm," she says and looks deeply into my eyes.

"Windstorm is here, Raven," says Maddie, bowing her head.

"So I see, Blackbird. Falconsong wasn't feeling well." She looks back at the house. "But we have Panthera here tonight." *Great.*

Mira jerks up and reaches toward the sky. She moves so fast that I'm startled. Her cloak falls back a little. I notice her large breasts under the folds of her cloak. She's naked underneath.

"Blessed be the gods who bear witness to our coven! To the moon, the stars, the trees. Earth, water, wind, and fire. We all gather once more under your arms!" She looks at me. "Come join the circle, High Priestess. I told you of darkness. I believe it is afflicting our blessed Falconsong. Let us summon the demons, wraiths, and will-o'-the-wisps tonight to fight them back and heal her."

"Why do you think there's evil?" I ask.

For the first time, I notice how wild-eyed she looks, and I feel dumb asking her a question. I'm wondering if she's taken mandragora. Mandragora, or mandrake, is a drug we sometimes take during ceremonies. I told Maddie that if anybody does that shit again, I'm out. I think Mira snuck some. And I'm not sure she understands what I'm saying.

"I've sensed evil ever since my long journey back from shadows in the East," Mira says.

That's silly. Mira just got back from her parents' house in Orlando, Florida. She makes it sound like she just arrived from Transylvania.

"I don't feel anything," I say. Then I look at Enora. "Do you?"

"There's left-sided magic here," Enora says with a nod, looking around the yard. "Raven's right. That is why Falconsong summoned me."

"Why don't we all sit down?" I say.

And they do because I'm their High Priestess. We all sit around the fire. The flames tower above us, and my chest tightens because it reminds me of my conjuring again.

"May I begin the evocation?" Mira asks me.

I'd rather you not.

She's sitting on my right, with three girls between us. I'm sitting between my BFF and my boyfriend. After I don't answer, Mira says, "We will manifest the spirits that threaten us. Then we will banish them from Falconsong's home."

"Why bring them here?" Maddie asks.

"We're not bringing them. They're already here. We're manifesting them. Windstorm, may we begin?"

"Do your worst," I say with a sigh.

Anyway, it doesn't look like Mira can "evoke" anything. Enora, who's glaring at me, could probably summon some mean spirits. Every time she watches me, I squirm and hold Bryce's hand tighter.

"If we face the shadow that lurks among us," Mira says rapidly, "we free ourselves." She's definitely high, might be mandrake, could be a dash of nightshade. "Everyone rise and hold hands. Walk single file, but face the flames."

And we do, just like we did during the eclipse.

"Spirits of Nyx!" Mira exclaims as we walk, "Gaia commands you to reveal the wraiths that you shelter. Here before the fire…" Then she lets go of Hope's and Marilyn's hands, takes a small metal flask from her pocket, and sprinkles water on the flames. It reminds me of a priest performing a blessing with holy water. "Water, and the earth under our feet, and the air we breathe, come to light. We demand you show yourself. Come forth." And then she puts up a hand for us to stop. She searches the yard as if she lost something. "Come forth!" Mira shouts. "Reveal yourself. Show yourself now."

But we hear crickets and the crackling fire. The silence is loud. But that's okay, because I'd rather feel like an idiot than have some spirit come forth.

"Come forth!" Mira repeats, as if yelling will invoke her spirits. "Show yourself! Now!"

"Perhaps we should just sit down and talk," I suggest.

"What do you think?" Mira asks Enora. "Do you feel this presence? Can you help reveal it?"

"I do," Enora says, with her arrogant smile illuminated by the flames. "I can."

"From the power of our coven, can you manifest it?" asks Mira.

Cordelia likes that question. Her scowl changes to a wicked, sardonic smile. She leans over and whispers something in Enora's ear while looking over at me. Enora nods.

"I can manifest the evil among you," Enora says. "But I don't think you'll like it."

"Does the spirit harm our beloved Falconsong?" asks Mira.

"The spirits harm all of you."

Mira looks at me. "High Priestess, will you allow Panthera to assist us?"

No. I don't trust Enora. I turn to Bryce, but he gives me a tentative nod. Then I look at Maddie. Maddie nods too and says, "For Alondra, Katie."

"I guess," I mutter. "Do...your worst."

My words sound so uncertain. It's one thing to let Mira babble; it's quite another to let this creepy witch conjure a spell. Bryce is anxious too. He's gripping me so tight now that I have to pull my hand away.

"Follow me," Enora says with a faint grin and a nod. Then, with her finger, she gestures for all the witches to leave the fire. She leads us toward Alondra's house.

"Gather around," Enora says, "but away from the flames. The fire is too dangerous."

The fire is too dangerous?

Then she does something really weird. As we circle around her, she crouches down on the wild grass in her dark cloak, gathering herself into a black ball at the center of all of us. We sit around her and wait as she's motionless for a long time. Then she whispers *"Spiritus"* quietly with her head cradled in her arms. I hear her words as if they're a gust of wind in the woods. She repeats them like a mantra. *"Spiritus. Spiritus, venite foras. Spiritus. Spiritus venite foras. Spiritus."* She continues to repeat the words, ever louder. *"Spiritus. Spiritus, venite foras."* Then she looks up and locks her eyes right on me. I lurch back as if one of Alondra's cats grazed by my leg. I could swear Enora's eyes have changed from blue to white.

"Spiritus, venite foras," she repeats ever louder. I can feel the words. They're cold and seem to be blowing around us. It makes me want to return to the warmth of the fire. *"Spiritus, venite foras."*

But the fire is the last place I want to be near. There's a howling. The fire rises higher. That freaks me out because it reminds me of my own conjuring. Then a swarm of black birds, not snakes this time but birds, bursts straight up from the center of the flames. Some of my friends shriek. A hundred crows caw as they take off into the starry sky.

A body forms in the center of the fire. A human form. I see a face, contorted, melting. It opens its mouth and screams inaudible words. It's silent. Too quiet. Only the sound of Enora's chant can be heard. Other than her words, it's just as quiet as it was when Mira was leading us into the forest.

I look at Bryce. He's spooked too. He's squeezing my hand again. Does he see the body in the flames? I follow his gaze and it only gets worse. More bodies twist in the fire. An emaciated old man with a long thin beard and limbs like sticks stands beside a child—maybe his son or daughter? The child's eyes are sunken in. A line of men and women march toward them from behind, in single file, with their heads down. The fire seems to be a portal, and beyond these bodies are hills and valleys and a crimson lake with blood-like tributaries flowing into a river. And everything is seen through a dark red filter.

The fire rises higher. Enora's words are now a whirlwind, as if they're not words at all but a tempest surrounding us. Another man's form appears distinctly in the center of this red vortex. His body is emaciated as well, but he's young. He's entwined with the body of another. A woman. The woman's body melts in and out of the man and, though she is terribly thin, her naked breasts and belly are full. Among the red hills, a shadow, a figure wearing a dark cloak like mine, approaches the couple from behind carrying a curved knife.

I've had enough. I shout for Enora to stop and am horrified when I find my lips paralyzed. I can't utter a thing.

"*Spiritus, venite foras.*"

The mouths of the couple in the fire are now wide open, screaming in unison as they suffer in pain. I can hear their scream now, but it doesn't sound like the noise is coming from them. I look at the other witches standing in the circle with me.

I realize that the scream is not coming from the couple but from my friends.

I see the torso of a man with a thin bone-like arm appear outside of the fire for a moment. Blood is dripping from melting flesh.

Enora points at the fire and, with her white eyes, cries, "*Ecce signum! Ecce diabolus vester! Ecce satanas vester. Ecce adversaries vester!*"

All the witches of my coven repeat her words as if reading them off a script. I don't know what they mean. Bryce is still holding my hands, and he's repeating her words too. His eyes are wide open, staring at the flames.

"Stop!" I say. The words explode from my chest, but my lips are still immobile. And yet Bryce and Maddie turn. The rest of my coven turns too. Somehow, they hear me.

Enora continues to chant. "*Spiritus, venite foras.*"

"Stop!" I repeat. This time the words echo throughout the forest. Oddly, my words seem to compete with Enora's. Enora rises from her crouched position and thrusts her hands toward me as if striking me.

There comes a terrible scream. At first I think it's one of my friends, but then I realize it's from the fire. All my friends stare at the flames. The fire rises, as it once did upon my command. It's two stories high, and the couple is now melting in the center.

"Stop!" I scream at Enora. My lips relax and I can move my mouth again. "Stop it, now!" I cry. "What are you doing? Stop!"

She turns and looks at the fire, as if curious about her own witchcraft. The flames are now spinning rapidly in a red vortex. And in the center of the fire is no longer a couple but bodies, hundreds of them, naked, melting, writhing, and circling ever higher in a fiery tornado. I know the fire is a doorway. Into hell? Occasionally, limbs appear outside the flames. The arms and legs are misshapen, with welts and open sores in their skin, and blood oozes. But most horrible are their faces. The faces are not of this world anymore. They are melted and contorted like wax on a candle. Some are missing eyes, ears, or noses. But they're alive, hollering in fear.

"Stop it!" I shout at Enora. "I command you! Stop this now!"

She turns to me and, in the midst of all the chaos, she smiles with those creepy pearl eyes. But the spell is breaking. The rest of the witches in my coven are stepping back toward the house, ready to make a run for it. No longer do their eyes appear glassy or in a trance. No longer are they blindly repeating her incantation. They're stepping back from the fire in horror.

"*Venite foras!*" Enora spits at me, as if challenging me with her words. Then she points at the fire. "Here is your evil!"

"What are you doing!" I scream back. "You're opening a door. Close it! Close it now!"

I rush to her and stare into those creepy white eyes. I feel an energy pierce the center of my chest. *Stop now!* I shout, but once more my lips don't move. It is a thought at the core of my very being. My soul. She shakes her head and closes her eyes tightly as if I've hurt her. She loses her smile and, for the first time, she doesn't look like she's in control.

You can stop this, Cadence. The words are not Enora's; they're felt by me. I don't know where they're coming from, but they sound familiar. Maybe my conscience? *You have the power to stop this. Stop it now. End the spell, Windstorm. End it now.*

Panic surges through my body. Then comes a flash of lightning from the sky. Enora looks up excitedly. A second bolt crashes down only a few yards from us, nearly striking her. She falls to the ground, covering her eyes as if blinded. When she opens them and turns to me, the creepy whiteness has left her gaze.

"*STOP!*" I shout. Not only the words but the thought springs from my body. Enora is thrown a few feet, rolling in the grass. A torrent of rain pours down. And then more lightning and thunder.

With the rain comes wind. A powerful gale strikes the ground, throwing my hood and hair back. Enora's hood flies off her head too, and her hair is blown horizontally. She slides across the grass, driven by a force as if a tornado has been summoned. A few witches stumble over, and for a moment the bonfire nearly burns out. Enora looks into my eyes, and her eyes are blue again. But she stubbornly yells once more, *"Venite foras!"*

"Apage, diabole!" I cry back, and my words are accompanied by more lightning. Each word is echoed by a crash from the sky. *"Vade retro!"*

I look over at the fire. It's spinning and bodies are still suffering in the flames. I run past Enora and land on my knees right before the flames. Then I raise my hands and repeat words never before uttered from my lips: *"Vade retro, diabolus!"*

A gust of wind knocks me over. It whirls around Alondra's yard and lands over the fire. A few wraiths nearly escape the flames, as if in a final effort to enter our world, but the wind crashes over them too.

The fire is snuffed out.

Then the wind leaves as quickly as it came. So too does the rain. So too does the thunder and lightning.

Everything falls silent.

I hear whimpering behind me. My friends are crying. They're in shock.

My breathing is fast and heavy. I cock my head back, and Enora's on her knees too. She looks exhausted as she stares at the pile of smoke, once our bonfire. She's in total shock.

"Get out!" I shout to Enora. *"Get out, now!"*

She looks at me and furrows her brow.

I despise this woman. She brought the same sort of magic

that I've been trying so hard to forget. She's made my nightmare come true.

But she does nothing. She just stares at the smoldering flames. I think she's in too much shock to move.

I feel a hand on my back. I spin around. It's Mira. She's reaching out to help me up, but I bat her hand away.

"Leave our coven!" I shout at Enora. "Leave, now!"

"You asked me to manifest darkness and the spirits from hell. I warned you." She didn't warn me. She didn't say anything about "spirits from hell."

"I didn't," I object.

"You did."

"You did, Cadence," Mira says gently. But for the first time ever, Mira is completely serious. She's shaking leaves and water from her cloak. All my friends are slowly rising behind us.

I run right up to Enora, and the woman backs up, scared.

"How could you do this!"

"I did what you asked, Cadence." Enora raises her hand. "I summoned devils to show you what threatens your circle. You saw them. They are here. Close the door or not, they are always with us. I did not bring the devil to this coven. The past did. I only manifested it. Made it visible. This evil is among you. You just don't want to see it. This is the threat Mira feels. This portal is so close to being open. I simply brought it out from hiding. I manifested what is here, I didn't create it."

"You brought it here! You brought something that shouldn't be here."

"And you made it go away," Enora says, finally giving me her stupid smug smile.

I look around. No one is saying a thing. Some have sat back down on the wet wild grass with their heads in their hands.

Bryce comes up to me, helps me up, and embraces me. I start crying in his arms. Some of the other witches are still crying too.

"How'd you do that?" Mira asks Enora in wonder.

"I will show you." Enora seems excited. "I can teach all of you. It is powerful magic that—"

"You will show nothing!" I say, jumping out of Bryce's arms. "Go away!"

She doesn't go.

I stare at her for a moment. So...I go. I run away from everyone.

Bryce calls out my name, but I ignore him.

5

911

I RUN UP TO THE SLIDING GLASS DOOR LEADING TO ALONDRA'S living room, and I see very little light inside. All the lights have been turned off. Perhaps the lightning knocked out the electricity. I struggle to open her glass door, which is somehow now closed, and the fight to open it makes me cry even more. Tears are streaming down my face.

I didn't even want to be here. Everything is reminding me of last year, and last year was seriously fucked up. I just want a normal life. What happened is precisely what I feared would happen.

I finally throw the door wide open, pull off my dark cloak, and toss it on her fluffy carpet. Why did I come? I'm so mixed up. Since my wandering through the forests of Hawthorne last year, I've accepted that I'm a witch. Fine. I'm a witch. But I haven't accepted a witch's magic. Especially dark magic. I just want to have friends and be a normal person. I don't want a boyfriend who's a warlock. And I don't want a best friend who calls herself *Blackbird*. I want out of this coven.

But see, I'm so confused because I know in my heart that

there is no way out. I'm a witch. And this is my coven. This is my family.

I rush down the hallway toward Alondra's large foyer. The lights are out everywhere, and it's dark and spooky. But I'm angry enough not to care. Of course, I could turn on a light, but I don't bother. I grab the brass knobs of Alondra's large mahogany doors to leave and am about to throw them open when I hear a groan. A sound of pain. It reminds me of the portal, but this is a solitary moan. It echoes through the dark, empty house.

I hear it again. It's coming from upstairs.

So? Why should I care? I should just go home.

But someone sounds hurt.

My feet disobey me, and I quickly make my way up Alondra's stairway. It only gets spookier as I ascend, in total darkness, away from the windows near the front door. And there's moaning again. A steady groan of pain.

I follow the moans down the hallway to an open door. I walk in and see a large window facing Alondra's backyard. If the window weren't there, I wouldn't be able to see a thing in this bedroom. The window overlooks the yard, where my sisters and Bryce are confronting Enora and her witches. It seems like a standoff, with the three of them shouting at the ten witches of my coven. Good. At least they're fighting her now.

There's a groan again. I turn and see someone in bed, in the shadows, clutching her stomach.

"Who's there?" I ask in the darkness.

The groaning stops. I don't think the person even knows I came into the room.

I find a light switch and flip it on, but the light doesn't work. The electricity is out.

I hear a soft, weak voice. "Cadence."

"Who's there?" I know who it is. Who else could it be?

"Cadence," the voice mutters again.

I kneel by the bed in the dark. Alondra slowly turns. She's wrapped in her sheets. She groans again, but more softly now knowing someone is listening.

"What's wrong?" I ask. "What's the matter?"

"Nothing...I...I saw everything."

"Enora?"

"Panthera," she says with a nod.

My eyes are adjusting.

Alondra looks awful. Her hair is disheveled, and she's wearing a simple T-shirt under the sheets. Her skin looks glassy and covered with sweat.

"Are you sick?" I ask. Of course she's sick.

"You've proven yourself once more. I knew your powers were great, but I've never seen anything like that."

"What's wrong, Alondra?"

"You are a powerful witch."

"So what?" I snap, shaking my head violently. This is so Alondra. One second wonderful, the next a complete bitch-witch. Who cares how good a witch I am? She's sick! I take a deep breath and say, "Are you hurting? I heard you from downstairs. What can I do?"

"I'm dying, Cadence."

There's silence after that. I feel a tightness in my chest, but I don't think I can cry anymore. My eyes are still wet from being so mad at Enora. The tightness in my chest rushes to my throat. She reaches out her hand and holds mine. Her hand is slimy. Her weak grasp makes me feel even worse. And her hand is shaking.

"You are our leader," Alondra says. "The embodiment of Escoba. And more. I shall give you my gift too. I will give you my power from Abigail. You will be the greatest witch that ever lived."

"Stop it, Alondra! I don't care." I reach into my pants pocket for my phone. "I'm going to call 911. You're sick."

"No doctors," she says. "I refuse any medicine."

"Bryce said you had an infection. Did you take your antibiotics?"

"A witch doesn't take antibiotics. Only herbs."

"You're so stubborn."

"This coming from you," Alondra says with a weak laugh. Then she shuts her eyes tightly. "I am close to the Summerland, Cadence. Let me go in peace."

I let go of her hand, jump up, and walk to the window. I'm surprised to see the fight is over. Enora's out there corralling my coven again. Somehow, she's organizing them around the smoldering fire once more, and my friends are following her. How does she do that? It is then I realize that this witch is sabotaging my circle. *My* friends.

Alondra groans. I think she's so sick she's forgotten I'm here.

"Why is Enora here still?"

"What?" Alondra asks weakly. She seems to have trouble even uttering a breath.

"Why is Enora in our coven? She's trying to take over."

Alondra laughs. I can't believe it. She actually laughs. But midway between a guffaw, she falls back, breathing heavily again.

"Wait. You brought her to take over, didn't you?" I ask in amazement. "You brought her here to lead the coven instead of me?"

Alondra takes a deep breath. Then she says, "Do you fight me even in my last days, Katie?"

"Am I right?"

"Of course, the Hawthorne coven must survive."

"Led by that witch!" I snap in disbelief.

"I can't...fight, Cadence...I can't..."

She has no energy. I rush over. Her eyes are wide open in the darkness, for a moment, as if she's truly about to die. She takes a deep breath and rolls to her side. But she's still breathing, thank God.

"You know what," I remark wickedly, "I know exactly how to get even with you." Even in her convalescence, she cocks her head curiously in the darkness. "No Western medicine, huh?"

I take out my phone and call 911.

6

——————

THEY'RE SO WEIRD

I'M RUNNING.

Whenever I'm stressed, I exercise. I got so fit last year that I had well-developed abs, calves, and quadriceps. Then summer came and Maddie and I gained weight. Now, in the second week of school, I'm exercising again. I spent three hours in the gym this morning and slept the afternoon away, and now I'm running all night.

Maddie never returned to our dorm. I think she went with Bryce to the hospital, but I shut the phone off. I suppose since I didn't go to the hospital, I should have at least been studying. But I wasn't in the mood to study either.

I'm winding down a hill, and I turn, nearly hugging a tree trunk. My shoes are sticking between rocks in a thick, muddy stream, and I'm worried that I might sprain my ankle. I can barely see the ground. There's only a crescent moon.

I make my way up an incline from a dirt path, and the trees disperse. I can finally see the ground beneath my feet in the clearing. Then I'm paralleling a river. Soon the forest surrounds me again. I'm still making my way up, and I hear a lovely waterfall (I wish I could see it) flowing to my right. I'm pretty sure that if I were to climb the rocks up the waterfall, I'd end up on a path that would lead me to Alondra's house. Her house is right by a tributary that flows into Hawthorne Lake.

I make it up to a hilltop and look out at a gorgeous view of the dark forest. Lights from campus are shining below me. There's no official name for this hillside view, but students are known to call it Hilltop Bluff.

I crouch down, breathing heavily, and lean my hands on my knees. I've been running for an hour. This is the third time I've been up here tonight. I must really be upset. It's a gorgeous view. There's not a cloud in the sky, and I can see the woods for miles. I can even make out the far-off mountains.

As dark as the night is, there's enough light in the clearing to see the field of wild grass at the summit. Last year, there were burnt logs in the center. This was where my coven did "ceremonies," sometimes the most wicked ones. Maddie was raped here. Well, Reardon and Alondra called it ceremonial sex, but I call it rape. They gave her mandrake, and the old fart had his way with her. It makes me nauseous thinking of it. I was never ceremonially raped and, thankfully, never witnessed it, but this is the other reason why I went berserko last semester and nearly killed all the witches in my coven. And that's why today I've weight-lifted, biked, run on the treadmill, and jogged over twelve miles. Do you understand? These are my friends. Now they're up to it again with hellfire. Why are these my friends?

There's a large boulder near the edge of a cliffside and, instead of returning to the trail, I take a small bottle of water from my belt and sit down on the rock, looking down at the lights from campus. I don't venture too far on the ledge, because the drop is treacherous and it looks like my weight could topple the whole thing down the sheer drop. I can make out the library in the woods. I suppose I should be studying there. That's the other thing my fucked-up friends did to me. I'm a straight-A student, and I nearly failed out of school the first semester of last year. I take the water to my lips and chug down three-quarters of the bottle.

And I sit here for the longest time. It's so peaceful—the beautiful wilderness under the stars. Stars shine brighter in Hawthorne. There's no smog to obscure the twinkling lights. I lean back on my hands and just stare up at the sky.

That's when I'm startled by the sound of something stepping on leaves in the bushes. I turn to my left and pull my phone from my pocket. I shine my cell phone flashlight in the direction of the noise. A deer's eyes shine white, reflecting the light. I don't like that. It reminds me of Enora's white eyes. Slowly, the animal approaches very close. I sit up and watch it as it timidly stands beside me near the cliffside. I shut off the light from my phone.

"Hey, girl," I say.

The deer walks right up to the rock, only a foot away from me. Then it turns its head and looks down at the view of the valley too. I reach out my palm and enjoy the touch of her hide. She seems to come closer under my palm. She closes her eyes as I pet her. Touching her fur not only soothes her, it comforts me too.

But then my hand jerks from the sudden vibration of my cell phone. The deer darts off, alarmed by the motion.

I had the phone off until now. My friends have been trying to reach me all day, and I've been ignoring their texts and voicemails. For some reason, I check it now and see my dad's number.

"Hey, Dad," I say.

I look at the side of the university furthest from Alondra's house. The oldest structure of Hawthorne, the Billington House, is barely visible among the trees.

"Hi, squirt." He sounds like he's in a good mood. "How are you doing?"

"Great," I lie.

"Hmm," he says. "You don't sound great."

I sigh. I lose myself for a moment looking down at the woods in the shadows directly below me. Then I wonder if my father would be happy to know that his daughter is running in the pitch dark of night, in the woods, by her lonesome. Probably not.

"I'm okay."

"What's wrong?"

"Why do you think something's wrong?"

"You know our deal, Katie. If things aren't going well, you're to come home. We'll make other arrangements at another school. Last year was too difficult. But...you were doing so well with Maddie this summer. I don't understand."

"What makes you think anything's the matter?" *Geesh, am I that obvious?*

"I got a call from Maddie. She's worried about you. She has no idea where you are."

"She's a bitch."

"Really?" He sounds shocked. No, she's not a bitch. But she is a witch. "You didn't think so this summer. You guys had such a great time."

"Well, she's a witch, I meant." I laugh. Dad doesn't understand. He doesn't know about my coven. He'd never understand. I barely do.

"Well, I'm glad to see you're all right."

"I'm okay."

"Katie...I know I'm not Mom. You know, when Mom passed last year I think you lost someone to confide in, but I can do the best I can."

"Don't worry about me, Daddy. I'm fine."

"Well, if there's anything going on, can you call me? Please? Can you let me know?"

"Sure, Dad."

There's silence. My deer is back. She dips her head down near my hand. I absentmindedly pet her hide again.

"There's one more thing, squirt. You know your brother is checking out colleges. I was hoping you could show Damie around campus. He really likes Hawthorne. I know it's more of a liberal arts school but, between you and me, I think he wants to do what you did. He looks up to you. And it's so close to home, you know." I'm letting him drawl on, but I'm squeezing my left hand really tight. I'm breathing fast and my chest is tightening. I'm about ready to scream. "So what do you think, Katie? Can he drive by the school and have you show him around with your friends?"

"No!" I shout. There's silence on the phone. I stop petting my deer and push myself off the boulder. "No! Don't let him come here. It's so weird here. Just have him go somewhere else. Somewhere where he can make normal friends."

"Kate...I...I thought you liked it there."

"I do. It's just...it's just a bad night, that's all."

"He really liked visiting you on campus last year. And he might have a few friends going there."

"Don't have him come here, okay? Please. Promise me. Just don't. Tell him... Let me talk to him. If he wants to be a doctor, he won't get anywhere with the science program here at Hawthorne. He won't get in. I'm a history major, for Christ's sake. This is not the place—"

"Okay," Dad says, disappointed. "Fine, Katie. Don't cuss. I don't want—"

"Please, Dad. I thought he was applying to Emory? And wasn't he thinking of Harvard? He's smart enough. Don't have him go here. Anywhere but here."

"Okay, okay. I shouldn't have mentioned it. It's just a nice town, Kate. He really likes how nice everyone is in the countryside."

"Have him go somewhere else."

"Sure. How about you tell him? I told you two I don't care where you go. If you can convince him, I'm fine with it. But I really don't understand. You two get along well, and Hawthorne has a fine track record for premed. It's a very good school... Well, you tell him. He wants to visit you."

"It's just weird here."

"I'm just glad you're okay. Turn your phone on so your friends and that boyfriend of yours don't freak out. Maddie said Bryce was worried too."

I walk to the end of the stone precipice beyond my boulder and look down at the shadows. If I were to jump, it'd be about a hundred-foot drop. Don't worry, I'm not stupid or suicidal. Never have been. But there's a weird rush when you're this high up. And I can feel the breeze brush pleasantly on my face. It's a cool wind. I shiver and grip my arms around my chest for a moment. It's getting cold. Running warmed me, but resting for too long makes me remember that winter is coming.

"How is Bryce, by the way?"

"Everything's fine, Dad." *Now please go. I can't talk anymore.*

"Okay, squirt. I love you."

"I love you too, Daddy. Bye."

My deer stands beside me and looks down into the abyss. I pet her soft fur. "All the witches are so weird here, aren't they, girl?"

$$7$$

THE VISITOR

HAWTHORNE HOSPITAL IS NOT REALLY A HOSPITAL. IT'S MORE OF a clinic. When people really have medical problems, they travel to Atlanta. This place is an ugly white two-story complex with concrete walls, a couple of bushes, and a silver metal overhang in front of the emergency room for their ambulance. The one thing that makes its ugliness bearable is the gorgeous surrounding trees of Hawthorne's forest.

After napping most of the day, I make my way through the electric glass doors into the lobby. It's Sunday. I should be studying, but the circle is fucking up my study habits once again. I know that sounds heartless, but that's the way I feel. Even Alondra seemed more interested in my magic jousting match with Enora than her fight with cancer.

The lobby just looks like a small clinic waiting room. A nice chubby nurse with curly brown hair takes my name and checks to see if I can come in as a visitor. She calls a room, probably Alondra's, and talks for a moment. She nods and asks me to sign a guest list. Then I'm off, down a really creepy dark hallway. There aren't many other people about, because the hospital closes in less than an hour.

As I get out of the elevator on the second floor and walk down another dismal, spooky hallway—even darker than the one downstairs—wouldn't you know it? My favorite witch, Enora, wearing a black lace shirt barely covering her boobs, is strolling down the hall, staring at the white-tiled floor. She looks snooty. She passes right by a doctor and doesn't even give him the time of day. I have every intention of ignoring her, but she looks up and says, "Hi, Cadence."

"Don't talk to me."

"She's in room 214," Enora says. I don't stop walking. "Cadence, I'm sorry."

"You're not."

"I am. Truly. I'm sorry for what happened."

I force my feet to move, avoiding her gaze. I hear a faint grunt and the bitch is gone.

When I get to room 214, the door is slightly ajar. I knock. The door opens and, of all people, Mira is standing there in her usual long black dress and thick black goth makeup. Her mascara is smeared. She closes the door behind her gently and shocks me by falling into my arms.

"She's so sick, Katie," Mira says with a cracked voice. "I don't know what to do. It's terrible."

"It'll be okay," I say. But I'm not so sure.

Mira pulls away gently and shakes her head. "I don't think so. She's inside. Bryce and Alondra are asleep."

I haven't answered any of Bryce's texts in over a day. I don't think he's going to be happy to see me right now.

"You guys have been here since—"

"Yes." Mira nods. "Bryce and I went with her in the ambulance. What about Maddie? Did she come back with you to your dorm?"

I shake my head. I haven't answered Maddie's texts either.

"Maybe she went home to Aunt Jane's again."

Then we're silent. I kind of feel like Mira should be sleeping; she looks so worn out.

"I just saw Enora down the hall," I say.

"She was here casting healing spells."

I bet.

"Together we tried herbs," Mira says solemnly. "I prepared feverfew with honey. She added sandalwood and basil for pain." Mira chuckles. It's the first time Mira has smiled, and for a moment she seems like her old sarcastic self. But then she gets morose again. "We had to sneak the stuff in under the nurses' noses. But Alondra's really suffering. I think the feverfew helped with the fever. Then we cast some spells. Enora chanted a healing incantation for hours. She's really powerful."

"I saw."

"She feels bad about what happened. Did she tell you?"

"Sort of."

Mira just shrugs. She looks so tired. Normally, she would really enjoy irritating me, but she's exhausted.

"Alondra's not very happy with you, Cadence," Mira says. "You know she didn't want this kind of help."

What? Doctors? Medicine? This is why they're all so weird.

"She was sick before we met for our Sabbath, you know," Mira adds. "She told us to still get together. She said..." Mira turns and wipes away tears with her black sleeve. "'If I die, Windstorm will lead the group and help me on my way to the Summerland.'" She looks at me and I have to turn away. I've never seen Mira so sad, and it depresses me. "She said that no matter what happens, the Sabbath must continue. So ..."

"She invited Enora?"

I'm recalling my fight with Alondra. Why was I such a bitch? I mean, what do I care if Alondra appoints Enora instead of me?

"She called Enora in the event that you refused to go," Mira explains. "She knew you didn't want to perform ceremonies anymore after what happened."

"I was mean to her," I say, looking down. "I told Alondra that she should never have had Enora come. Why do I even care?"

"Because you're our High Priestess," Mira says with a shrug. "I understand."

I don't. Mira accepts me. Why don't I? "Maybe you should be our leader, Mira."

Mira smiles her old sly smile for a second. "Not after what I saw you do to Panthera's spell." Then she touches the latch on the door. "Come in. Alondra might hate you, but she's been asking for you all day."

We walk in quietly. It's a single bedroom and the drapes are open, but it's dark because it's nighttime and the lights are out. Through the window I can see the forest. The shadow of my boyfriend is lying on a recliner next to Alondra. Poor thing. Alondra wakes up. She's wincing in pain again. She smiles when she sees me.

"Turn on the light," Alondra says.

I do. The room has drab and ugly whitewashed walls like the rest of the hospital. It smells like chicken. There's a plate half covered by plastic on a nightstand next to Alondra's bed. Alondra has clear tubes stuck in her arms. One is hooked into a plastic bag thingy on wheels. Her hair's a mess. That's not like her. Alondra's like Bryce. She always takes care of herself. And her face still has that sick glassy look she had two days ago in her bedroom.

"Hi, Cadence."

I choke up and almost cry. But I can't cry. I won't cry. I might be sad, but I'm also mad. It's this weird relationship I have with her, you know.

"Are you feeling better?" I force myself to say. It sounds formal.

"A little," she says, scooting up in bed. "No thanks to you."

"You were sick. I had to do it."

"I know," she says with a chuckle. I look back and notice Mira left us alone. "Don't worry about it."

"I wasn't going to just let you die."

"You should." Then she turns to the window. "It would be better."

There's a small wooden chair next to the window. I grab it, glancing outside again. The forest extends for miles.

I sit down near her bed. "It's stupid for you not to seek help. If you know the doctors can help you, avoiding them because you're a witch is dumb."

"Is it? Not as dumb as you not believing in us after all you've seen."

"I do believe."

She nods irritatingly slowly.

"I know I have to accept who I am," I say. "I'm a witch. But I'm also a girl who just wants to study history and graduate Hawthorne."

Alondra looks out the window again. She can see the trees, but they look like shadows now that the light's on in the room.

"Can you promise me something?" she asks almost in a whisper. Then she reaches out for me. I hold her hand. It makes me almost tear up again. I nod. "When I die, let me die out there." She points to the window. "Not inside a house or in a hospital. No buildings. Out there. In nature. One with Gaia and Selene. Can you grant me that one wish, Windstorm? You know how much I love the woods." I don't answer. So she says, still holding my hand, "When I was a girl, I grew up in wide fields on a farm. The fields went on for as far as the eye could see. That was nature too, and beautiful, but there's something about the trees that reminds me of magic. Not magic like a magician, but magic with a *k*. Magik. Mystery. The occult. That is what's out there, Cadence. I hope that you not only see through the eyes of your sisters but, one day, see through the eyes of Bacchus. Or, as the Norse call him, Vidar. I've spent my whole life studying his mysteries. Funny how women, witches, are most in tune with him." She turns and looks at my eyes as if to see if I'm listening to her, and I have this strange sense that she's teaching me again. "Vidar, the god of the woods, I mean."

I nod. She's still holding my hand. She turns back to the window. "Turn the lights off again. I want to see the trees better... Will you see to it that I pass away in the forest?"

"Only if you allow the doctors to treat your cancer."

She stares at me in amazement. Then she chuckles and shakes her head. "You are the stubbornest witch I've ever known."

"Do we have a deal?" I ask. "I'll be a bona fide witch if you start seeing a doctor."

"You already are a bona fide witch. Especially after the magic I witnessed with Panthera."

"Why didn't you take the antibiotics the doctor told you to?"

She takes a deep breath and lets go of my hand. She says nothing.

"You are feeling better," I say.

She nods.

And I'm glad. You see, I care about her. I might have been stubborn and childish and refused to go with my friends in the ambulance—that was mean—but I had just fought with Enora. I wasn't in a normal state of mind. And I know I didn't visit her for two days. Okay, I guess I was a bitch. But I like Alondra. I know, it's really weird, but I do. And that's why I couldn't go with her to the hospital. Do you understand?

I take her hand again.

Bryce is snoring in the recliner. God, he must really be tired. Alondra looks at him too.

"I don't like Enora," I say out of the blue. I have to say it. I've been wanting to say it since Alondra was sick in her bedroom.

"Panthera is a fire element, Windstorm. She's competitive, brash, excitable, and quick-tempered. Like you. Also, like you, she is a very powerful witch. And stubborn. You two are actually a lot alike." I shake my head, and there's a hint of a smile from her. "But, unlike you, she's not grounded. She's unstable because she's afraid. You are stronger because you are afraid. I know this doesn't sound like it makes sense, but it's true. Your fear strengthens you. You're careful because of your fear. Enora is conceited. That weakens her. But both of you are natural witches. Your magic comes from within. Your atman is strong. If you learned casting like Mira, if you both did, you would be greater than any of us."

"I don't trust her."

"I trust her." She lets go of my hand again. "I think you and she will turn around. Just like you and Mira. You two seem like friends now."

"Enora's evil."

"I told you last year that there is no such thing as good and evil. The world is not a simple dichotomy of black and white. That is a puerile view from the kind of people who judge others by their black or white skin. Only fools see the world in that way. Evil is really an illusion."

"I disagree. I think there is such a thing as evil."

"So you've told me. Your disagreements have made you an apt pupil... And an annoying disciple." But she smiles.

"Enora opened a hellish world in our firepit. It was terrifying."

"She was testing you, Cadence."

"What if she couldn't close it?"

"She could close it," Alondra says, completely sure of herself. "And if not, you would." She looks out the window again. "And if not, I would... Please, please, Cadence, turn the light off again for me. I so wish to look outside at the lovely trees."

It's then that the doctor walks in. He's a thin, handsome man, clean-shaven, with dark-brown hair—almost in a crew cut —graying on the sides. He's wearing an open white lab coat with a button-down shirt and jeans underneath. He's got a big smile. I don't know what he's so happy about.

"How's my favorite patient?" he asks and sits by the bedside.

"I feel like shit."

I don't like it when Alondra cusses. She was my professor. It always feels wrong. Usually she's so prim and proper. She's an enigma. There's no explaining her mystery. Like our relationship. It's...

"Well," the doctor says, "your fevers have stopped, Ms. Johansen. And you're able to use the restroom again." He leans down and checks a tube beside the bed. It's full of yellow fluid that looks like pee. Gross. Then he stands up and examines the plastic bags full of fluids. He checks them and measures them with a pen in his hand. "You're doing better."

"I'm feeling a little better."

"What's wrong with her?" I ask.

"Urosepsis," he says. "A little bit longer and we would have shipped her to the ICU. Or worse. She was so sick she wasn't able to use the bathroom."

"Is it the cancer?"

"Are you her relative?" he asks.

"As good as one," Alondra says.

"How bad is it?" I ask.

"Cadence," Alondra snaps.

"She hasn't told you?" the doctor says, furrowing his brow. Then he looks at Alondra as if waiting for permission.

"Is it treatable?" I persist. This is my chance to finally get to the bottom of her illness. The doctor probably thinks I'm crazy, but I'll never get it out of her any other way.

"If she's willing to get surgery. But—"

"No surgery!" Alondra snaps. Then she looks right into my eyes and says sternly, *"No surgery... Never, Cadence."*

Geesh.

The doctor takes out a pad and starts humming. He's so comfortable even though Alondra's dying that it's irritating.

"Will she stay another night?" asks another voice. It's Bryce. I think the doctor was finally loud enough to wake him.

"I think so. One more night and then she can go home. She'll have to take antibiotics after discharge. We have some running through the IV, but I'd like her to take the pills at home."

"She will," I say.

Alondra shakes her head at me.

"She'll take them if she can take them out in the woods," I add.

Alondra can't help but laugh at that. Bryce gives us a funny look, not getting it.

The doctor leaves.

I walk over to Bryce, reach down, and give him a hug. He hugs me, but it's like hugging a board. He's really mad. Why wouldn't he be? I haven't answered his texts.

"You could have at least answered your phone, Cadence," Bryce says.

"Sorry."

"I'm happy to see you together," Alondra says. "You make a good couple."

She's got that famous grin again and, for a second, it looks like the old Alondra.

"Why don't you go home with Cadence, Bryce? You need to rest in bed, not in a hospital chair."

Bryce stretches out his arms. Then he snarls at me. "Maddie's super mad at you too, Cadence. She kept calling me asking what your problem was."

"Where'd Maddie go?" I ask.

"She said she'd probably head to Aunt Jane's for the weekend."

"The light, Cadence," Alondra reminds me. "Please turn it off."

I get up and turn off the light. Only a crack of light from the hallway leaks in. But I figure our eyes will get accustomed. I see Alondra staring out the window again.

Bryce jumps up and grabs a pitcher. "You want some water?"

"No thanks, Bryce," she says with a chuckle. "Cadence, he's quite a man. He's been at my side every sleeping and waking hour."

The door opens wider, letting in more light from the hallway. I'm thinking it's Mira coming back, or the doctor, but it isn't. Another man walks through the door.

I jump back toward the window in shock. He's thin and bald, with a goatee and a black cape draped over a red-and-black button-down and slacks. Professor William Reardon. Alondra's estranged husband.

"What are you doing here?" asks Alondra.

"Go away, she's sick," I snap. But Alondra puts her hand up.

"I came to see my wife," Reardon says. "You don't mind, do you, Windstorm?" Then he looks at Bryce. "Disciple," he says with a nod.

"I thought you expelled him," I say.

"I did. I haven't seen him since, Cadence. I swear."

"She expelled me from the coven, not from our marriage, Ms. Cadence Hawthorne. And now, I would ask that you two leave. I'm taking her home." Reardon looks around with disgust. "As if anything in these plastic walls can help our beloved Falconsong."

"Why are you wearing that stupid outfit?" I say. His cape makes him look like a magician. It's so dumb and weird.

"Alondra," he says, ignoring me. "Let's go. This isn't a place for us." He looks around the room again. "Why come here? Why not stay home? Why would you ever agree to commit such a sacrilege?"

"I'm on medicine."

"I'll give you medicine. *Our* medicine." He sits down by her bedside, like the doctor just did, and I'm completely grossed out. I scowl at him again.

"I was sick, Bill," she says. Then she turns her head. She looks as disgusted to see him as I am.

"Was this her doing?" He points at me. I can swear I almost hear a snarl.

"Cadence did what she had to do," Bryce says.

"You agreed to her being taken by an ambulance, disciple?" he asks Bryce. "After everything I've taught you?"

"Stop calling him that!" I snap.

I hate him. He thinks I destroyed his comfortable little fuck-cult and stole his wife. It's times like this that I think I should have burnt him alive—sorry. It's just that he infuriates me. He gets up and walks over to me, just a foot away from my face, staring right into my eyes.

"Back off," I warn.

"Bill, stop," Alondra says weakly. "Both of you. Please."

"Get away from her," Bryce says, jumping up.

"Just leave, Bill," says Alondra, exhausted. "I didn't ask for you to be here. Leave the kids alone."

"*Kids?*" he says to her. "Maybe that's it. What you and I were never—"

"Bill!" she snaps. I'm surprised she has the energy. "That's enough!"

"You will pay for what you did," he says to me. Then he looks at Alondra. "I wasn't prepared for her inferno. I am now. Any magic she plans to throw at me and you, I can assure you, I'm prepared for."

"I never prepared for anything," I say. "I didn't need to. I just wanted you to drop dead for being such a perverted sick snake!"

"A snake, am I?"

That's when Mira walks in. She must have heard the yelling. Mira's in as much shock as I am at the visitor. She hates him too.

"What's he doing here?" asks Mira.

"Sister," he says, cocking his head back.

"I'm not your sister," Mira says.

"Get out," I yell. "Alondra doesn't want to go home. She needs to get well first."

"Are you going to stay in a hospital?" Reardon asks Alondra. "Are you serious? Let them poison you?"

"Bill, I..." Alondra's eyes close. It's too much for her.

"Girls, get out," Reardon says. He sits back down at Alondra's bedside and takes her hand. I want to throw up. "Leave my wife and me alone. Whatever fights we have, let's put it aside... for her. But ask her herself. She doesn't want to stay in a hospital. Do you?"

Alondra nods. Then she shakes her head. Weakly, she turns and looks out the window for a moment, then looks at me.

"Cadence," Alondra says, forcing her eyes open to look at me. I'm still looking at the satanic devil's hand clutching hers. I'm trying my best not to light it on fire. "It's all right. Thank you for your care. But this is between Bill and me."

I can't believe it. She's weak and sick, but she wants me to leave her with her nasty, perverted husband. This is why I can never like her. We have to endlessly fight, hating and loving each other.

"Let's go," Bryce says, touching my shoulder. I shrug him off. Bryce touches my back, trying again. "Let's go, Cadence."

"This is what you want?" I ask Alondra. "Are you sure? You need to get well."

"It's all right," Alondra says. "Now leave, please."

"Leave us," Reardon says, still holding Alondra's hand.

Alondra nods with her eyes closed. She says feebly, "Thank you, Cadence."

~

Why did we leave him with her!" I shout at Bryce after the elevator doors close. We're alone on our way down to the first floor. Mira's still back there in Alondra's room. As much as Mira drives me crazy, I get comfort in that. I know Mira always has Alondra's best interests in mind, and she'll fight fiercely for her. And she hates Bill Reardon more than I do.

Bryce doesn't answer. He scowls but looks down.

I'm so mad I grip my hands tightly. When the lights in the elevator flicker, Bryce looks at me in shock, because he knows I'm doing the flickering.

"Why didn't you answer your phone last night?" he snaps. "Alondra needed you."

"I didn't—"

"I needed you."

"I ..."

"You what, Kate? Why would you do that? What's gotten into you?"

We're silent as we leave the elevator and walk down the hallway. We're walking fast because we're both pissed. I don't think we've ever been this mad at each other before. But I'm still thinking of Alondra and that beast. And his hand on her. How dare he come back for her.

We walk outside through the automatic glass doors. Outside it's really dark and cold. There aren't any lights beyond the streetlights in the parking lot. The wilderness is pitch black.

Being outside is Bryce's excuse to unleash full throttle on me. "Leave me a note!" he snaps, a foot from my face. "Or voice-mail. Something. Don't just walk away and not tell me where you are. Don't abandon me like that. I can't...I can't trust someone if they just close off and run away."

"It wasn't because of you, Bryce. It was—"

"What? You're always running. You run from our group. You run when Alondra's sick."

"I got her to the hospital."

"I know," Bryce says, finally simmering down. He runs his hand through his short hair. "But then you left."

"I'm sorry."

Bryce has his hands on his hips. He's staring at the hospital parking lot, shaking his head. "It's not enough. I can't trust you when I can't get a hold of you."

"I couldn't get a hold of you when you weren't at the eclipse." *Yeah. So there!*

"For the hundredth time, Cadence," he says with a sigh, "I was there to help Alondra. And I did answer your texts. But...I didn't tell you I was in town because I wanted you to go to the ceremony with the circle. Tell me, honestly, if you knew I was going to miss the eclipse and go to Atlanta, wouldn't you have gone with me?"

I don't want to fight. Bryce looks exhausted. I want to take him in my arms, but I can't. Now I've got him worked up.

"I'm sorry I didn't answer your texts," I say. "But it wasn't because of you."

Bryce shakes his head again. "I'm not so sure. I'm part of our coven. You turned your back on us. And so...you turned your back on me."

"I don't know what else to say. I'm sorry."

He shakes his head.

I force as wide a smile as I can muster and open my arms wide. "Still friends?" He hugs me, but not close.

I look back at the hospital. I'm still thinking of Alondra with that creep. "We should go back and get him away from her."

"He's her husband. It's up to her."

Outside surrounding the light of the hospital entrance is the dark forest. But the darkness isn't scary. It's inviting. I'm thinking of what Alondra said, and I'm enjoying the shadows of the trees too. I love the trees. And I like the darkness, even on a clear, moonless night like this one. I yearn to smell the leaves and touch the soil. I understand Alondra's wishes. I know that out there in the wilderness is peace. Gaia. The earth mother that we worship. And the moon and the stars. When I die, I want to die out there too.

"Just don't do it again, okay?" asks Bryce.

I nod, looking at the trees.

"Why didn't you answer me?" he asks.

"I just want to have a normal year, Bryce," I say with a shrug. And I look in his eyes. He runs his hand through his hair again, all flustered. I flash a slight grin.

"Oh, Cadence. What's *normal*?"

"No drugs, nakedness, and magic." He laughs, and I laugh in spite of myself. "Just a junior year in college. I just want to be a normal student."

"Alondra needed you." He shakes his head. I look outside at the shadowed trees again. "I needed you."

"Okay, Bryce," I say, turning back. "I'm sorry. I said I was sorry. You're right, I should have answered my phone. Okay? I'm sorry."

"You're going to have to make a choice. You have to accept who and what you are and help your friends. I saw what you just did to the lights in the elevator. You have more magic in your fingertip than Mira has after three weeks of ritual. I...I know what happened with Enora upsets you." That's an understatement. "It upset me too. I get it. But it's done. You stopped it. You have to help us and be the leader you are... Ceremonies again. Sabbaths. All of it. You have to accept this and lead us as our leader. As our witch."

I hang my head and nod like an admonished child.

"It's okay." Bryce raises my chin. "Let's go home, babe. I'll drive you back."

"No," I say. "I want to walk."

That's how I got to the hospital. I followed the sidewalks to a dirt path through the forest. It's about a mile walk from campus. Only about fifteen minutes. Of course now it's the middle of the night, so Bryce is squinting at me like I'm insane.

"I need to walk," I repeat.

"Katie, it's pitch black outside. Don't be ridiculous. I'll take you home."

"No, I need to walk. I'll meet you back at your apartment. It's not that far."

"You want to walk? Alone? In the dark? Are you sure?"

I'm absolutely sure. "I'll be fine."

He looks like he's about to object, but he nods while running his hand through his hair. He's completely exhausted, and I think he doesn't have the energy to put up a fight.

"Katie, I love you, but don't get mad when I tell you this."

"What?"

"You want a normal year but...you're not normal."

I laugh. "I'll see you back home, lover," I say and I kiss his cheek. "Go get some sleep."

8

———

WANDERING

MAYBE BRYCE IS RIGHT ABOUT THE DARK NIGHT. I DON'T REALIZE how bad it really is until I make my way deep into the forest. Then I lose the trail pretty fast. But the walk is such a joy to me. I can't see the ground, so I have to grope my way through the trunks and branches, but I know that if I keep walking in the direction I'm heading, I'll land in Hawthorne U. I think.

Crickets are everywhere. They're loud and soothing. I love their sounds.

I hear something in a bush to my right, and it sounds big. I'm guessing it's a deer. I don't really care. I like the sound of her, whatever she is.

The trees open into a large field of thick wild grass. I don't think I've ever been in this field. The grass is tall, up to my ankles, and muddy. For a moment, I realize I'm muddying up my white tennis shoes. That's okay, I don't really have a choice. I even walk through cold, shallow water. I can't see a thing. But I cup my hand and reach down into the water. I bring the water to my mouth and taste it. It's metallic and chalky. Cold. It's refreshing.

As I find myself under another canopy of trees, I realize that

I am completely lost. There are no trails, only thousands of trees with thin, leafy branches hovering over me. But I move forward. It seems to only get darker. I think for a moment that perhaps I should reach into my pants pocket for my cell phone for a flashlight, but I decide against it. I'd rather just walk in the shade under Nyx—the arms of the night god. Alondra was so right. There is so much peace in the woods. I wonder if this is the direction she was looking from her window.

I take a deep breath. The fresh air is refreshing too.

In a different state of mind, I might be afraid. But I'm not afraid. I feel a rush of energy at the pit of my chest under the arms of the leafy branches. Such joy. Such blissful joy. I can't explain it. I am so happy to be among the trees, alone in the forest. I wish to never leave. My loneliness doesn't bother me, for I am not alone. I am one with the woods.

A bird flutters by me. Then another. A whole school of birds fly by me, touching my back and shoulders. That's okay. I can sense that they want me to leave because they have a nest nearby, but when I don't, one lands on my arm. It's a large, heavy black bird. A raven. I extend my arm and pet the bird slowly, marveling at the softness of its feathers. It turns its head. Its eyes flash white. Then it closes its eyes as I continue to stroke its back, as if I am soothing it.

"Amica," I say. Amica is her name. I don't know why, but I know her name.

The bird opens its white eyes and nods. "*Et nos unum sumus.*" The words are not uttered by the raven, but felt by me.

"Atman," I say. *Amen.* "Come with me, Amica," I say with a giggle.

And I walk, holding a large black bird on my outstretched arm.

The brush becomes thicker and more difficult to cross. Then I approach a slope leading down. It becomes treacherous, getting so steep that I cannot see the bottom. For all I know it's a sheer drop. All I can see are twigs and branches falling into nothingness below me. Above are leaves underneath a gorgeous starry sky.

I smell smoke. And a burning light appears far off in the distance. I turn away from the precipice and look to my left, where the light is coming from. It's a bright red flickering light, like fire. And it's growing. Is the forest burning?

It comes closer. Soon the red light is only a few feet away. Between three trees, it has become a burning pyre—I don't know who started it, but it's raging. It rises like Panthera's fire. Yes, exactly like that. And I smell sulfur. But this time I am not afraid. I look down at Amica and laugh. I think it's really funny. The raven doesn't seem to have any fear either. I pet her.

"To the door and away, turn my back from light, and into the night sky," I say, as if reading lines from a book. "Past flames that light the forest and trees, make sacred to my knees. Forgive and forget. As Gaia and I are one."

I kneel before the precipice and gently put my bird on the ground beside me. Then I pull my coat and T-shirt off my body. And my bra. I remove my dirty shoes. Then I pull down my pants and underwear. I stand naked before the precipice beneath me and stretch out my arms as wide as I can in the darkness.

As Gaia and I are one.

I look down at my bird. "Are you afraid, Amica?"

"You shall be my sacrifice." The words are not from my bird. I quickly turn and recognize it to be Reardon's voice. My eyes narrow. I search around me, ready to strike the man down in fury. I remember my anger in the hospital.

The fire and smoke have spread in the forest, forcing me to walk down the sheer precipice. Where else can I go? I understand that the villain is pulling me to meet him down there, in the darkness. Good. I shall greet him.

I grope my way down the hill. My feet guide me down the

incline. I slide a few times, slipping along and slowing any fall with my hands, as I maneuver around twigs and undergrowth. Never would I normally descend such a dangerous cliff, but I am in a trance and at peace with Gaia, so I don't mind. My new friend, Amica, flutters close to me as I make my way down.

When I've descended twenty feet or so, I crouch on my knees and catch my breath for a moment. Amica lands on the ground and I pet her. Then I touch the soil and bring the dirt to my nose. I touch it with my tongue, enjoying the earthen fragrance.

I feel burning. And I see red smoke surrounding me. The flames have spread down the hillside. They warm me, but they appear to be transparent, like an illusion.

"You shall be my sacrifice," repeats Reardon.

"Fuck you, goddamn liar," I whisper. "I belong to no man. I am one with Nyx. No devil. How dare you bewitch me. In darkness, I am one with the inner shadows. Thanatos, Erebus." Then I shout out, "Wait! I'm coming, lover. Your sacrifice awaits to bring you pleasures."

"Come closer, Windstorm," says the air. The air sounds hungry.

"I'm coming!" I shout with laughter as I continue down the slope in darkness. Then I whisper ruefully, "I have the ground below, and Astraeus above that shall guide us, Amica. Gather around our poisons so that we may rub sumac leaves over his loins, stab him in the chest, or gouge out his eyes with the splinters of tree branches."

Clouds thicken—a red fog blocks the light. I can see nothing. My feet feel my way down to the bottom, stepping over bushes and through gaps between sticks and stones. Some branches cut the skin on my feet. I bleed. But I feel no pain. I will myself to feel no pain. I am spurred on by a feverish desire to hurt this man.

The incline ends and Amica returns to my shoulder. I reach

down and touch a part of my leg that stings. It's sticky. Blood. I take the stickiness to my mouth and lick the saltiness with my tongue.

It is then that I see my foe. The darkness fades between two nearby trees to reveal the devil himself as he cometh clearly before me in the red mist. It is Bill Reardon, but he appears stronger, younger, and more virile than he did at the hospital. His goatee is perfectly manicured. His face is clean. He stands up straight, wearing his cape and red-and-black magician outfit, but everything is pressed and neat. He almost looks desirable, if I didn't know who he is and what a prick he is. He is leaning on a cane, waiting for me between the trees.

"Make love to me, Cadence Hawthorne, great-great-great-ancestor of Escoba and Maverick Hawthorne. Make love so I can impart my semen and together we can feel the power of your lineage."

I come close to Reardon and I embrace him. Amica darts off my hand and hits his face, making Reardon twist back for a second. I laugh and I place my lips on his. I cannot stop my laughter as our lips touch. I'm practically biting him, chewing on his lips. He breathes heavily. I rub my breasts against his body and watch as his wicked eyes stare down in rapture at my naked chest. He clutches me tighter, grabbing the crack of my ass. He's strong; his shoulders are as broad and his chest is as fit as Bryce's. This is not the aged Reardon but a conjured-up younger version of himself.

I place a finger on his lips and say quietly, "You call on family? I invoke them. I ask for Maverick and Escoba to appear by my side." I walk ten paces back from him and smile. Precisely ten. Ten paces are what is required for the spell. I don't know how I know that; I just do. He stares at my naked body ravenously, and I raise my hands high and move my fingers about through the fog as if touching the stars above. As if I'm dancing to Bacchus. "I ask that they devour you," I say with a giggle. "I, Windstorm, take you down into the shadows you so covet." And I drop my hands before him.

Two ghosts appear. Maverick, a boy, in his suspenders, and the voodoo witch Escoba, holding his hand. I look down and a snake brushes against my leg. Then another. For a flash, I lose my confidence and am afraid. Like the pile of snakes above the pyre, they swarm by my legs. It's as if they are a part of me, but they disgust me. For a moment, I fear that if I'm not careful, I could be consumed by them. Reardon stares with wild eyes at the slithering black serpents covering my feet.

"If you ever try even a taste of my skin again, these serpents shall devour you," I say, raising my arms again. "*Ishtar, Hecate, Amare.* I cast this spell, make it so, now and forevermore. I shield me from you. And I warn you—if you try to touch my skin with magic ever again, you shall feel poison from my fangs and choking from my skin that will draw you down to hell."

Amica falls on him like a stone. She pecks and claws wildly at his face. Then I drop my arms once more, as if officiating a race, and Maverick charges him from behind me. Maverick is a child in suspenders, a black boy, my ancestor, who lived two hundred years ago. His spirit transforms into a wraith with fangs that runs on all fours and jumps on him like a lion. And beside him is his mother, Escoba, the famous voodoo witch of New Orleans. She too transforms into an animal-like creature and leaps on him. They pull him to the ground. Reardon squints at me and cries out in rage. I raise and drop my arms again, to the darkness of night, and the serpents covering my feet fly at him and writhe all over his body, feasting upon him. He cries out in terror as I laugh joyously, cackling like the witch that I am.

In the recesses of my mind, I understand now. My wandering is my protection, and all this is a spell. I have been in a trance. I am unsure if it is from Alondra or myself, but the wandering was a shield protecting me against this demon. So was Amica.

Amica still sits perched on my shoulder, watching the old man being devoured by my spirits and snakes. I feel like it pleases her.

He intended to take me down, lie with me, or poison and kill me, but I resisted with my own magic and reversed his spell. Even the precipice could have meant the end of me if I hadn't used magic of my own. Without my trance, I could have rolled and plummeted down the cliff to my death. But his spell has backfired, and now I am shielded from him forever.

I turn and leave. But Amica tugs at me with her claws to go back.

"Finish him," my bird says. She doesn't talk. I *feel* her words. "Finish him."

I shake my head.

"Finish him, now. This is our chance. He will hurt you. Hurt him. Do it now!"

I laugh and pet my bird, shaking my head, and walk away from the man's screams. "This is enough."

But the bird doesn't stop tugging at me.

Somehow, I know if I return I will have no more control over myself. Indeed, I might kill him. My bird's claws begin to irk me, so I push Amica off my arm. The bird responds angrily by fluttering her wings at my neck and face and then flying off.

The fog lifts. I am still surrounded by trees, but I can see the forest more clearly now, even though it is dark. Reardon is gone. So is my bird. All that's left is the shadows and the forest. But as I gaze down, I realize that I am naked. I cover myself with my arms and feel ashamed. I search around me and realize that I don't even know where I left my clothes. I feel a rush of terror in the center of my chest. I am so confused.

∼

When I knock on Bryce's door, I'm not sure what time it is. Not only have I lost my clothes, but I've lost my phone. When he opens the door to his apartment, I fall into his arms.

"He tried to kill me!" I say, crying in his arms.

"My God, Cadence, what happened?" Bryce pulls me quickly inside and shoves the door closed. The lights are dim in his apartment. I figure he was sleeping. "I've been calling you for hours! I knew I should have taken you home. You didn't answer me again. What happened?"

I'm crying.

He holds me. "What happened, baby?"

"Reardon tried to kill me. With his magic."

"Come inside. Where are your clothes? And..." He looks down at the floor. I'm tracking in blood. "God, Cadence, you're hurt."

He lets go of me and runs over to the kitchen, grabbing some paper towels. He wets them and pulls me over to his sofa. Then he kneels down and carefully washes my feet. He is so gentle. It's okay if he hurts me. The fact that he cares for me is so sweet. My heart is racing. My hands are jittery. I am so charged. So alive. It's like I'm on some kind of drug. I only wish I were still out among the trees. And I have lost my beloved new companion. My bird. Where is she? My new friend, Amica. Where did she go? She tried to protect me too.

After a few more trips to the kitchen, he's done washing my feet and legs. My cuts aren't deep, and he's managed to wash off all the blood. But he's still on his knees when he looks up at me.

I touch his hand and bring it to my upper leg. Slowly, I guide his hand over my skin and press it into my thigh. He looks at me funny. I feel so aroused. I bring his hand up higher. He jerks his hand back, but I catch it and press his fingers in and around my pussy. He stares into my eyes. I close them, enjoying his touch, pressing his hand up and down along my privates.

"Cadence, we should—"

I lift his finger to my lips and suck it. Then I move to another finger and slowly lick my tongue along that digit. Then another. I suck, gripping fingers between my lips with my eyes closed. When I open them and look down, Bryce looks bewildered.

My sex drive is so overwhelming. I don't feel like I can control it. It's the spell. It must be. I want Bryce so badly. His taste. His smell. His touch. I didn't want Reardon. I wanted to kill him. I wanted to lure him, even have sex with him, only if it meant I could destroy him. Bryce is different. But even with Bryce, I hold an irresistible desire to devour him.

I lean back against the couch cushion, take a deep breath, and guide his hand between my legs again, rubbing me once more. Slowly and carefully, I guide his fingers. He enters me with one of the fingers I was sucking. I moan, and he does too. I look down again. He gazes into my eyes, looking hungry. I groan and, for a moment, he closes his eyes in pleasure. But it's almost as if he's in a trance too. I don't like that. I want love, not magic. And so I snatch his hand from between my legs.

Holding his hand, as if I caught him stealing a cookie from a cookie jar, I shake it and ask earnestly, "Do you love me?" I search his eyes. He's taken aback and he laughs, looking at me like I'm crazy.

Well, I did just wander alone in the forest naked. Maybe I am crazy?

"Do you?" I persist.

"Yes," he says with an amused smile. "I love you, Cadence. I love you."

He's not wearing a shirt. He usually sleeps in just underwear during this time of year. I look at his rippled hard chest under the shadows, and I reach down and massage it. Then I massage his stomach and run a hand along his strong arms. He's so hot. I kneel down and violently yank down his underwear and shorts, staring at his long, erect penis. When I lift him up, he doesn't resist me, and I help lay him down on the couch. I lie on top of him.

"Wait. Cadence, I need to get something."

I kiss him on the lips ravenously. I don't want to let him go. It's like I want to eat him like an animal. I want him raw and inside me *now*.

He has to literally throw me off the couch. I land on the carpet and laugh. He's so nice, so Bryce, that he pauses while running to the bathroom and asks if I'm all right. I laugh again. It's not long before he returns. He lies on top of me, stroking the hair along my forehead, and I love his weight on me.

"Oh, Cadence, I think you are under a spell." He cocks his head, unsure.

"So," I say. "Fuck me, Bryce. Do it to me now." And I pull him close to me.

He shakes his head, but before he can object further, he's already inside. I'm pumping my pelvis slowly up and down and moaning. I love how he caresses me. He rubs my breasts and the sides of my hips. He moans too. I can just make out his face, and he looks right into my eyes again. We touch lips, and I taste him with my tongue as I continue to lift into him. But then he tries to pull away. I don't let him. He's stuck, tight in my grasp. I don't want him to ever let me go again.

"Cadence, I don't think we should," he repeats hesitantly. "I think you're under some kind of spell."

I answer by jerking up against him even harder. It feels so good. I feel his warm breath against my cheek. His breath near my ear. He finally gives in and presses up and down. I encourage him by moaning even more.

He's so deep now. It feels so good. It's like the forest. It's like we're a part of Gaia. We are one. *Et nos unum sumus.* In the wilderness, I derived comfort and safety from the trees. Now I find comfort in my lover's arms.

He stops and falls to his side on the couch, but I'm still in his grasp with him inside me. He's breathing heavily.

"Don't you love me?" I ask again.

"Yes," he says, furrowing his brow. "More than you can imagine. But this is wrong. You're under a spell."

Yet I hear hesitation in his voice. It makes me laugh—not to be mean, but because I know he's saying this more to convince himself than me. I feel like there's no stopping us anymore.

"I *am* under a spell, Bryce... My spell. Don't worry. Take me. Make... love to me. Do it now."

He gently rubs my cheek. I answer by pressing my whole body hard against him. I moan in pleasure as I thrust while we're facing each other. He touches my lips and I suck his fingers again, one after the other, as I continue to rock back and forth. Then he pushes into me, hard and fast, and I cry out in pleasure.

He's all in now, doing all the thrusting. He's moving faster and faster and I'm loving every push, every touch. Our love-making has become a spell of its own. And as I look at his face, he is in too much ecstasy to object to anything anymore. He digs deeper in me, loving me.

"Yes, I am your succubus," I say, breathless. "You...are under my spell, Bryce... But...it's okay. Because you love me. And I love you. I love you so fucking much."

"Oh, Cadence. I do love you. I do."

9

———————

MADDIE AND THE DORM ROOM

"Where were you!" Maddie's pissed. I mean really pissed. She's clenching her fists and scowling, practically growling at me, by the door of our dorm room.

It's morning and time to get ready for school, but I've been at Bryce's all night. Luckily, I had a change of clothes in his room. It's not the first time I've stayed with my lover. It is the first time I came to his place naked, though.

"What?" I ask sleepily. That was the last thing I should have said.

"What do you mean, *what*? I was calling you all weekend."

"I was at Bryce's."

"Then why didn't you answer my call!"

I think the whole dormitory can hear her screaming. And it's not like Maddie. She's a carefree girl. She's really that mad.

"Sorry," I say with the cutest guilty expression I can muster. "Anyway, I thought you were at your house."

"It's Monday morning. I'm back because of, you know, *school*? We're in school, Cadence." Maddie shakes her head and sinks into my bottom bunk, burying her head in her hands. "I can't believe you just left her like that." I sit beside her and put my hand on her back. She looks up at me. "You left Alondra. I know you sent for help, but then you just vanished. I figured at least I'd catch up to you later that night."

"I know. I didn't call you and I forgot—"

"About me. You forgot about me. When I got back, I at least thought you'd be back in the dorm, Kate. When I called Mira and she said you weren't at the hospital or with Bryce, I thought you'd been kidnapped or something. So I called the police. I even filed a fucking police report. They searched all over campus for you. I should have known better. You don't like answering your phone anymore, apparently."

"I'm sorry," I say, rubbing her back. "I'm so sorry."

She starts crying. "I thought something terrible happened, like you were kidnapped or something."

"I kinda was."

"Huh?" That stops her tears and she looks up. "What?"

"I was under a spell. I had another wandering. But it was really weird. It was with Reardon. He cast a pervert spell on me."

But was it Reardon? As I relate the story to Maddie, I wonder. The problem with our wanderings is they're so mixed up with fantasy that some of it isn't real. Some of it is an illusion. She softens and I'm amused that talking about a witch's trance is enough to defuse her anger and make her calm down and not hate me so much. Only in Hawthorne.

"That fucker would cast a spell on you for sure, Kate. He blames you for everything."

"Then I lost my phone," I say, looking away, "and walked through the forest naked, ending up at Bryce's house."

"Wow, Katie. You walked all the way across campus, to his place, without clothes?" She's looking at me like I'm nuts now. I'm not sure that's much better than her being pissed.

"Sorry," I say again with a shrug and lean into her. "I'm so sorry I didn't call or text you, Maddie. I felt so bad after what Enora did. I just needed time to myself."

"You're really screwed up." She pushes me away, staring with wide-open eyes. I think she really believes I've lost my mind. "Next time, just text me. Tell me you're okay, at least, and I won't worry."

"Okay."

"We have to go."

We do? Where?

She jumps up and grabs a book from our desk. It's her art history textbook. Then she grabs her phone and starts texting.

She's smiling, back to her bubbly self. How does she do that? She's the only one I know that can be furious and then just let everything go as if nothing ever happened—the only one except her mom, Aunt Jane.

"The evil that Mira was talking about is Reardon," I say.

She nods absentmindedly as she types on her phone.

"He tried to touch me last night using his spell."

That gets her attention. "What a fucking creep," Maddie says.

I'm still sitting on my mattress. I just nod. Then I yawn. I came to Bryce's pretty late—it was probably three in the morning—and I didn't get much sleep.

"I'm just glad you're okay," Maddie says.

"Who are you texting?"

"Mira. She wanted to know you're safe."

Maddie shoves the book under her arm and grabs my copy, stuffing it in my black backpack for me. She doesn't have a backpack. She lost it. You know, she's the irresponsible one out of the two of us. At least she used to be.

"Time for lecture, okay, bitch?" Maddie asks with a rueful smile, handing me the backpack. God, it's already ten?

"Friends?" I ask, still sitting on my bed.

She rolls her eyes. "I'm mad because you didn't answer your phone, Katie. Not because I don't love you."

10

ART CLASS

MADDIE AND I ARRIVE AT OUR ART HISTORY LECTURE. I'M IN THE front row in order to sit near Bryce. There aren't any seats left, so Maddie sits directly behind us. Bryce is leaning over the stage in front of us, rummaging through papers in his big brown leather bag, while the professor, Dr. Riker, is prepping his computer at the podium.

"Feeling better?" Bryce asks absentmindedly as he looks through some essays we wrote last week.

"Yeah. After seeing you last night."

He raises an eyebrow and smiles. Then he returns to rummaging through papers. "I don't see your essay in here."

"I was going to get it done but something distracted me." *Like running through the wilderness naked and then making love to you.* "Look at it this way," I say with a shrug, "now you don't have to worry about unfairly grading my work."

"Yeah," he says with a nod, flipping through another page. "I can just fail you, Ms. Hawthorne."

I shove his shoulder toward the aisle on his right and he laughs.

"Seriously, Cadence, ask Riker for an extension."

"Can I get an extension, Dr. Wallace?" I ask Bryce, stupidly blinking my eyes.

"No." He takes a deep breath and shakes his head. "Ask your professor."

I stick my tongue out.

Dr. Riker clears his throat. The noise is magnified by a microphone on the collar of his gray shirt. He's wearing an informal shirt with jeans, but Dr. Riker can pull that off because—with his spectacles and clean-cut hair, like my Adonis boyfriend, sitting to my right—somehow he always looks formal. The lecture hall's nearly full. And noisy. Class hasn't started yet. Dr. Riker's history class is really popular—the second most popular class, next to Alondra's last year. He picks up a laser pointer. The lights dim and everybody becomes quiet.

"We're going to discuss Leonardo da Vinci."

Again? We seem to always be talking about Leonardo da Vinci. I love his artwork, but I was hoping to cover a lot more artists this semester. A slide shows the *Mona Lisa*.

"Leonardo is the quintessential Renaissance man. His genius crossed so many fields, including art, anatomy, architecture, and physics." The slide changes to a drawing of water. "But most amazingly, he incorporated his studies of science with art. This is his drawing of flowing water."

"Are we going to Alondra's tonight?" I whisper to Bryce. Bryce told me that dickhead Reardon took her home. I want to check on her. And pay a visit to Professor Reardon.

Bryce leans over and whispers in my ear, "You want to?" His breath smells like spearmint. I turn and look dreamily into his baby blues.

"We can bring the coven."

He shakes his head. "Don't think they'll come. Everyone's mad at you for abandoning Alondra that night." *Oh yeah.* "They assume the circle's broken. Well, we can go, but I'm not sure Bill will let you in."

"Why?"

He shushes me. Dr. Riker is looking directly at us.

"Note that the drawing is similar to his drawing of flowing hair," continues Dr. Riker. There's a close-up of a woman's hair from a painting. "*La Scapigliata.* The flow of the lady's hair is striking, but so is Leonardo's love for the curves and his yearning to understand the flow of water."

"Water, one of the four elements, right, Katie?" Bryce whispers in my ear. "Like Alondra. I want to see her so much too... Of course... But—"

"But what?" I say a little too loudly.

"The point I'm trying to make," continues Dr. Riker, glancing at me, "is that Leonardo brought a combination of science and art."

This time I put my finger over my lips and shush Bryce before he answers me, but it's too late.

"Mr. Wallace," my professor says. "Will you be so kind as to accompany me on stage? I'm having some difficulty with my slides. I'd like to move on a hundred years to the Netherlands. We're going to discuss the Dutch artists, including my second favorite painter, Rembrandt."

Bryce runs up the steps to the podium. Dr. Riker turns off the mike on his collar and starts arguing with him. He gestures toward me. It takes them a long time to get the slides to come up on the screen. Of course an art class without slides is totally useless.

The murmuring behind me gets crazy. This would be the perfect time to check my phone. I touch my pocket but then remember I lost my phone. Dad's going to seriously kill me.

As I'm sitting, getting bored, Maddie taps my shoulder from behind.

"Going to Alondra's tonight?" She probably heard us.

"Yeah. Can you come?"

"I want to."

"The sisters are mad at me?"

"Yeah. But do you care? I mean, no one is expecting you to lead another session after what happened. Anyway, a lot of us want to skip this Friday. Too spooked."

When a painting of a group of guys in black hats and ruffled white collars—pilgrim clothes—appears on the large screen above, Bryce jumps back down the steps and sits next to me. Then he turns to me and Maddie and, this time, he's the one who puts a finger to his lips.

Maddie taps my shoulder again. "What time?"

"I'm not sure if we can," says Bryce. He's talking carefully while watching the professor. "Bill's not allowing any visitors."

"*Fuck Bill!*" Maddie is really loud.

"Please," Dr. Riker says, looking down at us from the podium, "please everyone be silent during lecture. If you have a question, you can come up after class."

If you have a question—that's so nice. Dr. Riker's such a nice professor. He reminds me of Bryce. I feel bad for talking. I sink down in my chair, turn to Bryce, and cover my mouth. Bryce puts a finger to his lips again.

"Here's a self-portrait of Rembrandt. Notice the significant change in style from the Renaissance period. The dark brown and yellow tones."

"We should go anyway," Maddie says.

"Fuck yeah," I whisper to her. Maddie laughs.

Bryce leans his head on his hand, closes his eyes, and shakes his head.

11

PICKING LILIES

I grab my boyfriend's hand after getting out of his BMW in Alondra's dirt parking lot. There are no cars in her driveway. Even Alondra's swanky Jaguar has been moved. There's just her decorative antique red carriage.

I'm wearing a loose-fitting black dress. I'm regretting not bringing a sweater. It's cold. Mr. Handsome is in a button-down and slacks. The leaves are turning, and that reminds me that it's almost my favorite holiday: Halloween. As we walk onto a grassy field of weeds, an animal scurries along dead leaves and it makes me jump. I grab Bryce's arm and he laughs.

"What is it?" he asks.

"Nothing."

"Can you explain to me why you can wander through the forest naked and commune with the trees at night but you're afraid to walk in Alondra's front yard?"

Good point. Honestly, I don't know, but when I'm in a trance, things are different. I feel so confident and strong. Now I need a little help from my boyfriend.

Alondra's house is not usually creepy, but a fog rolled in this afternoon, causing a white cloud to cover everything. It's humid too and my cheeks are moist. There's light coming from one of the windows upstairs. The light spreads out in the fog like yellow smoke over her elegant mansion. The lawn is browning a little with the turn of the seasons, and under the fog at twilight, it's creepy.

"Hey, guys!" cries Maddie from behind.

I jump in the air. "Don't do that!"

"We didn't hear you," says Bryce, chuckling.

"I walked from the dorms," Maddie replies. Then she hugs me. "Hey, bitch."

We make our way up onto Alondra's elegant white columned deck. The lights that usually illuminate the steps are not on, and it's dark under the fog. Maddie knocks on the door, and who do you suppose answers?

Bill Reardon. He's dressed in ancient clothes. I've seen them before in ceremonies. They're baggy, wrinkled, and brown and held by a rope, making him resemble a Capuchin monk. He's glaring at us with the door half-open.

"I told you she can't have visitors, disciple," he says to Bryce, ignoring Maddie and me. "You have to leave."

He might be a little more cordial to my boyfriend, but I know Bryce hates him. Bryce told me that the two of them had an abusive relationship when Reardon was our High Wizard. He bullied Bryce into doing gruesome satanic work like some kind of ceremonial janitor: cleaning blood, pieces of tissue, and sinew from animals, cleaning up after sex, cleaning feces off instruments and planks, and a number of other unspeakable things that I stopped Bryce from elaborating on. Bryce said he tried to leave the circle a few times, and Bill threatened to curse his family. Since being "freed" when Alondra and I cast Reardon out, Bryce has recovered from his brainwashing and hates Reardon as much as I do.

"We just want to see Alondra," Bryce says.

"No."

"What of the Sabbath?" Maddie asks Reardon. He's just about to shut the door on us. "Can we hold it in the backyard this Friday? We can even go around to the side yard."

"No. No more meetings. Not now."

"Is this what Alondra wants?" asks Bryce, squinting.

"It's what my wife shall have," Reardon snaps. "You all nearly killed her with Western medicine." Then he looks at me. "And you nearly killed all of us."

"We saved her life," I say.

I'm ready for this. I think this man is taking advantage of Alondra because she's sick and weak. I also want to tell him off for what he did to me the other night. It gets rid of my fear of him. He disgusts me.

"Good day to you, Ms. Hawthorne." He sneers. "And the rest of your young friends."

"Have her come down," I say. "If she asks us to leave, we'll go."

"This is my house, young lady," he snaps. "I think sometimes you forget. I will care for my wife any way I see fit. She cannot be seen. Now go!"

"You probably hope she dies so you can claim her inheritance." My statement is so nasty that Bryce lets go of my hand and looks at me in shock.

"Cadence!" snaps Maddie.

"Go away!" Reardon says with wide-open eyes. "Now! Get out!"

I squint and he locks his eyes on mine.

He is about to shut the door, but I weaken him. I don't know how, but I stop him from closing the door. Then I raise my arms into the air.

I don't say anything. I don't need to. Instead, there's a flutter of wings behind me as if my arms are flapping like a bird. A chilly wind blows and clears some of the fog. My arms are not wings; the sky becomes a shade darker, not from fog, but from a torrent of black birds flying from behind me. Reardon unlocks his stare and looks around me in amazement. Then one bird—my companion, Amica—lands on my outstretched arm. Amica caws at Reardon. I distinctly hear her say, *"Back. Back."* I feel a trance coming on. Bryce grabs my shoulder and shakes his head, warning me, but it's too late. I feel elated with a sudden surge of power.

What a sense of peace and tranquility. Any sense of anxiety has faded, and I hope Reardon will try to do something stupid so I can hurt him. I dare him to. I challenge him with my glare.

"Cadence, calm down," warns Maddie.

Surrounding us are a hundred black birds, circling or walking around Alondra's front yard. Some are standing on the porch, others are fluttering and making noise above the deck, and still others are walking beside my feet.

"Get back, black witch!" cries Reardon in fear. "Stay away from me."

"I asked you to keep her in the hospital," I say. "You've hurt her. She needs medicine. Now I simply ask that you let us in so we can see her. If she wants us to go, we'll go. Open the door."

Bryce touches my shoulder again. His eyes are wide now. He looks afraid. Afraid of what? Me?

Amica repeats, *"Back, back."*

"Leave me and my wife alone!" snaps Reardon. "She's too sick, I tell you! Leave her fate to the moon and stars."

I walk right up to Reardon and push him inside the house.

It's dark in there, with only a dim light upstairs. I could just walk upstairs and see her. But I don't. Because I know now she's not even there. It's been unveiled to me by the trees in the forest. I don't know how I know, but I know.

I approach Reardon the same way he approached me in the

hospital and press a fingernail deep into his chest. Bryce touches my shoulder for a third time, but I bat him off.

"Watch yourself, liar," I say, "I know the spell you cast on me. Do something like that to me again and I will torment you a hundred times over. Got me?"

"I never cast a spell on you," he says, shaking his head.

I walk back out onto the deck. Amica is still with me, and I pet her as she perches on my arm. With my other arm, I gesture toward the door and say indifferently, "*Clausus.*" The black birds around us leap into flight and swarm the door, forcing Reardon to throw the door closed. A hundred black birds collide, one after the other, pounding against the closed wooden door.

My friends are speechless. They're looking at me the way they did when I conjured the bonfire spell and nearly burned the other witches alive last year.

"Let's go," I say.

Behind me the birds continue to throw themselves against the door. I look back and see a stack of the birds piling up, bloodied and shaking, as more and more birds crash down on them.

"He's a bad man, isn't he, Amica?" I ask my bird, petting her. "A bad, bad man."

"Cadence?" Bryce says.

I push the bird from my arm and she flies off. "Huh?"

"You all right?"

"Wonderful," I say with a furrowed brow. "Why?"

"You're scaring me."

Maddie doesn't say a thing. She's already down the hill, rushing back to our dorm.

"I'm just glad Alondra is feeling better," I say as Bryce turns on the ignition. He drives us out of the dirt parking lot.

I'm looking out the car window at the shadows in the wilderness. I can see her in my mind, gathering herself like a ball in her black cloak—the same way Enora did—meditating on feeling better. She's still sick, but she feels peace out there.

"How do you know she's better?" he asks.

"I can see her in the trees. She's telling me so." Bryce shakes his head in total confusion. I laugh and shrug. "I can *feel* her telling me, you know?"

12

ALL HALLOWS' EVE

HALLOWEEN AT HAWTHORNE IS MORE POPULAR THAN CHRISTMAS. The whole university goes nuts with everybody wearing costumes all week, including the professors. Dr. Riker wore glasses with tape, carried an old 1980s calculator, and slicked his hair back. He was a total nerd. Well, people say costumes fit them. Bryce has been wearing an old person's mask with wrinkles and long thin white hair. I'm not wearing any costume— sort of. As of late, I've been using darker mascara and even wearing black lipstick. I've had black nail polish since last year, but the facial makeup is new. I look totally goth. My best friend, Maddie, does too. Like Mira, all the sisters of the coven wear black. Someone who's never seen us around campus might think we're wearing witch costumes. Or even guess what we actually are.

Every year there's a huge bash at the Psi Kappa Psi frat house. The Billington House. It's one of the oldest buildings in Georgia. It's perched on top of a hill surrounded by the shadows of the forest. It's haunted. People say Alondra's ancient relative, Abigail, stands alone by the window facing the hilltop, holding a candle by her chest, late at night. Escoba, *my* relative, roams the halls too.

The story of the haunting tells of the voodoo witch Escoba taking a fancy to Josiah, Abigail's husband. Escoba and Josiah had an illegitimate son, Maverick. Then Escoba cursed Abigail, killing her family. Well, Escoba was later found dead in her rocking chair in the Billington House with a knife in her chest. No one really knows if Abigail murdered her, but it's suspected. It's a really awful, grisly tale of revenge; that's why their spirits roam the halls. And that's probably also why Alondra, Abigail's distant relative, and I, Escoba's descendant, never completely got along.

I've never seen Escoba and Maverick in the haunted house. But I did see them roaming my dormitory and dining hall last semester.

Anyway, while we're walking up the hill to the house, I hear shouting and laughter. The party's already raging, but the raucousness is a good thing, because the paths between the woods and the house are rather spooky. Bryce is holding my hand.

"Why are you standing so close to me?" Bryce asks with a chuckle.

"I am?"

He nods.

"Must be love," I say stupidly.

"Or you're afraid again." He shakes his head.

"I don't like this place, especially at night," I say with a shrug.

"I'll try to keep you from hurting anybody."

He opens a creaky old wooden gate and we head up to the front door. I look at the window in the center of the three-story brick building and think about Abigail again. That's where legend says her ghost holds her candle. But now, rainbow-colored lights are flashing from the haunted window. And the noises inside the house aren't scary. I hear heavy metal music. I recognize Ozzy Osbourne's voice, which I love. We don't have to knock on the door. It's ajar; Bryce just pushes it open.

A guy dressed like an axe-murdering clown greets him by the entryway.

"Bryce!" shouts the clown. "How you doing, man?" He puts both hands on his shoulders. Then he reaches down into a barrel full of ice and hands us each a beer. A few other people shout, "Bryce!" He's very popular here. He was a member of the fraternity when he was a student. A few more people say hi, and I get lost in the shuffle. Bryce turns and looks back with concern, but I smile and gesture for him to go enjoy himself.

I enter a cramped living room. It's a big room, but it's full of bodies, shoulder to shoulder. A large wicker chair is occupied by someone in a purple dinosaur suit holding a bong. The dinosaur stands up and gestures for me to sit, then lifts off its head, with the ripping sound of Velcro, and takes a hit. It's Nick, Maddie's old boyfriend from last year. He offers the bong to me, but I shake my head.

"Enjoy the party, Katie," Nick says with a slur. He reeks of the musky weed and he walks like he's also tipsy. I sit in the large wicker chair. It's dizzying, and a bit surreal, watching so many costumed bodies dancing before me. Or maybe it's the marijuana in the air. I don't know. I sip some beer.

"Hey, Cadence," says a voice I recognize. Standing above me is Mira. She looks around but there's nowhere to sit, so she just kneels down next to me. She's holding a chocolate pastry that looks like an éclair. And she's not in a costume. She's wearing black like me.

"How's Alondra?" I ask. It's hard to hear my own voice over the blaring music. I recognize the song. It's "Sabbath Bloody Sabbath" by Black Sabbath—very appropriate, looking at her.

"She's okay. The infection is gone but she still has pain."

"How? If she's not sick?"

"The cancer."

"Is Reardon still keeping her prisoner?"

"He sure is scared of you," she says with a sly grin. She looks at me as if I'm some kind of rock star or something. I think that's stupid. "All the sisters heard about the birds. We talked about it at our last Sabbath. We're just so sorry you and Bryce couldn't make it."

"What last Sabbath? I thought Reardon forbade meetings in the house?"

"Enora ran it on Hilltop Bluff," she says, touching my hand. I can't help but think she's touching me with a handful of chocolate frosting and white custard. And as I think of it, she takes a big bite of her pastry. Then, with her mouth full, she says, "There's a bunch of cakes and candy in the kitchen. You should get some."

"I've already eaten."

"Your dress is pretty," she says with a lascivious smile.

I drink more beer from my bottle. It's an IPA. A bit too sharp for my taste.

I sway to the music. Mira doesn't. She remains on her knees, stiff as a board.

"I love this house, Cadence," Mira says. I recall last year when I watched her run a séance here. It's amusing how she hated me back then. Now I'm the only one she wants to talk to. "You can feel the haunting presence." Mira lights up as she looks around the room. "The ghosts. Your family, Katie."

I shrug and drink more beer.

On the floor is a vampire wrestling with someone in a white sheet, who is supposed to be a ghost, I think. A couple of other guys, sitting on the floor dressed in football uniforms, are cheering them on. But as the white sheet rolls off, I see a girl in a red bikini, and the wrestling seems more lewd than combative.

"Why is Enora still here?" I ask. "I thought she was just visiting."

"Do you care? I mean, I thought you wanted us to stop meeting anyway."

"Only because of Enora. I don't trust her."

"I don't trust her either. I wish you'd run our meetings. Your power is greater." Mira licks her fingers and stands up. "I'm gonna get something to drink. You want another beer?"

I shake my head.

"I'll be back."

Someone screams. A dinosaur nearly tackles Mira to the floor, shouting, *"Drink and stack!"* I jump. It's Nick acting like a complete idiot. *"Drink and stack!"* he shouts again. Mira nearly punches him in the face, but she pulls her punch and pushes him onto the wrestlers on the floor instead. *"Who wants to drink and stack?"* he shouts, trying to get up. He's so drunk that he falls on more people.

I've completely lost Bryce. I said it was okay for him to see his friends, but I meant for a few minutes, not the whole party.

I watch people clear a table on the other side of the room and decide I don't like sitting all by my lonesome anymore. I get up and make my way to the table. The music changes to something techno, and the lights swirl a bit. I chug down my beer. There's another bucketful of ice and beer bottles. (They're everywhere.) I grab another.

That's when someone throws her arms around me. A girl with a big fluffy velvet top hat and a brown suit with purple buttons and a purple collar—the Mad Hatter—squeezes me tightly. It's Maddie. Her breath reeks of alcohol. She came with Rock, but I don't see him.

"You want to play, Katie?" Maddie asks. The techno is only getting louder.

"Play what?"

"Drink and stack. We're gonna stack blocks. Come on, it'll be fun."

My friend Tammy, dressed in a white bunny suit, is arranging all of us in line. The line is zigzaggy and crazy, but by this time, half the people here are too inebriated for order. But it frustrates Tammy as she tries to gather people together. She waves excitedly when she sees me.

"Drink up, bitch," Maddie says, raising her beer in a toast to me as we get in line.

I do. I drink a lot of my beer. This one isn't a tangy IPA.

"Everyone," Tammy shouts. "Hey... Hey... Hey, *SHUT UP!*" Someone turns down the music. Tammy laughs. "Listen, this is gonna be so much fun! This is a block game. You're gonna build and then remove and you're gonna be timed. Okay? You each need to stack four rows of three blocks—for those who can't do math, four times three makes twelve. Stack them and then remove three blocks, one at a time. But you only have thirty seconds, so be quick about it. I'll keep time. If you can't set up four rows in time, you have to chug. If you pull out three blocks and the blocks fall, you have to chug. Got it? The person behind you goes and adds another four rows. You have to keep stacking the rows on top of each other until they come down ..." She takes a break, and by now I have no idea what the hell she's talking about. But this should be easy, because many people in line are a lot more drunk than me. "Technically, you can remove from the lower rows, but that would be riskier. Right? Whoever knocks down all the blocks has to chug beer. Then the next one stacks another four rows. And so on. And so on. Got it? 'Cause if you don't...guess what?"

"*Chug!*" shout a bunch of people stupidly.

"Right," Tammy says with a laugh.

I'm looking around the room. Where's my Bryce?

"Ready?" asks Tammy.

The table has a pile of blocks and a bunch of empty Jenga boxes.

I look around at all the costumed bodies dancing and swaying to the techno music. Then my eyes fall on something I can't believe. Near a corner of the room, I see Bryce. He's standing beside a woman with dark makeup, wearing a black dress similar to mine, who's leaning against a wall staring at me. It's Enora.

Mira stands beside me in line. She has no interest in playing; she just wants to watch. I grab her by the elbow and point at Bryce. But when I look back, my boyfriend and my arch-enemy are gone.

"What?" Mira asks, furrowing her brow.

"Did you see her?"

"Who?"

"Enora."

Mira looks at me funny. Then she gives me her stupid sly smile. "You casting a spell or something?" I think she's hoping I am.

"Maddie?" I turn around, but she's got her arms around Rocky and the two of them have stepped out of the line.

I look at the table. The first person is Nick. He places his blocks on top of each other without any order, turns, and bows to our line, and instead of removing three, he purposefully knocks his rows down. Everyone laughs and Tammy hands him his beer. Nick chugs down a beer; then a few people help carry the purple dinosaur away from the line.

I turn back and Enora's there again. Again, Bryce is talking, but she's ignoring him. She's glaring at me. She places a hand on his arm and runs her fingers down it—*while looking at me.* Then she closes her eyes with pleasure and laughs.

I practically shove Mira and point again.

"What?" Mira asks.

They're gone again. Replacing Bryce and Enora by the wall

are a girl in a cheerleader outfit and a boy with torn clothes and zombie makeup. I reach into my pocket and take out my cell phone (I got my dad to buy me a new one) and text Bryce's number. "*Where are you? Come back. NOW.*"

"Was Enora coming to the party?" I ask Mira.

She shrugs.

"I just saw her with Bryce."

The next player in line is a short blond girl in a vampire costume. Unlike Nick, she's actually playing for real, carefully but quickly aligning the four rows while Tammy stares at her stopwatch. This young girl's sober and easily stacks four columns and removes three central blocks.

Maddie comes over. "Hey, guys," she says. Rocky's holding her by the waist. "Looks like you're almost up, Kate. You playing, Mira?"

"No. Just watching Windstorm cast a spell."

"I'm not casting a spell," I say, shaking my head.

"I think she's going to," Mira says to Maddie, cupping her mouth as if whispering.

I turn to Maddie. "Did you know Enora's here?"

Maddie shakes her head.

"Who's Enora?" asks Rocky. With his free hand he drinks beer.

"A witch," I tell him. Well, it is Halloween. He doesn't think anything of it.

The next player is drunk. He's a senior named Nathan. I know him from my economics study group. A nice guy. Nathan stacks the blocks carefully. Everyone's amazed that he manages to add four rows. There are eight rows stacked and I'm next.

"Nervous, Kate?" asks Tammy with a chuckle. "It looks pretty high."

I shrug and drink more beer.

I almost spit out my beer. From the corner of my eye, I see Bryce and Enora again. This time Enora is standing close to him. Real close. She reaches up and kisses him passionately while running her hand along his chest and waist. Bryce gropes her ass. Then she brushes her long dark hair back, laughs, and looks right at me again.

All the colorful, swirling lights cut off for a second, and it turns dark. There's a scream in the darkness and people laugh. Then the lights turn back on.

"Just a circuit break," says Rock. "It's amazing this old building has any electricity at all."

"Where's Bryce?" Maddie asks me.

"That's what Cadence keeps seeing." Mira seems excited. "Did you shut the energy off just then, Windstorm?"

I did, but I shake my head. My heart is racing and I'm grinding my teeth, wanting to kill them. But when I'm about to do the deed, Bryce is gone. I quickly pull out my cell phone. No answer.

I'm next. I walk out of line to search for my boyfriend, so I can inflict bodily harm on him, and Tammy grabs my elbow. "You're next, Katie. Come on."

I shake my head hesitantly.

I'm surrounded by costumed boys and girls I don't know, staring at me, shouting for me to play. I'm dizzy. Sick. As if I am drunk, but I'm not. I look back at the corner of the room and, thankfully, my boyfriend's not there.

"Are you okay?" asks Maddie. As drunk as she is, she looks concerned.

"I saw Bryce."

Maddie looks in the direction I'm looking, squinting.

Mira has a really wide smile.

"Katie," says Tammy pleasantly, "come on, we're all waiting for you. You ready?" She raises her brow. "You okay?"

I look down at the stupid table. Then I look back one more time but don't see my boyfriend. It must be a vision. The past? That's probably it. It's probably a vision of the past, like seeing a ghost. Right? I'm not so sure. But everyone's waiting for me to play their stupid game. So I walk over to the table to get it over with.

On the table is the column of blocks. It reminds me of the white columns that stand along the wide patio before Alondra's house. It's like the light wood blocks are holding up her house. It's delicate. It could easily topple over and fall apart like a deck of cards. And now it's up to me. I have to keep it together. I finish the beer I'm drinking, and everybody cheers stupidly and wildly. It's like I'm already chugging before I lose. Then someone in a gladiator suit hands me another.

I haven't felt my phone buzz. Bryce hasn't answered me. Why? Is this payback or something? *Or is he really with her?*

A couple in black robes and white masks are holding hands behind me. Funny, I didn't see them before. Their get-up reminds me of a secret society. Beside them is a girl in a deer mask with antlers. She's in a tight red bikini. That looks weird. And behind the deer is a girl in a purple cloak. I've never seen this girl before. She has spooky red contacts and a black mark on her forehead that reminds me of Ash Wednesday, but it's in the shape of an upside-down cross. She's licking her lips. She lifts an open palm, and there's a red pentagram painted on it.

"Go ahead, Katie," says Tammy.

Get it together, Cadence. Just put the dumb blocks on top of each other and be done with it. Then go search for your boyfriend. If he's still your boyfriend.

My eyes stray toward the corner again. I'm not expecting to see them, but this time I do. My body shakes. Bryce is standing there in Enora's arms, and the two of them are kissing passionately. Enora only has on her bra and, as the lips of my lover touch Enora's, she's still looking at me, as if taunting me. Challenging me. Just like she did when we had our last Sabbath. Enora is slowly unbuttoning Bryce's shirt while he massages her tits underneath her bra.

"Are you ready?" asks Tammy again, confused.

Yeah, I'm ready. I'm going to fucking kill them!

I touch the pile of blocks. One of them rises an inch over the table. Tammy is staring at it.

"Here we go," says Tammy a little more cautiously. She presses a button on her watch.

I take a block from the middle, leaving only one block at the center holding up the tower. Physics dictates that the column should collapse, but it doesn't. People look in wonder. I set it vertically at the top.

"You can stack your rows first," Tammy says, trying to help me.

I turn back and watch Enora and Bryce making out. They are bare-chested and pressed close to one another, French kissing, sucking, and practically fucking right before my eyes.

I put a block vertically on top of the column without even looking.

"You only have to make rows," says Tammy. "Why are you laying them on top of each other?"

"They're gonna fall if you do that!" shouts someone behind me, laughing.

"She's already out! She hasn't stacked her rows!"

The column doesn't even teeter. I add a few more blocks standing vertically. Then I look at the tower. I start working quickly, stacking the blocks up in a single column on top while taking them out of the center of the tower. There are now about twelve standing on top of each other, up to my forehead, with large gaping spaces in the middle of the structure. There is no way, under normal dynamics, that the column would still be up.

"That's not what you were supposed to do," Tammy says, shaking her head. "Now how are you going to remove three more?"

"She wants to drink!" says someone.

"How is it still up?" asks another.

Bryce runs his fingers along Enora's naked back. He bends her down, still kissing her, and runs his other hand along her breast. Enora opens her eyes, throws her hair back, and glares at me once more.

All of a sudden, with mindless speed, I remove blocks from the bottom of the structure. I take them from the sides. The blocks should collapse, but they're not falling.

"I can't believe it's up," says Rocky behind me.

The blocks don't even sway. A couple of people who were ignoring our game are now surrounding me. In fact, most of the people at the party are staring at the table. It looks like the greatest feat of balance of all time.

I'm done with seconds to spare. I take my beer and start chugging it down anyway, because I really don't give a fuck anymore, and my crowd goes wild. Everyone is touching my back and congratulating me. As I drink, Mira looks at the corner that's been holding my attention and suddenly loses her amused smile. Her eyes open wider. But it seems she's the only one seeing what I'm seeing.

"What the hell?" Mira says.

I feel a rush of energy from my legs to my throat. Absolute raw fury.

"And thirty!" says Tammy. She looks at the blocks in shock. Not only is there a column of twelve stacked on top of each other, but there are three or four rows with gaping spaces on the sides. It is absolutely impossible that the structure is not teetering and collapsing onto the table.

"YOU BITCH!"

The words are screamed through the air, but nothing is coming from my mouth. They're uttered from my mind. But everyone hears the words and is searching the room. And then a whirlwind, like a gale, rushes through the Billington House. The blocks fly from the table all over the room as if from an explosion. A few of these projectiles hit my face and chest.

The lights shut off again. But this time, they don't turn back on.

I quickly make my way to the door, groping in the dark. A few people yell and scream, and this time it's not a joke.

Outside the Billington House, it's quiet. Cold. I'm running as fast as I can down the hill and onto the dirt path through the forest.

"Cadence!" cries Mira from behind.

"Leave me alone!"

"It's a trick!" yells Mira. "A spell. It can't be real!"

I don't believe her. It looked real. Very real. And I still haven't gotten a text from him. Bryce would never ignore my text or call. Unless...they were together. It was real. I know it was real. Because I'm a witch. It was not a hallucination or an illusion. It really happened. And Enora, that disgusting monster, wanted me to watch. She wanted me to see it. Did she bewitch him? Bryce told me he hated her. Maybe she cast a spell? Why would he touch her like that? Put his lips on her? Hold her tits! Naked and...

Mira runs close behind me, in her long black dress, gasping for air. I whirl around and she backs up, afraid. "Stay away! I'll hurt you!"

"Cadence," she says with her hand out.

"Keep away! I can't control myself!"

"It can't be Bryce," Mira says, shaking her head. "I'll talk to Enora."

That was the wrong thing to say.

"*Talk to her!*" I shout. My voice is guttural, inhuman. Rain starts to pour from the sky. "If you're my sister, you'll never even look at her again! Or Bryce! I hope they both...God." I start to cry. Mira steps forward, but I warn her again. "How could he! Why?"

"Cadence, it might not really have happened."

"You saw it, right?"

Mira nods.

"I want to kill him," I say, my eyes narrowing. My heart is bursting in my chest. My God, if Bryce were here now, I think I would. I would strike him down dead.

I'm afraid. I'm afraid I don't have control of myself.

"I'll tear him apart! ...I will."

Mira just nods.

Maddie runs over. She's out of breath too. I've run so far that I'm almost down the hill, near the lights that border the walkways on campus. It's pouring. Behind Maddie, far up the hill, I can see shadows leaving the Billington House. No electricity means no more party. Everyone's leaving. I ended their stupid party. Good.

"What's wrong with her?" Maddie asks Mira, out of breath. "What did she see?"

"Enora," says Mira, still catching her breath, "holding Bryce."

"Oh my God," Maddie says. "She'll kill him."

13

BUT I SEE FRACTALS

WELL, I DIDN'T KILL HIM.

I'm sitting alone in the back row of the one-hundred-seat auditorium where my Economics 101 class is held, sipping a latte—it's my second this morning—trying to keep my eyes open while I take notes. My economics professor, Dr. Garson, is really boring. His voice lulls you to sleep. I see a few students nodding their heads beside me. I'm doing that too. That's why I chose the back row, but that doesn't help prevent my professor from noticing me because there are only about thirty seats occupied in the entire room.

Prerequisites. What's one to do? I'm already halfway through my undergraduate major. I could have chosen a basic math or science class, but I figured that one day I'll have to make money. I'm not sure Dr. Garson's talking about money.

"We're going to take a look at comparative advantage." As boring as he is, he does love his subject. He gets excited. But it's over *comparative advantage*, for God's sake. He's a short, pudgy, bald man wearing glasses, a white T-shirt, and brown slacks. He's pacing like Dr. Riker's been known to do. He aims a remote toward the center screen on stage, but nothing happens. Then he starts fumbling with his remote.

I get a text. It's Bryce. Does he actually think I'm going to fucking talk to him? I think it's the twentieth message since last night. Funny, I didn't see him returning my text while he was fondling Panthera's tits. I ignore yet another message with the naughty pleasure of knowing how much he hates it when I don't answer his texts and calls.

"You must understand how comparative advantage calculates labor with units produced and can show favor of one agent over another in free trade."

What? Like *W-T-F?* This is why I came to the lecture. I have no idea what the hell he's saying.

"In the early nineteenth century..." Finally some history. "David Ricardo put the law to use, comparing two countries: England and Portugal." He walks up to the whiteboard and starts jotting down equations. *Isn't this math?* "If you take these two countries and observe their production of wine and cloth," he drawls on, "you can see that England can produce more cloth than wine and Portugal can produce more wine than cloth. The subsequent trade between the two countries allows for more goods to be available to both nations than autarky would. Right? Now let's move on to Harberler."

He is speaking English, right? And now he's moving on as I'm falling behind.

I can't stop seeing Bryce and Enora together in my head. It's like the vision is imprinted in my mind. Especially the bitch's sardonic smile. Oh, how I hate her. And I hate Bryce too.

My phone buzzes again. *Fuck off.*

Of course not all the calls and texts are from Bryce. A whole lot of them are from Maddie. And one, last night, was even from Mira. But I didn't call her back either.

I angrily throw my hair back and stare at Dr. Garson again. He's gesturing to a large graph on the center monitor. He's smiling and looks really excited about it. I take a deep breath and rub my eyes.

"Harberler's ideas were essential in creating a better understanding of the growing international market of the early twentieth century."

I look up. The lights are dimmed. I wish they weren't.

To my right, an exit door cracks open, letting in the early-morning sunshine.

A boy catches my eye. I know him. Kurt. Kurt's chewing gum and smiling at me. With his crew cut and well-built body, he's a total jock. His girlfriend, Veronica, is staring at Dr. Garson in confusion. I don't think Veronica knows what Garson's talking about either.

My phone buzzes again. I get it in order to finally answer him. My plan is to tell him off.

"I get it," Bryce texts. "U won't answer. But Alondra's sick. Call Maddie. Call her now."

Alondra's sick. So? I know she's sick. She's been sick for months. So what?

Maddie's calling now. *Oh, God.*

I take a deep breath. When I see Dr. Garson's remote get stuck again, it's enough reason for me to walk out. I mean, does it really matter that I miss the lecture? I think I can discern more from staring at my textbook than listening to him. I shove my book into my backpack and make my way out.

Outside the lecture hall, I answer my phone.

"What!" I snap.

"I've been trying to reach you all morning. Where were you? I'm sure it wasn't with Bryce."

"Yeah," I snap. "You guessed it. It wasn't with Bryce."

I make my way to the main drag of campus. Predictably, it's not busy. But give it another week or two and everybody will start studying for midterms.

"Well—"

"I'm never going to talk to him again."

"Whatever, Katie. I'm not calling you about that. You always think everything's about you."

"What? Just tell me. I'm heading back to our dorm now."

"Well, I'm not there. I'm at Alondra's. Didn't you at least answer Mira?"

"No."

"Come here now, Cadence. Please. It's not good."

I finally get it that she's worried. "What?" I ask, softening for the first time. "What is it?"

"Just come to Alondra's."

"Will Bill let me in?"

"I'm sitting across from Reardon right now."

I take my beat-up Honda to Alondra's. It's only eleven in the morning. When I get there, I'm surprised to see her dirt parking lot packed with cars. I jump out of mine and make my way to her door. Her grass has browned even more, and the leaves on the trees around the property, as elsewhere throughout the college, are orange and brown. I muse that if I weren't in such a state, I would enjoy it. Fall is my favorite season. But now, I'm thinking about Alondra.

I pound on the door with her large knocker, and Tammy opens it. She's wiping tears from her eyes. Inside it's noisy, almost like one of her parties, with the house packed with people. Many are my sisters of the coven.

Reardon walks to the foyer. He's wearing his stupid monk robe. He looks terrible and I fear the worst.

"Where is she?" I ask.

A bunch of the witches hear my voice and rush to the front of the house. No one's smiling. It's like they're holding a wake.

"She's very sick, I'm afraid," Reardon says.

"No thanks to you," I snap. I'm full throttle at this point, pissed at my "boyfriend" and in no mood to disguise my disgust at this sick, satanic creep. I look around the house. Then I nod toward the stairs. "Is she in her room?"

"We don't know where she is, Cadence," Mira says. "She disappeared."

"He knows where she is." I point a thumb in disbelief.

"I don't," he replies with seemingly equal hatred of me.

"Where's my disciple?" asks Reardon.

"You mean Bryce?" I ask. "Why don't you call people by the names given by their parents instead of your stupid cult names?" I walk up to him and he steps back, afraid. "No, I haven't seen him. Last I saw, he was with Panthera."

"He's not here," Maddie says. She's walking over from the kitchen. She looks terrible. Not at all like her usual happy self. "Hi, Cadence. We were waiting for you."

"Why? For what?"

"We thought you'd know where she is," says Mira. "She kept telling me she wanted to talk to you. That was before she disappeared."

"You can't find her?" I ask Reardon. I don't want to talk to him, but there's just no choice. He shakes his head.

I make my way into the living room. Marilyn and Hope are crying on the sofa. I pull at Alondra's glass door. Of course it doesn't open, so I have to push on it hard. Outside, on a wooden rack on the outdoor patio, are our black cloaks. I put one on.

Mira and Gilda put on cloaks too. I didn't even notice Gilda. They must have called her from Savannah.

"If you want me to find her, I have to go alone," I say.

"How do you know where she is?" asks Gilda.

"She knows," says Mira.

I do. I don't know how I know, but I do.

I make my way into her backyard. Mira walks beside me.

"Mira, I said I have to go alone."

"She's really sick," Mira says. "Just bring her back to the house with you."

"Why?" I ask.

"Because ..." Mira's voice cracks and she turns away with tears. "I want to say goodbye."

And that's a terrible thing to say. I take a deep breath and embrace Mira, and she falls apart in my arms. I feel choked up too. As I look toward the house, I see all the witches of my coven have gathered outside, watching me.

"Katie, I don't know where the evil is," Mira whispers in my ear between tears. "Bring Alondra back. Please."

14

THE ONYX STONE

I'M WALKING THROUGH THE DENSE BRUSH OF THE FOREST, NOT FAR from Alondra's backyard. In fact, as I cock my head back, I can still make out her house through the dense trees and see my friends, still standing outside talking about me. Everyone wants me to find her. I acted so sure I could, but now I'm not sure.

After walking downhill for a while, I enter a clearing. The ground looks darker between the trees. I step in mud and water. There's about thirty feet of water in front of me—Alondra's water hole. I've never seen it, but I remember it. When I had my initiation last year, I saw it from above, in the air, under the influence of mandrake. At the time, I thought the drug had caused a hallucination. Later, I found that it was real. Bryce and I had flown. And, with a bird's-eye view, I had seen this water hole.

Something tells me she's across the water. There's a small tunnel made up of twigs and branches. And the only way to get through the tunnel is to walk across the water hole.

The water is about two feet deep at its center. It's not deep but it's cold. I tread slowly with my cloak and dress floating near my arms. It gets shallow again, and I crouch down and pass into the tunnel. It's only about three feet high.

I feel as if I enter a tunnel under a canopy. It is then I realize that this is a secret area. It's a natural tunnel and, maybe because it is so unique, I feel like it will lead me to her.

The tunnel is so beautiful. And as I walk, it feels like nighttime under so much yellow-and-red foliage. It's like a nest and, for a second, I wonder if it's man-made. Perhaps Alondra built this?

The end of the tunnel leads me to a field not all that different from Alondra's backyard. But this field has a ceiling of branches and leaves, making it like a natural amphitheater. In the center of the wild grass is a black figure crouched in a ball. This is the same stance Enora was in when she opened her hell portal. I take a deep breath and sigh. I found her.

I walk slowly to her. She doesn't stir. She remains crouched in a black ball, wearing the same cloak as me.

I remove my hood.

"Alondra," I say.

"You're a powerful witch." She sounds like she's amused, but she still barely stirs.

"What are you doing here?" I ask.

"Dying."

And that's horrible. I feel my breath leave me and my legs weaken. Now that I've found her, I don't want magic. I don't want any of it. I want to just run home to my dorm and study. Read. Try to discern Dr. Garson's *comparative advantage*. Anything but witchcraft.

"Please, come with me back home," I say. "Mira wants to see you. We all do." She doesn't move. She remains crouched like a black boulder, immobile. "Why are you sitting like this?"

"I am gathering my energy from the ground. I am grounded with Gaia. I feel peace in her arms. My only concern is you and your friends do not."

"Why did you ask to see me?"

"Because I'm dying," she says again. "Will you forgive me?"

"For what? For dying?"

"No. For what I did. I've asked you before, now I ask you one last time. Can you forgive me for what happened last year?"

"No." When I say that, my words sound as terrible to my ears as they probably do to hers. She says she's dying. Why can't I accept her last words? Or at least lie about it? She's talking about the "ceremonial initiation" of my friend. The deception of her circle, when the circle meant taking drugs and having sex ceremonies with Maddie and her sick husband.

"I'm sorry, Cadence," Alondra says. "I am fortunate to have talked to all those I love before I pass to the Summerland. You are my last."

"Don't say that." I choke up. "Just come back with me to the house."

"Don't be sad. I told you I wanted to leave under the trees."

"Just get up and walk back to the house."

"I don't have the strength."

There's silence. I don't know what to say.

"Do you believe that some things can never be forgiven?" she asks. It is so Alondra. She's acting like Socrates, trying to make me think at the last breaths of her life. I don't think she has an answer herself.

"I'm the one who's sorry," I say.

"For what?" she asks. There's a sense of amusement.

"Because you're dying."

"Ah. But I believe death is an illusion. It does not hurt the dead. It's one's loved ones who suffer. What do you think of that, Cadence?"

She's doing it again with a second question. It makes me almost angry. It seems like her teachings cover her real feelings.

"No, I can never forgive you for what you did to Maddie," I say, ignoring her philosophical questions. It's mean, but I feel like being honest is the right thing to do. Probably not to her. Probably not to someone who spent a lifetime avoiding the truth.

"All right, Cadence."

"You knew I'd say that. Is that why you wanted to see me?"

"No, Katie."

"Then why?"

"Because I love you. I feel like you are the daughter I never had."

That does it. I fall to my knees beside her in tears. But she's still sitting in a weird black ball, not even looking at me. Now she's calling herself my mother. It's so sad. And so upsetting. It's the confused relationship we've had ever since we met.

"Why do you do this, Alondra?" I rub my tear-filled eyes.

She lifts her head to me for the first time. Her hand unfolds and shakes as it touches my face. She runs her fingers along my long black hair. Her jade eyes are glassy. Her face is covered in leaves and dirt, as if she has been swimming in mud. She looks so weak. And yet she seems serene. She is dying.

"Don't worry."

"I...I thought you could help me," I say. "I'm so confused. I don't know how to use my powers. Every time I'm upset, crazy things happen."

"But you don't see ghosts anymore, do you?"

"No."

"At least that haunting has left you."

"But I see other things. I saw Reardon." I start talking fast. There's so much I want to tell her, and I need to tell her now. And quickly. Because...well, she's dying. "I was lost in the forest and I saw Reardon. He cast a spell on me. And then, last night, I saw Bryce kissing Enora. I wanted to take down the whole Billington House, and I know I could have if I wanted to. That scares me. I don't have control over myself." Tears stream down my face. "No ghosts, but I can't control my power. I'm a monster."

A tear runs down her cheek too, but she smiles. "Your power is greater than any of ours. Stop running from it. You can be Cadence. And you can be Windstorm. But whoever you choose, choose nothing anyone ever gives you. Just be yourself."

"But I saw evil. I saw visions of devils and Satan. And it was from *me*, Alondra. I'm evil."

"I told you there's no such thing as evil. It's easier to focus on what you think is evil, because evil is driven by fear. But your power isn't evil. You're not a monster."

"But I might be going crazy."

She closes her eyes and lowers her head. She's as still as a rock. I become panicked.

"Alondra! Alondra!"

But she's still breathing. So weakly.

"Bill isn't attacking you," she says, her head now buried in her chest. "And Bryce loves you more than anyone. I brought Enora back to the circle to make amends to her. I don't think you're seeing things right. Have you talked to Bryce about what happened? Or Enora?"

No.

She shudders like she did that night I called the paramedics. I think she's in pain.

"You told me last year you could help me control my magic," I say.

"I told you that to bring you back to the circle. And you came back—but not for your powers. You came back for me. Even when you almost hurt me and my husband, you did it all because you were upset about what was happening to me. Because you cared about me. So know that I forgive you." She pauses, as if to gain strength. "Windstorm, it doesn't matter if I show you magic. Tarot cards. Potions. Cauldrons. Spells. None of that makes you a witch. The earth does. Your power is from your heart. Give your heart to our mother. You keep manifesting your energy when you're upset. Learn to find it when you're good. A witch's wisdom is like that of a yogi. It's easy to practice black magic. It's much harder to practice white. It's harder to be good. Try to be good and you may find balance. A weak witch and a weak man only practice evil. You are not weak. Learn the harder path. Learn the balance and you will no longer feel unstable. Or crazy, as you said."

She takes a deep breath. It seems strained.

"I have to go. I don't believe there's an answer to my questions. Not here. Perhaps where I'm going. I love you. And I know you love me, whether I'm forgiven or not. Goodbye, Cadence. I wish you well. I've been so happy to have been your teacher. Yatu."

She slumps over into her chest. It is silent for a moment; then she says faintly, only to herself, "I'm afraid."

Her breathing stops. She's immobile.

I fall on her, sobbing. "Oh, God, Alondra, don't go! I forgive you! I do! I forgive you... Don't, don't go. Please. I forgive you!"

I touch her hand and her fingers move weakly. She squeezes my hand for a moment. But then—nothing.

When she lets go of my fingers, it's quiet. Birds chirp. Clouds move shadows over the grass. The woman I hated for so long is dead. But I loved her. She was right. She was not only my mentor; she was my mother. And now both my mothers are gone.

I stand and look down at this black orb on the grass. I realize that if it were up to Alondra, she would let the earth consume her body like this. Her wishes would be for no funeral. She would be happy to just fade here in the forest. But I need to get back and tell the others. My witches need to mourn. And we will need to hold our Sabbath to help her spirit cross to the Summerland.

15

THE BILLINGTON CEMETERY

I DON'T LIKE FUNERALS. I DON'T CARE FOR CEMETERIES EITHER. I mean, I never visit my mother's grave. I'd rather honor her in my heart, you know?

Mom died around this time last year. That funeral was closer to Atlanta. This time, I only drove about forty miles from the university. It turned out that Alondra's family, the Billingtons, don't live very far from Hawthorne. So we all meet in Flintwood, a small farming town about thirty miles east of the college.

The funny thing about Alondra is that she was so mysterious I've learned more about her over the past hour, at their farm, than I did when I knew her. That is so irritating! I especially learned a lot from her garrulous uncle, Hanley. Uncle Hanley has been talking to me for the last half hour beside a large red barn close to the Billingtons' family cemetery. All the witches and a bunch of well-dressed strangers have convened here to shelter from the rain. My friends are wearing black dresses and actually look like witches today, but it doesn't seem inappropriate right now.

Uncle Hanley is giving me a history lesson on the Billingtons. He doesn't know yet how I knew Alondra. He just brightened up when I asked how Alondra had such an incredible house.

"Well, Alondra's relative was Abigail Billington, you know," he says. "Figure she was living in high cotton, *literally*. She was born in a rich cotton plantation in Tallahassee, Florida. She had an arranged marriage to Josiah Billington and, well, Josiah cheated on Abigail, having an affair with a slave from Louisiana: Escoba Hawthorne. Escoba was a voodoo witch. And she was black. The Hawthornes weren't such a distinguished family." *Okay. That sounds a little racist. Not to mention Escoba happens to be my distant relative.* "So Escoba ended up on their farm and wooed poor Josiah. They had a mixed-race boy named Maverick. But the fact that he was illegitimate and that his mother was a slave was scandalous. And yet, you know, folks were so understanding in these parts back then that the town of Hawthorne grew under his family name just the same."

The fact that "folks are so understanding" probably has something to do with the Billington family. I'm struck by how nice Uncle Hanley is. Alondra always told me I had a great heart when, in fact, she did. I think her good-heartedness runs in the family.

I know all about my family tree, but he's talking so excitedly that I don't want to interrupt him. As Hanley's relating all this —and I find it amusing because, in suspenders and spectacles, he looks like he'd fit right in in nineteenth-century Georgia as a farmer—I just politely listen. But when he starts talking about how Maverick set up our university town, and he speaks with pride about it, I can't resist telling him my relationship to Maverick. He surprises me by scooping me up in his arms and calling me family. I laugh. It's really cute and it reminds me of Alondra.

Maddie catches the whole thing from the corner of her eye

and smiles. But it's a sad smile, and her sadness reminds me of Alondra passing away.

As we're still waiting for the service, I ask Uncle Hanley a question Alondra never answered. "Why is her last name Johansen?" *Why not Reardon?*

"Well, that was her first husband's name. She got her teaching degree and figured she'd never change it."

Yeah, because then it would be Reardon and he's a total asshole.

Then I see the asshole walk into the barn. The bald devil is wearing a white shirt with a black vest and black slacks. Even though he knows my friends well, he stands alone near a snack table beside a stack of hay.

I pick up an hors d'oeuvre from another table. It's basically a cracker with cream cheese. Then I lean back against the table, by myself. Frida and Hope have drawn Uncle Hanley away. He's got quite a magnetic personality.

Then Bryce walks in alone wearing a navy-blue suit. That's a good thing, because I think my temper would have boiled over if he were with Enora. Sad or not, I would have lost my mind. I don't want to do that. Not at Alondra's funeral. He sees me but I don't walk over. I just remain leaning against the table. He doesn't approach me. Instead he walks over to comfort Mira. Mira leans into his arms, bawling.

"Katie," I hear beside me. I turn and see a thin guy with graying hair and matching gray eyes giving me a faint smile. It's Dad. I hug him tightly.

"Hi, Daddy."

"Hey, sis," says a broad-shouldered boy in a collared shirt and slacks. Damien. My brother. Damie is looking at my face funny. So is my dad. We've been talking on the phone, but they haven't seen me for a while. Not in witch attire, with all this black makeup. I look totally goth. But if they understood, they'd know that Alondra would have liked me dressing like this.

My brother hugs me. My dad and brother came because

they know how important Alondra was to me, and their presence makes things a little easier.

"Hi, Mr. Hawthorne," says Maddie, coming over.

"Rocky couldn't make it?" I ask Maddie.

She shakes her head dismissively. "You must be Katie's little brother." Maddie reaches out to my brother.

"Damien."

"Damie," I correct him. "Damie for short."

"Well, he's not short, Katie," says Maddie with a chuckle. She checks him out from head to toe and, for a flash, she loses her frown and smiles. "And he's not little."

That's true. Damie's about six foot three.

"How're you holding up, squirt?" Dad asks me.

I can't say anything. I just shake my head.

"Kate and Alondra were probably closer than any of us, Mr. Hawthorne," explains Maddie. She's somber again, which almost makes me tear up. "She loved her. And Alondra really loved her back."

"You guys were in an honors program, right?" asks Damie innocently.

"Yes."

"Sure," Maddie says with a smile to Damie. "Hey, you're graduating this year? Right?"

"Yep."

"You should come here. It's—"

"He's going to an Ivy League school," I interrupt.

"You're smart, huh?" Maddie asks my brother with interest.

Uncle Hanley comes over and starts talking up a storm. Apparently, I must look like my dad and brother, because he starts talking about our relationship to Maverick Hawthorne. I'm not sure he believed me.

Eventually we all gather outside with umbrellas on white wooden chairs in a wild grassy field. The service goes fast. Too fast. It's pouring rain and, from under a huge umbrella, I watch my teacher and mentor, my friend, lowered into the ground. That's awful. I think I should have just left her in peace in the woods.

The worst part about watching the casket being lowered is that Bryce is standing across from me. Twice he meets my gaze. I wipe my eyes pretending to cry but, really, I don't want to look at him. I'm furious. I know my "vision" at the Billington House was no vision. I know he was with her that night.

I don't cry. I don't shed a tear during the whole service. After Alondra died in my arms, I think I emptied all the water I had left in my eyes. I stayed there with her, alone, for at least a half hour before I went back to the house to tell my circle the horrible news.

When the ceremony ends, Maddie comes up to me and asks if it's okay if she stays at her house instead of the dorm for a little while. She says she needs some time alone with her mom to grieve. I nod. Her mom is the coolest mom I've ever known. If anyone can cheer Maddie up, it's her. But I really don't like it, because I'm fighting with Bryce. I'll be very alone.

Then I watch my cheating boyfriend walk across the grassy field and back to his BMW in the parking lot. He has a really small umbrella, and the rain just splashes on his short dark hair. For a moment, I have the urge to leave my dad and run to him with my umbrella, which is huge, but someone stops me.

Enora. I didn't see her during the whole service, but now she's walking across the grass toward me. She doesn't have an umbrella. She doesn't seem to care about getting wet. I really hate her. I hate her so much. She's even wearing a slutty black lacy dress. It's so inappropriate. And she doesn't look sad. Why is she even here? Did she really care about Alondra?

I turn to my brother. Damie's got his eyes on her too, but for very different reasons.

"You guys, I need to go. I'll meet you at Lacey's." Lacey's is a nice steak house my dad wants to take my brother and me to. "There's someone I have to talk to."

"Sure, Katie," says Damie. He hugs me.

"Thanks for coming."

My dad hugs me too and kisses me on the forehead. "I'll see you at six, okay, squirt?"

I nod.

My brother and dad leave with not a moment to spare. Enora walks right up to me. I'm ready to crack a hole in the ground and send the witch back to the hell where she belongs.

"Sorry for your loss," Enora lies with a sly smile.

I just give her a hard stare.

"I know this is difficult for you, Cadence. All the witches in your coven told me how much Alondra cared about you. And your mother died around this time last year, right? It must be hard for you."

I know all this. I'm living it. The last thing I need is for this bitch-witch to spell it out for me. She's only angering me more.

"I also heard from Mira about something you saw at the Halloween party," Enora says with a grin. "You realize that there's nothing between Bryce and me. Not anymore, anyway. He's yours." *Thanks. I appreciate your permission.*

"I know what I saw. What you *wanted* me to see."

My feet are about ready to turn and walk, but Enora puts her hand on my shoulder. I throw it off. Then, of all people to rescue me, Mira walks over. Mira, who's been crying her eyes out, who gave a speech and ruined it by crying too much, runs up to Enora and me. And she's not acting like Enora's friend. She's acting like mine.

"Is this really the time?" Mira asks her. "Why don't you leave her alone?"

"The time for two *real* witches to talk, you mean?" Enora says.

"You should be careful, Panthera. If you anger Windstorm,

who knows what she's capable of?" Then Mira snatches my hand. "Come on. Let's go, Katie."

"Wait," Enora says to Mira. Then she turns to me. "You did see Bryce and me. I'm not saying you didn't. Bryce used to be my boyfriend, Cadence, when he lived at the Billington House. I think, for some reason, you conjured up a vision of our past."

"Boy, did she," Mira says.

"I don't believe you." I shake my head. "It wasn't the past." I turn, with Mira holding my hand, but Enora's not done.

"I have one request, Cadence. You are the leader of the Hawthorne coven. I ask permission to pay my respects to Falconsong at your next meeting." She looks around the cemetery in disgust. "Not in a Christian burial, but through the rites of a witch's funeral. I was Alondra's friend too. I—"

"That's not what she said," Mira interrupts.

"We had our differences," Enora says with a nod. "That's true. But we made up in the end." Enora nods to me. "Cadence, can I join your circle for her going-away ceremony? I too wish her a swift and pleasant journey to the Summerland."

"No."

Enora is shocked at my response. It's like I struck her across the face. She's not smug anymore. She's pissed. She frowns and her dark skin flushes enough to turn red.

"How dare you," Enora mutters. "You don't know what this means to a witch." Then she looks at Mira in contempt. "A *real* witch."

"I don't want you near our circle ever again," I say.

"Think it over. If you don't let me pay respects, you might as well call me her enemy. That will undo all the things Alondra did, at the end of her life, to make peace with me. And I know this is not what she would have wanted."

"I don't want you holding Sabbath with us again. You don't belong in my coven."

"I'm not asking to be a part of your weak coven, you stupid

cunt," she snaps. "I'm asking you to permit me to pay my respects to the dead. A fellow witch who, although we had our differences, I admired."

"No."

Enora stares at me. Then she grunts like an animal and rushes off, seemingly humiliated.

Mira watches her with concern. I'm happy to have gotten rid of her, but just when I think she's gone, she turns once more.

"Oh, Katie," Enora says with a smile, cocking her head back. "I'd have a talk with your boyfriend about his college years. You seemed so upset when you saw him touching me that night. Perhaps you should ask him about all the other girls he touched while he was in the fraternity and when he was working with the High Wizard. Bryce was a very popular frat brother. And very useful to Alondra's husband." And with that, she spins around in her wet dress and leaves.

I can't stop staring in her direction. But I'm too sad and angry and in too much pain to do anything. I feel like just giving up and falling to the ground.

"Are you okay?" Mira asks.

I shake my head.

Mira surprises me by hugging me. Then she walks off alone.

It rains harder. I reach into my pocket and check my new cell phone. It's four thirty. I have a half hour to get back to campus and an hour to get ready for dinner.

I walk back to the freshly dug earth. Alondra's resting place.

By now, the cemetery is vacant. Down below lies Alondra, and I'm alone with her. I pick up some of the wet, muddy soil and let it run through my fingers under the rain. I bring it up to my nose. Touching the mud gives me pleasure.

I think of her two questions. One was her request for forgiveness. The other:

I believe death is an illusion. It does not hurt the dead. It's one's loved ones who suffer. What do you think of that, Cadence?

"You're so wise, Alondra," I say out loud, choked up. "You told me once the word *witch* means wisdom. You were a great witch. The answer to your final question, teacher, is...*yes*."

I kneel in the mud before the mound and finally cry.

When I finally get control of myself, I stand up. I'm alone in the cemetery. The farm has fields for miles, which is a pretty break from the forest surrounding Hawthorne. I enjoy the beautiful view. In the distance, near my college, mountain ranges rise. But here the fields go on and on.

The clouds are clearing. I'm not sure how long I've been out here, but I don't want to leave. I even see the pastor who ran the service. He walks by, shakes my hand, and gives me condolences again.

I have to go or I'll be late for dinner with Dad and my brother, so I will my legs to move back to my car. The parking lot's now empty. As I unlock my door—by the handle, because my key fob doesn't work anymore—I see something in the fields. A figure in black. I whirl around to get a better look. She's a witch in our black cloak, walking the fields alone, about a hundred yards out. I can't make out her face because she is wearing a hood. I walk closer to see who it is. Enora? She seems to be walking toward me. Maybe she wants to curse me? I don't know. But then, as quickly as I saw the witch, she vanishes.

16

KINDA ALONE

I'm alone, but that's okay because I want to be. I'm reading a textbook on the Sumerians of ancient Mesopotamia on the cement stage in the center of campus. It snowed last night, and ice is still thawing in patches on the lawn. I'm wearing my red-and-gold sweater—school colors—over another sweater, a button-down undershirt, thick underwear, and jeans. Yeah, it's cold. But I want to be outdoors. Especially since Maddie's still at Aunt Jane's. She told me she was just too depressed to return to campus.

It might be cold but it's also nice outside. The nearby trees are losing their leaves, and many branches are leafless. The gorgeous orange, red, and brown leaves that I love have fallen, but there's an early-morning dew that smells fresh.

I look down at the textbook on my lap. There's a picture of a statue and a guy with a beard. I take a deep breath and read.

Did you know that the Sumerians were thought to be the first great empire in the world? Some religious scholars think they were descendants of Abraham. *They lived around the Tigris River in modern-day Iraq.* Aha. It says that on page forty-two. Personally, I prefer learning about the Egyptians and their pyramids, but the Assyrians are neat because I don't know much about them. Well, no one knows a whole lot about them. They're an ancient, ancient civilization.

I sit straighter, stretch my arms, and take a deep breath. Down the lawn, I see another straight-A student at a bench, reading. He's a thin boy with glasses. He nods at me. Cute.

We had our Sabbath memorial a few days ago. Reardon was there. How could he not be? It's his house and his wife. Bryce wasn't. I'm such a bitch for not letting Bryce come. But hey, it was enough that I met with my sisters at all after the night Enora nearly brought hell into the backyard.

I gave Mira the memorial candle. In our tradition, whenever we mourn, we light the candle in memory of the deceased. I still have one for my mother's death. Mira was shocked at the honor. Everyone was. They all thought I should take the candle, since it's given to the witch closest to the deceased, but I argued that Mira had the greatest love for Alondra.

I look out at the trees. Beyond a few red brick buildings, I see a water tower, with the words "Hawthorne University" painted on it, beside a few rolling hills, and farther still is an old farmhouse. The buildings are old, but they'll be gone eventually. The buildings come and go, but the trees never change. If a tree falls, another takes its place. Just like their red and orange leaves. They haven't changed since I first came to Hawthorne two and a half years ago. They probably haven't changed since Maverick and Escoba walked here. There's a comfort in their permanence. Alondra was right. When I die, I want to die out in the wilderness too.

I thumb through some more pages and realize I have no interest in reading about Assyria. So I reach into my black backpack and replace it with another book: *Broomstick*. This is my Book of Shadows.

Alondra gave me *Broomstick* during my initiation ceremony last year. The first half was written by Alondra. That's why I take it out. This morning, I don't want to write an entry in it. I want to hear her words again. She's written so many entries in small writing or in the margins that I haven't read all the sections of her writings. Reading it now makes me feel like she's still here with me, you know.

I thumb through the pages, avoiding sections on feces and vomit—yeah, that stuff is really in there—and the equally ridiculous poetry on garden flowers, until I come across a page that intrigues me because it's about Sumerians, interestingly enough.

~

ASSYRIA, WITH PERSONAL DISCOVERY, ON THE SUBJECT OF GHOSTS

The spirit world is so close to our realm that it is easy for the dead to become trapped. As in life, most of these spirits are good and merely need to be nudged to find peace. They need you, witches, your friends and family, to show your love and guide them swiftly to the Summerland. Your help will ensure that one day, when your time has come, they might help you on the other side. And so our funeral rite is so important for a true witch.

Other ghosts remain in our plane for personal reasons. They are not trapped, they know the way, but they haunt the living for reasons that may not be apparent until a later time.

Finally, there are some that, as when they were living, delight in hurting others. Poltergeists. These spirits haunt the living. They have been spoken of ever since the most ancient of civilizations. In fact, it is the Sumerian sorcerers who wrote of the evil spirits we see today.

There are two main devil spirits referenced in ancient Akkadia: the Ekimmu and the Alu. The Ekimmu are the ghosts most commonly found haunting homes. These ghosts refuse passage from the spirit world, usually after dying a violent death. They are the most common, and potentially dangerous, poltergeists. Like modern vampires, they feed off the energy of the living. The Alu haunt victims at night, but usually during sleep. Doglike spirits, these ghosts are often erroneously thought, in modern times, to be simply nightmares experienced during sleep paralysis.

A witch can ward off these evil spirits with her usual remedies: salt and sage, burying small figurines of Lamassu, or speaking the words of Nineveh. Surely any witch knows this, but for true success, I tell you, there is no incantation of greater power than one's soul. Atman.

The failure of the mind is equal to the failure of a witch's spell. Our thoughts cannot fully comprehend the universe that surrounds us, so how can a witch do justice to the power of Selene? Practice with atman, sisters: no thought, one's heart. Approach with confidence in yourself and the power within will flow.

I had unique opportunities to rid my coven of poltergeists. One Ekimmu haunted Loraine, who joined the circle after my success. She had traveled from Wichita, Kansas, upon hearing of my reputation. The other was Winona, who ...

I hope my witch-ghost isn't an Ekimmu. Alondra never told me how to get rid of my ghost, Maverick. He just disappeared. But now I'm seeing a transparent witch around campus. I've seen her a couple more times since the funeral.

I stop reading for a moment and laugh out loud. Only Alondra would teach extra-credit Sumerian demonology right after her death. And, typical of her, she makes it sound so much more interesting than my early civilizations professor. I'm thinking maybe I should incorporate all this shit into my Sumerian essays for the final for extra credit.

And I really like reading Alondra's words. It's like she's here with me still.

But I yawn and close the book. I'm also really tired.

I lean back and look up at the cloudless sky. It's beautiful. The yellow sun blinds me, but I enjoy the hot rays hitting my face and warming me in the cold.

My eyes close. I haven't slept well for days, since the funeral. And before that, I wasn't sleeping after my fight with Bryce. And before that, I wasn't sleeping well because Alondra was sick.

I let myself lie on my side on the cement stage and drift off.

I hear footsteps that stir me. I think I hear my name.

I'm surprised when I see a young man walking across the grass carrying a big leather bag. I recognize his neatly pressed preppy clothes. Bryce? It is! And I think he sees me.

I catch him furrowing his brow, but he quickly turns his head. He's wearing a dark gray button-down and black slacks. He's sporting a beard now, or trying to, which is new. Usually he's just a little unshaven.

I shove my books in my black backpack and run to him.

"Hi, Bryce," I say. I'm surprised at how sheepish my voice sounds.

He stops, shuffles his heavy brown leather bag over to his other shoulder, and turns around under an ugly silver awning. His blue eyes look at mine over thick bags—he's not sleeping either—and, for a moment, I remember our old flame in those hypnotic blues.

"Cadence," he says professionally.

"I...I just feel bad because I didn't let you come to...our ceremony." I can't say sorry because I'm not. I mean, if I were sorry, I would have invited him. Right?

"I loved Alondra," he says. His voice is strained. "I asked Maddie because I just wanted to pay my respects."

"I know. I just couldn't see you there." That sounds really bad. And I'm wondering where I'm going with this.

"Okay," he says with a sigh. He pauses for a moment, but then he shakes his head and walks on.

"Wait," I say.

He stops again.

"I want you to know that I always liked you, you know, other than just as a date. You know. I like you as a friend. Because you're so nice. And I think you're really a good friend too, and—"

"Then why didn't you let me go to Alondra's memorial?"

Uh, yeah. Why? Shit.

"I didn't want to see you."

Is that supposed to make sense? He looks right into my eyes, baffled. My heart jumps because I'm still mesmerized by his baby blues, but that seems to disturb him more. It's like our old flame upsets him. His eyelids flutter and he quickly looks away.

"Okay, Cadence."

"Wait, I didn't want to see you," I stammer, "because I thought I'd hesitate. I like you, you know, but I...don't like you, you know. Because of what you did at the party. Ya know?"

"No, I don't know." He looks angrier than I've ever seen him. "I called you. I reached out and you ignored all my texts and calls. You just ran away. You abandoned me just like you abandoned Alondra. The moment something happens, you run away, Katie. You never let anyone explain. You just shut down."

"But you didn't answer your phone at the party." *Yeah. So there!*

"You accused me without letting me explain to you what happened."

"Okay, what happened?" I shake my head. "I saw you with Enora. And she told me about the other girls." I look down and bite my lip. "That disgusts me. You lied to me. You said you didn't do anything with the other—"

"Again, Cadence," he snaps. "You never let me explain."

He turns and walks off, and this time he's not about to turn back.

I don't know what to say. I can't apologize because I think I'm right. But I want to apologize. Just to be with him.

"Didn't you lie to me?" I holler. "Weren't you with all those girls?"

"Shut up!" He's never yelled at me like that. I'm shocked. Then, in a forced whisper, he snaps, "We're on campus. You don't know what happened, and now you're accusing me in public!"

But there's no one around us. I think the only student is that boy on the bench about fifty yards away.

"Well, were you?" I insist, searching his face.

"I already told you my activity is in the past. I don't owe you anything. How can I be with someone who doesn't listen and allow me to explain?" And that's it. Then he says, before turning from me a final time, "You need to grow up." I think he was going to say something far worse, but he hesitated when he glanced into my eyes again.

And he's gone.

I don't cry. I've done plenty of that. But I feel uneasy and a little sick to my stomach. And I don't believe it. Is he gone now?

I still feel I'm right to have done what I did about Alondra's memorial, but I guess he's right that I should have let him explain everything. But what he doesn't understand is that I knew if I let him talk I would accept whatever he said. I'm that attracted to him. That's also why I didn't let him go to Alondra's memorial. I knew I'd just get back together with him.

I watch him walk all the way down the long walkway and turn a corner. As he turns, I could swear he looks back for a moment. Maybe he's not gone from me?

I'm tired. My whole body feels like it has a two-ton truck on its shoulders. I just want to go home and sleep.

I reposition my backpack on my shoulder and head back to the dorm, alone, to take another nap. But I know I won't nap. I won't be able to sleep at all. Maddie's still away, so I can't talk to her. And I've lost Alondra. And now Bryce.

I'm so alone.

17

ICED COFFEE AND A LIGHTER

I'm not sleeping and neither is Maddie, so, even though we should be having fun shopping in Atlanta, we decide to grab coffee on campus at seven in the morning. Maddie and I have a tradition of shopping over the weekend after our midterms are over, but neither of us wants to do anything. I'm just thrilled she's back. The university coffee shop is empty, with all the two-person tables along brown-painted walls and windows, and the four large tables in the center, being unoccupied. In fact, the whole campus is empty right now. People are still recovering from their exams.

Maddie didn't cry much during the ceremony, but she cried last night in bed. She tried to keep her whimpering quiet, but I heard her.

Right now, Maddie's staring into her cup as she absent-mindedly stirs the cream, cradling her head in her hand. It's so depressing.

Maddie's been wearing black ever since the funeral, and this morning is no different. So I wore a black dress to match her. The clothes and our black lipstick, eyeliner, and nail polish make us look like real witches.

The grassy hill outside is not green. It's white. That's the other reason it's empty in the coffee shop. I hate snow and so does everyone else at Hawthorne University. It's icy cold. Slippery. Dangerous to drive on.

She's still stirring her coffee. I'm sipping a green tea latte, my absolute favorite.

I did well midsemester. It was the first time I'd gotten straight As since my first year. I think it's because I didn't have much to distract me. Enora ruining our Sabbath and Alondra's passing meant that I stayed away from our circle and studied. You know, my mother used to tell me to be positive and look at the cup as being half-full.

"I'm done with Rocky," Maddie says, finally looking up from her cup.

"You're kidding?"

Maddie shakes her hair out. I thought she was crying about Alondra last night, but maybe it was over her boyfriend. "He's a meathead. Do you know what a meathead is, Cadence?" She looks up with a flash of her famous whimsical smile, but it vanishes as quickly as it came. "It's an expression for jocks. You know, no-brain morons. All-muscle jocks. That's Rocky."

"He seemed nice."

"He's an asshole." She looks out the window pensively. "Like all men."

I nod.

"And he was cheating on me."

Oh.

"And..." She takes a deep breath, trying to smile again. "He's a loser. You told me that."

"I didn't." All I said was she should be going out with a doctor or something.

"Men are all the same. It really doesn't matter if they have brain cells or not. They're all goddamn assholes."

Two sorority snoots, wearing their letters on their red-and-gold sweaters, swing the glass door open and prance in, giggling stupidly. One has a long blond ponytail and is perfectly manicured, wearing a plaid skirt. (She must have been freezing outside). The other is a short dark-haired girl with flawless makeup. They both order something at the register. The blonde looks over. I could almost swear she's happy we look so miserable.

"How'd you do on your art exam?" Maddie asks.

"Ninety-four."

"Jesus, Cadence," she says, brushing her hair back. "How do you do that?" She lifts her cup, shakes her head, blows some mist, and sips some coffee.

"What'd you get?"

"Seventy-six. Guess I passed."

"It was a difficult exam," I say with a shrug.

"Stop being nice. It wasn't that hard."

"I hate this," I say and hit the table.

"What?" She furrows her brow.

"Everything's depressing. Why do we have to feel so down?"

"Alondra just died." Oh, yeah. She has to say it like that.

And that's when the two girls across the coffeehouse look at us and laugh some more. They think something's really funny.

"Excuse me, but aren't you two friends of Mira?" asks the blonde between giggles. She thinks that's really funny too.

I roll my eyes and look away. "Why do they have to be here?"

"Can't have the place all to ourselves." Maddie shrugs, sipping more coffee.

I take a deep breath. "What was I saying?"

"You asked why we were sad. I said it was because Alondra just died."

"Why do we have to dwell on that?"

The sorority girls laugh harder. I feel my face flushing.

They're really pissing me off. Of course, the two strangers have no idea that this is the wrong time to mess with me.

"You're cute, Katie," Maddie says, touching my arm and distracting me from glaring at the snoots. "I don't know. Maybe you're right. Maybe we should have gone shopping. Alondra probably would have liked that."

"And now you broke up with Rocky? When?"

"He and I broke up before the funeral," she replies with a shrug. "I just didn't want to tell you. After the Billington House party, Rock asked if I wanted to go to another party off-campus. Being that you shut off all the lights..." I stick my tongue out at her and she laughs. "We went to Violetta's house. Violetta is Rocky's old girlfriend. I already had a bad feeling about that."

"Can I ask you two something?" interjects the blond-haired girl across the café. I really don't want her to. When we don't reply, she says, "Mira's so weird and she always dresses like you two dress now. Are you guys...what everyone says you are?"

"What?" asks Maddie.

"You know," the blonde says. Then she covers her mouth and looks at her short-haired friend. "Witches?" And that makes the two sorority sluts completely lose it. They're just laughing their heads off.

When they quiet down from whatever the fuck they think is so funny, I say, "I tell you what." They look at me. "If you keep bothering us, you'll find out."

The dark-haired girl loses her smile. See, we've developed a reputation through the gossiping channels around campus, and the press isn't very good. Usually, I just get a stray glance, but I suppose our black mourning clothes are just too much today. I knew I should have just put on a sweater and jeans.

The blond-haired girl chuckles again, but it sounds nervous.

"Don't do it, Kate," Maddie warns. She looks worried.

"What?"

"Whatever you're thinking about doing."

I roll my eyes. "So what else happened?"

"Well, Violetta…" Maddie continues after sipping more coffee. "She's not a meathead, she's a pothead. You know, she even wears a rainbow Rastafarian hat and braids her hair. But…" Maddie points at the girls sitting across the café. "She's like them. Hardly Rastafarian, ya know, more like a rich spoiled kid. The house is apparently hers, even though she's never worked a day in her life. She graduated Hawthorne three years ago.

"Anyway, Violetta has all her weed-smoking friends there, and they're nice but—it's not that I mind pot, but the whole house smells skunky. And no one's in costumes, unless you count Violetta's hat. So, I'm toking away with three of her girlfriends, and actually having a pretty good time. I mean, you know I had already drunk a lot. Everything's going swimmingly until I see Rock near the stairwell. And he's with Violetta, which I don't think much of, until I see her put an arm around him."

"Sorry," I say.

"I'm not finished, Cadence… I think everything's fine. I figure he's drunk." The bitches across the room are laughing again. "And the way she looks at him, she's lost in his eyes, you know. The way I've seen you and Bryce look at each other. So I begin to think we're there for very different reasons than to just get stoned with my boyfriend's friends."

"At least you didn't see him making out with her like Bryce."

"Right, Katie. I'm not done." Maddie pauses and sighs, staring outside at the white hillside for a moment. "An hour later, after I've gotten more fucked up, I have to run to pee. So I walk down a hallway, relieved that there's less smoke, and open a door, thinking it might be a bathroom. Well, it wasn't a bathroom, it was a bedroom. And there before my eyes… I don't have to give you the details. You can guess the rest. Needless to say, I didn't see him making out with her. They weren't wearing any clothes."

"Oh God, I'm so sorry."

"I wouldn't be surprised if Violetta planned the whole goddamn thing. You know, get me screwed up, distract me, and then have her way with him. The bitch. What do you think, Katie?"

I kinda register her words, but I kinda don't, because the sorority snoots are laughing really loud again, and I distinctly hear the word *witch*. Maddie touches my hand. "Whatcha think?"

"It's terrible, Maddie. What a jerk."

"It's okay. Honestly, I felt like we were moving too fast. It was, I don't know, too good. We never got to really know each other. I just loved doing stuff with him. He was fun. And he was a really good lover, you know." She giggles. "But it wasn't deep like you and Bryce."

"Bryce and I aren't deep."

"Hmm…" Maddie looks at her coffee. "You and he go really well together. I think you should give him another chance."

"Seriously?" I snap, hitting the table hard with my palm. The sorority snoots turn. Even the barista behind the counter, a large old woman with thin gray hair, who I've seen working the register since I first enrolled in Hawthorne, looks over too.

"Calm down," Maddie says.

"I tried to talk to Bryce, and he was just cold." I take a deep breath. "He's a player. Worse than Rocky, I think. I never thought he was, but he is. I should have guessed it, being that he was some kind of 'honoree' of Psi Kappa Psi. With all the girls there, imagine the supply he gave to Reardon. It all makes sense. I think he lied about that too. He told me he never had sex with the other girls in ceremonies, but Enora suggested he did. He fooled me. He fooled all of us, Maddie. He's not nice. And there's no way—"

"Don't get so upset. I like him. Why don't you ask him to explain himself? He told me you weren't answering his calls. Why don't you talk it out? You can't trust Enora. So they were making out. They weren't fucking like my asshole boyfriend. Maybe Bryce can explain himself."

"Ya think so, Madison?" I ask sarcastically, shaking my head.

"Yeah, I actually do, Cadence. What happened doesn't sound like Bryce. He told me he would explain himself, but now he's pissed that you didn't talk to him. And even more furious that you didn't let him go to Alondra's funeral."

"That was mean, I guess," I say with a nod.

"It was." She nods and lifts her eyebrows. "Very."

"Well, why didn't you tell me that when I didn't invite him?"

"I don't know, Katie. I've got a lot of shit I'm dealing with right now."

"I know." I touch her arm. "Sorry."

"It's okay," she says with a faint smile.

Then the two snoots are at it again. I'm angry at them, but part of me isn't. I get why they're laughing. Sometimes I think I should be at the other table, laughing at us. Why are we wearing these long black dresses and goth makeup? If I had seen us a year ago, I would have thought the same thing I thought when I first saw Mira: *freak.* If I hadn't joined the coven, maybe I would be over there laughing too.

I stare at the wall. The walls have murals. There are various drawings from an artist on campus. They're quite good. There's a sketch in white paint on a black canvas of a soccer player kicking a ball. We have a soccer team, not an American football team. We don't have a stadium large enough for American football. There are also drawings of two basketball players fielding a rebound and a swimmer swimming freestyle.

My eyes fall on the sorority girls. I can't believe they're still laughing. It's not that funny. I squeeze my hands. Maddie looks over too. They're like hyenas.

"Easy, Cadence," Maddie warns.

The blonde's cute red-and-black plaid skirt reminds me of a dress code skirt. It must be freezing outside with the snow. She looks like a whore. I'm sure her clothes were super uncomfortable out in the snow, but I doubt her ego cared.

So what I decide to do is help warm her up a little. Just a little kindling. Actually, I set her skirt on fire. A small flame, like a lighter, you know, but enough to make her jump up from her chair and brush the smoke from her heinie. Her friend jumps up too and starts slapping her ass to put out the smoke.

Then I laugh. I even cackle a little like a witch just for them.

"Cadence!" Maddie snaps.

The two girls are out of the café quicker than I can respond to my friend.

"What?" I ask, feigning innocence with a shrug. I drink some tea. "She looked cold."

"That was mean."

"I'm not in the mood to be nice, Maddie."

It looks so cold outside, and now that I've burned a hole in the sorority girl's skirt, she's going to be colder. But for now, her ass is hot. Her friend waves her hand over the smoke as they rush down a sidewalk paralleling the snowy hillside. I've really given them something to gossip about.

"Sometimes I don't know who you are anymore," Maddie says.

"A witch."

"Today you're being a bad witch."

As the two sorority girls rush around a corner and make their way to the main drag of campus, my jaw drops. There in the middle of campus, on the ice-patched asphalt walkway, stands a black figure. The same ghost I first saw at Alondra's funeral. The girls are rushing close to her, but it doesn't slow them down. She's a shadowy black hooded figure, wearing a black druid-like cloak just like we wear in my coven. I can't see her face.

"What's wrong?" asks Maddie.

"I see my ghost again."

"What?" Maddie jumps. She looks where I point but doesn't see anything. The two sorority girls walk right through her.

"Shit." I tear my eyes away and put my head in my hand. "You don't see her? Really?"

"No."

I used to see ghosts. I used to see Maverick and Escoba, but this figure seems different. Alondra said my haunting was over, and I was quite pleased she told me that. It had been torture going through months of seeing Maverick and Escoba. Am I going to be haunted by this new specter?

I look back out the window and the ghost is gone.

"I saw a witch. A witch...that ghost witch, I think. I don't know. Those girls walked right through her."

"Not good, Katie... Do you think it was Panthera?"

"I don't know."

"Maybe Alondra."

18

HIKING

I'M HIKING. THAT'S OKAY BECAUSE I ENJOY WALKING THE PATHS around campus at night, only it's three in the morning and I'm alone in the dark forest. Well, I couldn't sleep. And staring up at Maddie's mattress from my bunk bed, I felt a trance coming on. Maddie was sound asleep, so I didn't wake her. She's finally sleeping again after a few weeks of mourning. Time always heals, right? Anyway, I just quietly threw on some clothes, a heavy coat, and boots and stepped out.

I'm ascending a path and it isn't too dark. There's a full moon. I hear running water to my right. My waterfall. My destination. I figured since I can't sleep, I might as well visit my favorite stream. It's so pretty with water flowing over stones and reflecting the moonlight. The sound is so tranquil. I reach down and touch the water. It's icy cold. I crouch down and cup some of the running water in my hands. It might be cold, but it's fresh and clean. As I gather more and pour it over my face, I hear a noise. I can't tell if it's a yell or even laughter, but I hear it coming from the top of Hilltop Bluff. There's a red fiery glow on the summit. I skim my fingers along the cold, flowing water one last time; then I walk back onto the path to see where the light's coming from. It couldn't be my coven. It's past the witching hour.

I feel drowsy as if in a dream. But the trees around me seem so vivid and real. My senses are heightened as I walk up the grassy hill. There isn't any breeze, but I feel the air brushing along my cheeks. There's a dampness too. I smell a pleasant odor of wet mud, dead leaves and blades of grass. My heart's beating fast. It's a weird mix of somnolence and excitement that I've only ever experienced when casting spells. I must have slipped into a trance... But why?

There's a flutter of wings and a black bird lands on a tree branch about a foot away from me.

"Amica!" I'm so happy to see her. I reach out my right hand, and the raven lands on my outstretched arm. I haven't seen Amica since before Alondra died. I pet her wings. The feathers are a little damp. Perhaps she's been in the lovely waterfall too. I walk towards the summit of the grassy hill as I pet Amica's wings. Up at the top is where I saw my deer. I wonder if she'll be there now.

The light gets brighter and I can smell fire. Then the light becomes redder. And I smell something like ceremonial incense. But then I smell something else that makes me stop. Something putrid and sulfur-like. I stand right below the summit, afraid to ascend to the top and approach the flames. Now it feels like I'm in a bad dream and, though I know I'm in a trance, I don't feel my usual sense of peace. I'm afraid. But Amica's tugging me forward with her claws.

"*Venite foras*," the raven croaks. "*Venite foras*."

"*Profecto*," I reply hesitantly.

Somehow, my feet follow my friend's claws. The burning of ash, frankincense, and myrrh fills my nostrils, but it fails to cover the stench of sulfur, which I associate with dark magic.

At the summit, girls are dancing naked. A group is circling around three witches on their knees. The circling witches' heads are snapping up and down as they dance, showing the whites of their eyes—they're quite drugged. I thought they would be from my coven. They're not. I don't recognize their faces. Except one. My skin crawls. Alondra. Alondra is standing close to a bonfire, naked and covered in camouflage paint. She is not worshipping. She is simply standing and watching a round wooden totem lying flat at a slight angle from the ground. Two men wearing black cloaks stand beside her.

I climb the last steps to the summit and walk behind the circle of nude dancing girls. They don't notice me. The totem in front of the fire is made of large wooden beams. Circling the wood is a thick burgundy velvet cloth. And on the wooden beams, facing the fire, lies a nude woman, strapped to the totem by ropes on her wrists. She is blindfolded with a strip of the burgundy cloth. When I back away from the fire and the witches, I notice that the beams and the circle of red cloth form an inverted pentagram, glowing in the firelight. I begin to tremble.

Then I recognize the men. I wish I didn't. Bill Reardon's devil face flickers in the red dancing light of the flames. Standing beside him is his "disciple," Bryce.

The woman on the pentagram squirms and pulls at her restraints. She's crying out in fear, but I can't hear her screams. I can't hear anything. In fact, the witches dance and chant, but I can't hear them either. I'm not sure if the captive is afraid because she's unsure where she is—for she's blindfolded—or if she knows where she is and fears what they're doing to her.

I run up to the pentagram and Amica darts from my arm. I pass Alondra and Reardon and run right up to Bryce. He just stares at the pentagram. His eyes are glassy—drugged.

"*Free her!*" I yell. But Bryce doesn't seem to hear me.

He looks different. His face is fully shaven, and he appears maybe five years younger. He walks right past me, ignoring me, and hands Reardon a curved knife from his cloak.

I move to the naked woman and tug at her ropes, but my hands pass right through them. I look at my hands. They're solid. I can feel warmth and smell the fire. But as the woman continues to clench her hands and fight against her restraints, my fingers can't even touch the ropes. My eyes drift down to my body, and I'm shocked to see that I'm not dressed either.

Is this a trance? A nightmare? It feels like both. I squeeze my hands, even pinch my hip, trying to snap out of it. I must be dreaming.

The witches are still circling a few yards away from the pentagram. I hear a steady drumbeat, but I don't see any drums. In the center, they continue to bow to the unholy totem.

Alondra walks over to the totem and pulls out a metal pentagram the size of her palm. She kneels and raises it to the moon. I run to her.

"Alondra! Please. Stop! What are you doing? Free her!"

She doesn't hear me. She just stares up at the moon.

I hear a scream. The woman is screaming and tugging on the boards, and I hear it this time. Reardon is gliding the curved blade along her bare skin.

"Stop!" I yell.

No one can hear me.

"Stop!"

But Alondra appears to be in a trance too. I've seen it before. Under the influence of mandrake, her eyes are wild. She is still staring up at the sky, drugged and unaware of everything. Then she looks toward the forest. I follow her gaze and see a shadow approach. It could be an animal. My deer?

I hear a scream again. I turn back to the pentagram.

"Alondra, help me!" I shout to her. "Is this a trance? Am I asleep? Help her!"

But she can't hear me.

There are more screams. This time it seems to come from the witches. They are all kneeling before the effigy. They've succumbed to madness, throwing their bodies on the ground, rising, and falling to the ground again. And now the totem is burning. No longer is the fire lighting the effigy from behind; it seems to be consuming the woman. And as she burns, the High Wizard runs his metal knife along her naked hips and breasts.

"Stop!" With all my might, I scream, *"Vade retro!"*

Lightning flashes from above and thunder quakes. The witches look to the sky for a moment and freeze. A shadow approaches from the trees, and I recognize it as the ghost I've seen on campus. She's a witch, transparent but wearing the same cloak as my coven. But as she moves closer to the fire, she vanishes.

Reardon removes the red cloth from the captive's eyes. Her eyes are a piercing blue. I recognize the face. Enora. But just like Bryce, her features are younger, much younger.

I run to Bryce. "Stop him!"

Reardon turns to Bryce, mouths words I cannot hear, and hands him the curved knife. Bryce nods, walks over to her, and runs the knife along her body. I see flashes of images, the same red images of a couple lying together that I saw at the eclipse. They surround me for seconds at a time as if transporting me back to Alondra's backyard. Every time Bryce runs the metal along the curves of Enora's body, flashes of their lovemaking reappear.

This is the sacrifice for my coven. This was their sick perverted way before I joined. They killed animals and "sacrificed" women by having sex with them. Images of Bryce having sex with Enora on the grass flash before me.

"End this incantation," says a very calm voice from the forest. I almost recognize the voice, but I can't quite place her. "End it now. Leave Cadence alone." I look to the woods, but I see no one.

Enora looks into my eyes as Bryce continues to run the knife along her body. She stops struggling and turns her lips toward his. They kiss passionately. Then she pulls away to look at me. "Witness what he did," Enora says with a smile. "I shall take my revenge on your Hawthorne coven. *Et nos unum sumus.*" And she bursts into laughter as Bryce continues to run the blade along her body.

I'm sick. The scene swirls in circles around me, and I am surrounded by Enora's laughter echoing on the hilltop. A chilly wind blows along the hilltop, and all the witches, the bonfire, and the effigy are scattered into the wind as if they were never there.

I'm left alone on top of the summit.

I fall to my knees, crying. But it's over. Hilltop Bluff is just a hilltop overlooking the university. It's dark. I'm naked. And cold. And alone.

I feel my raven land on my shoulder. That soothes me. Absentmindedly, I pet her.

"Oh, Amica," I say between tears. "What have they done?"

19

WHAT'S HAPPENING?

I'm knocking on Bryce's door once again without clothes. I'm well aware that I have now completely lost my mind. I'm a total fucking lunatic. I figure I either talk to my old lover or run through town and commit myself to the hospital. But I have to know. I have to know what this vision meant.

Bryce and Enora looked younger. It was my coven, but years ago, performing one of their "sacrifices." Yet the fact that Enora was struggling but then kissed Bryce, taunting me, made the whole thing feel like a message from her. Either Enora was showing me her past or the whole thing was her conjured-up illusion. It was just like the Billington House. Enora claimed the vision on Halloween of my boyfriend cheating on me was from the past too. I don't know. I have to know.

He opens the door in shock. I'm sobbing. He doesn't touch me.

"God, Cadence, what happened?"

"I saw you. I saw what you did."

"What? Do you have any idea what time it is?"

"I don't care!" I snap. "Look at me! I'm cursed! That bitch did this to me. She took off my clothes and made me watch her have sex. Have sex with you! Made me watch Reardon direct his disciple to fuck her. *How could you do that!*"

"My God. Just come inside."

But I don't want to. I'm so confused I don't even know what I want anymore.

So I curl up like a ball outside his door and sob more. If someone comes home in the middle of the night and sees me like this, they might very well call the cops. But I figure it's Bryce's fault. And Maddie's. Shit, I wouldn't be losing my goddamn mind if it weren't for my best friend and boyfriend.

Just when I think Bryce is going to close the door on me, he doesn't. Instead, in his pajamas, he just sits next to me by the threshold.

And I cry. I cry and cry. And the crying disgusts me.

I don't know for how long. Finally, when I stop, I look at him. He doesn't seem very nice. He looks angry.

"Come inside," he says impatiently.

I shake my head.

He just looks down.

"Enora threatened me," I say quietly. "And after what I saw, I don't blame her."

"What did you see?" It doesn't sound like he wants to know.

"I saw Reardon and you raping Enora."

"We never did that."

"Did you have ceremonial sex with her?" I can't believe I'm even asking that.

"Yes," he says. And that is far worse. I was hoping for a no.

"How is that not rape!"

"Calm down, Cadence." He puts his hand out.

"You said you never had sex with any of the girls in ceremony. You swore to me that it was only Reardon who did."

"I did swear and I meant it."

"Then what do you mean?"

Bryce takes a deep breath and runs his hand over his short

hair. "If you really saw the past in a vision, you were watching the ceremony where I had sex with Enora."

"At Hilltop Bluff. Yes. *And ...*"

"At Hilltop Bluff," he repeats. But he hesitates and that almost makes me scream. He looks away, shaking his head. "It was years ago, Cadence. When I was dating her. I didn't have sex with anyone else in ceremony, ever, except her. At the time, I was having sex with her outside the ceremony too, because we were going out together. Reardon convinced me to do it and told me it was a requirement to join. He said since I was going out with her, it would be okay to do the public sex ceremony with her. She was also being initiated into the coven." He takes a deep breath again. "I know now it's wrong, Kate, and you've stopped our circle from doing this stuff."

"It's disgusting. Why did I have to be the one to put a stop to it?"

He nods with a sigh. "I'm not proud of it. I see that vision almost every day. You saw it just tonight... I wonder if I'm truly damned."

"Why didn't you tell me?"

"I did tell you. Just...not about my initiation."

"*Initiation?* Try rape. You had sex with Enora during a ceremony with her hands tied down with ropes!"

"She was never raped." He furrows his brow. Then he quickly shakes his head.

"With a curved blade and in front of the whole coven," I insist with a nod.

"Yes. There was that. But she was never tied down."

"You roped her to a pentagram with her screaming!"

"We never tied her." He shakes his head again. "And she never screamed. She never objected. She was fully able to get up and walk away at any time. You know that. That was always Alondra's code. She even told you the same thing on your initiation. She always told us that we could go if we became uncomfortable. Yes, she was on a pentagram—if that wasn't horrible enough. But she was never raped."

"That's not what I saw." I can't believe I'm even having this conversation. I don't want to and, looking at his forlorn face, he doesn't seem to want to either. "You said you never had sex in ceremonies. You said you just helped prepare and—"

"Preparing isn't a whole lot better, is it?"

I put my head in my hands.

"I didn't tell you because I was afraid I'd lose you, Cadence. That's it. I didn't want to lose you. I know how you felt, and you were right. I didn't want to disappoint you."

"So you lied to me. Just like you were afraid, last year, you'd lose me after telling me about Maddie, so you avoided telling me all winter? How many other virgins did you fuck ceremonially with Bill?"

That question makes him very angry. But he's too nice to lash out at me. He just doesn't look like he wants to fight. He wants to go to sleep. "Come inside, it's cold. Please."

It all fits Enora's story. It kinda absolves him...or does it? No, not really. So he had sex with Enora in a ceremony while going out with her. So? That's supposed to be okay? On a pentagram? Right. Oh, God.

He *claims* Enora wasn't tied down. That she wasn't suffering. That's not what I saw. But Bryce has never lied to me—he's hidden things but never lied to me. It's hard for me not to believe him. And I'm in a trance. Our witch trances are always mixed with illusion. How much of all this wasn't real? How much of it was Enora's spell? I mean, she was touching him while laughing at me again. But even still, he admits that the two of them did engage in public sex, and, as Bryce so disgustingly admits, it was on a satanic pentagram.

He doesn't look angry anymore; he looks awful. He probably hasn't been sleeping much either. How can he with Alondra's passing? And then I didn't let him go to the coven's Summerland service. That was mean.

I'm feeling bad for him.

"With no other girls, Katie," he insists, looking at me. "Not rape. Whatever you saw didn't happen that way. Enora consented and even wanted me to do it. Think about it. Alondra wouldn't have allowed Enora to suffer in ceremony...I told you, I did wrong. I've been struggling over this for years. Even before you joined. I've tried to apologize a million times. It was a long time ago. But there were no others in ceremonies with me. I swear it."

I get up and walk into his house. It's so warm and inviting. My raven, Amica, follows me in. Bryce would find that really weird if he weren't a warlock and member of our coven. It doesn't even faze him. I think he's too shocked at me being here.

I'm in my trance still. I can feel it. My heart is still racing. It's like I've drunk three cups of coffee. When in a trance, I feel a mix of sleepiness and power. But during tonight's vision, I was under a spell and felt weak. I must have been fighting Enora. Now that her conjuring is over, my power feels stronger. I feel confident. And all my senses are still in overdrive.

The smells in his apartment are overwhelming. I smell leftover pizza probably eaten by Bryce for dinner. I smell his cologne, which is odd because he usually applies it in the morning, but now it seems to permeate his entire apartment. It's irresistible. And even the mud and grime on my own body, from walking in the nude in the wilderness, is a pleasant earthy smell that reminds me of the lovely scent of fresh rain.

My anger fades, and as I walk around his kitchen naked, it's replaced by an odd feeling of arousal. I feel the warm air from a vent blow against my naked skin. And I feel his eyes watching me. I miss him. God, I miss him.

I open his refrigerator and grab a bottle of beer. I'm

thinking he must be looking at me. I take out a bottle opener, snap off the cap, and drink it. It's cold. As I lift the bottle to my lips, I'm thinking he's checking out my silhouette, from the curves of my breasts down to my naked hips and ass. It's wrong, very wrong, especially with our fight, but somehow that makes it even more erotic.

I hear the door close. He must have kicked it shut because he's still sitting, leaning against a wall, watching me stroll around his kitchen in the nude.

"Enora?" I ask after drinking more beer. "Were you with her when I was at the Billington House? Feeling her up? That's what I saw." I'm being a bitch. But I want to be. Somehow, it's not anger anymore. It's almost playful. I smile at him lasciviously. He seems to squirm from my gaze.

"Yes."

I almost drop the beer bottle. I convinced myself that I was watching a scene from the past. This is not turning out to be a good night.

He quickly puts a hand up. "She tricked me, Cadence. She took me into a private room in the house." I'm not sure I want to hear this. "We talked. She apologized for things not working out. She said she missed me. Wickedly, she even congratulated me on finding you."

I walk over and crouch down beside him near the door. I drink some beer and then offer him the bottle, but he refuses. I catch him staring at my breasts for a moment, but he quickly looks up at my face. I smile and gaze into his eyes. That seems to make him more uncomfortable.

"Go on."

"Then she closed the door and pinned me against a wall," he says with a nod. "She used a love spell. She almost had me." He shakes his head. "I was so confused." He sighs and looks horrible. I feel bad for him. "I pushed her away. I thought of you. I was so upset. Then I heard she used magic to show you the whole thing. I was mortified hearing that. I felt so bad that I hurt you. I was so worried that I'd lost you, Cadence. Then I couldn't talk to you. I...can't lose you. I love you, Cadence... Enora's doing this. Panthera. I told you, she's not to be trusted. She wants us to break up so she can have me again. Or she just wants to make us miserable."

I jump on top of him. The beer rolls somewhere on the carpet, probably spilling, but I don't care. I want him so badly. I'm naked and I want to feel his warmth beside me. And there's nothing that's going to stop me from fucking him *RIGHT NOW*.

I'm in a trance. I must be. There's no way I'd ever do something crazy like this. I'm dirty—literally. There's mud on my feet and leaves and dust on my body. My hair is probably a complete mess. But I'm so aroused. I'm pushing my thoughts of the disgusting rites in his past and everything that happened during the Halloween party to the side. I don't care. The desire to touch him again is irresistible. And he's said enough to make me want to make up and be near him again. I believe him. I'm sorry for fighting. I want to touch him. To feel him touching me. Smell his cologne. It's everywhere. I want to feel his perfectly kempt hair. And...feel him inside me again.

I'm alone. I'm so unhappy. So sad. I have no one. I feel cold. And he's here. I'm in his house, touching him.

I run my hand along his new beard as my naked groin glides along his leg. The dark whiskers are thin, but cute. He neatly manicured it—that's so Bryce-like. I admire his hard cheek and his ever-so-slight dimple. And, of course, his blue eyes. Well, they may not glow like Enora's but, while hers are haunting, his are adorable.

I roll with him on the ground until I land on top of him again with a laugh. His blues look into my eyes with a mixed look of confusion and hunger. He wants me too. He looks shocked, but he doesn't push me off. I roll once more, roaring with laughter, until we hit a wall. I straddle him and my laughter stops. We look at each other, deadly serious. I close my eyes and move my hands along the curves of my breasts and circle my erect nipples. Then I bring one of his fingers up to my lips and suck it while slowly gyrating my naked pelvis up and down on the bulge under his soft pajama bottoms. He moans. I run the other hand through his short hair and down one of his arms. I clasp his fingers and lean down and kiss him passionately.

"Katie," he says between kisses. "Wait. You're still in a trance, baby, fighting Enora. And ... we...were just fighting too."

I open my eyes and look at his beautiful blues again. Even though his brow is furrowed, his pupils are dilated. I shake my head. I run my hand under his nightshirt, over his thin chest hairs and hard pecs. Then I lock my lips on his again, kissing him hard. I let go of his hand while he squeezes my tits.

I giggle and pull up his nightshirt; then I run circles on his hard chest. As my skin grazes his, I feel his breath, and I can feel his heart beating fast. I want to be close, so close. God, I miss him so much. I want to feel someone close to me again. I move up and down along the bulge in his pants, nearly orgasming on his cock.

"Cadence, wait," he says again. It's a weak objection, but because he's repeating it, it makes me pause. I don't want to. I know what I want. He answers the silence by reaching up and touching his lips to me again.

Quickly, though we're still at the threshold of the doorway, I yank down his pants and underwear. I'm so violent that I might hurt him. I don't think he cares. Then I grab his cock and rub it with my palm, up and down. I jerk him fast while he closes his eyes and moans. But I don't let him orgasm. Quickly, I mount him and take him inside me.

I'm riding him. Everything is happening so fast, but that's arousing me even more. We've never had sex like this before. It feels so good having him inside me again. We don't lock eyes. I just keep moving up and down, with one hand against the wall and the other on top of his chest. All my angst is gone. I feel alive being with my man. I'm not even sure what all the fuss was about. My senses make me feel more than I ever had before —a glimpse of his gaze, or the touch of his skin. Each thrust drives me to press harder into him. I grip his cheeks with both hands and rub his hair as I bounce up and down. Then my head dips down and we lock lips passionately once more. When I release his lips, I shout out his name. I love him so much. I press my fingers in between his. I think he objects again, but I'm in a trance and it only spurs me on harder. Nothing can stop me. Fucking and being in a trance have removed all concerns. It feels wonderful.

He groans. That makes me grind harder. I moan too.

I don't think either of us is even aware of what's going on until my raven, Amica, flutters right between us. This awakens Bryce and he shouts, "*Stop!*" and throws me off him. I fall and bang my head against the wall.

"Ow."

"What are you doing!" he shouts. "I said stop! What's gotten into you? Jesus, you're putting a spell on me too, Cadence!"

"I'm not," I say. *I think I am.*

"Get out! I don't want this! You haven't talked to me in weeks, and now you want to have sex with me?"

I snap out of my trance. I feel ashamed. I've never done anything like this before with Bryce. All my confidence, all my joy, all our love collapses like those blocks in the Billington House. I feel like I can barely move. And then I remember that we were fighting. I feel awful.

I lean against the wall naked. Bryce has already pulled up his pants and is standing over me. He's never looked so angry. Amica is still fluttering around Bryce, hitting him, but Bryce is too focused on shouting and hating me.

"Get off him, Amica," I say to my raven. "Stop it!"

I crawl over to the door and open it. Amica flies outside. Then I jump up. I have every intention of running away in shame, but Bryce snatches my wrist.

"Christ, Cadence, wait! Let me get you some clothes!"

"I'm...sorry," I say, shaking my head at him. I yank my hand back. "I'm...really sorry. I don't know what I was doing. I'm so sorry. It was a trance. I'm—"

"Just come back in," Bryce says, shaking his head. His voice is calmer. "Please. It's so cold outside. It's okay."

I shake my head, running out of his apartment in tears.

What was I doing? Having sex with him? What the hell's the matter with me?

20

AS IF IT COULDN'T GET ANY BETTER

I DON'T KNOW WHAT TIME IT IS WHEN I REACH MY DORMITORY. Four? Five? Six in the morning? I don't know. All I know is it's foggy and dark outside. And I'm freezing. I touch my naked hip to the dormitory entrance and realize that, obviously, I am not carrying a card key. I should have remembered.

When I reached campus, I was running from tree to tree to avoid prying eyes. But no one was out there. Just the streetlights, shining down yellow curtains of mist. The touch of my wet, cold hip reminds me more of a toad's skin than anything human. I'm muddy, wet, and cold. I wrap my arms around my naked breasts and shiver like crazy before the glass door to the dorm. I sorely miss being in a trance. Being awake makes me aware of my horrible predicament.

I hesitate, look back at the trees lining the walkway, and look through the glass. The lights are on, but they're very dim. This is the one time when I'm not too keen on one of my neighbors opening the door for me.

Of course, there's only one thing for me to do. I stand on the walkway. The large high-rise, Krunner Hall, is across the road, and I'm wondering if any boys are gazing out their windows, seeing me naked in the shadows of the trees. Then, as if things could get much worse, I notice someone across the street, beside the entrance to the neighboring dorm. At first I think it's a guard or a student. Then I wish it were. It's a shadowy figure in a dark cloak staring down at the ground. Well, honestly, this is the one time I don't mind seeing my new witch-ghost.

I get to my dorm room window, squeeze myself into a bush, and rap hard on the glass. The lights are off, and I assume Maddie is sleeping. She turns on the light. I crouch down, doing the naked dance, moving about trying to cover my breasts and privates. I whirl around to Krunner Hall again, realizing that if no one could see me before, in the wee hours of the morning, they can now. My black figure's gone. Of course.

"Jesus, Cadence!" Maddie is looking out our window. Well, if people couldn't see me, now they can hear my indiscreet roommate. I gesture, telling her to run across the hallway and open the fucking door.

You can't imagine the relief I feel walking into the dormitory. The heater is like heaven. So is Maddie's hug.

I don't cry. I walk into her embrace, wearing her long coat. I think one or two people walk out, attracted by the commotion, but I don't turn to look. When they see me cradled in my BFF's arms, with mascara running down my face, probably, and mud on my arms and naked legs, they quickly run back inside their rooms.

I'm shaking. Freezing.

Maddie gets me inside our room. She turns off the light. Our drapes are open, and she gets that we shouldn't be showing all of campus our business. She pulls up the wooden desk chair —she probably doesn't want my dirty body on the bedsheets. Then she turns on a small lamp by the desk, along with our Keurig to brew something hot. I stare outside. My witch is back, facing our direction.

"I don't think he's going to talk to me ever again," I say finally.

Maddie sits on my mattress, facing me. All I hear is the percolating Keurig cup. She can't say a thing. We're silent until the drink is ready; then she jumps up, fills her Donald Duck mug, and hands it to me. I just blow the mist from it, enjoying the warmth. I still have her coat over my arms.

"I saw a vision," I say. I drink from the cup, still shaking. "Just now, out the window." I point at the witch across the street, near the entrance to Krunner Hall. Maddie opens her eyes wide, jumps up, and throws the curtains closed.

I chuckle. Maddie doesn't think it's funny.

"I had another vision earlier tonight. It was Enora," I say. "She was being ceremonially raped. And my boyfriend was in line. You know, Maddie, it was in the past. But it was as real as you are now."

"If it was in the past, Bryce already told you he was involved in those things."

"I know. But it was so horrible watching it. And then Enora looked at me. It was like a dream. I was in a trance, and I think she was too. She wanted me to see it. It was her conjuring. Then she threatened us because this happened to her."

We pause and I drink more tea. It's good. It's Earl Grey. Maddie knows I like Earl Grey.

"Then I came to Bryce's house. At his house, it was my turn. Naked, I jumped him and had sex with him. It was...I wanted so bad to get close to him again, you know. It felt good. But then I felt awful. Well, I don't think he's ever going to talk to me again."

Maddie's looking at me like I'm completely insane, and that doesn't make me feel any better. I sip more tea.

"Did you hurt him?" she asks.

I laugh. That makes her squirm. "No, I said I had sex with

him. It happened so fast, I wasn't even sure how I got on top of him. I was in a trance. He threw me off. Then I ran."

Maddie gets up and walks over to the window. She's wearing a very cute blue lace robe. I recall buying it last year.

"What's outside the window, Cadence?" Maddie pulls back the drapes and peers out across the street.

I don't like the way she asks me that. I know Maddie, and she sounds really scared.

"The ghost I was telling you about."

"Are you all right?" she asks, looking back at me.

I chuckle. Because I'm thinking, *Sure, I'm fine. I just got transported to the past to watch a satanic witch ceremony, attempted to make up with my boyfriend by fucking him, and then ran across campus naked. No, I'm not fine, Madison.*

That's when someone knocks on our door. The noise makes us jump. I'm thinking it's the campus police.

Maddie walks to our peephole and looks out. "Shit," she says.

"What?"

"Reardon." She looks back at me, and now I'm the one with eyes bulging. "Did he follow you?" Maddie asks.

"No. Of course not."

She puts her hand on the door and locks it.

"Answer it," I say.

"What? Why?" She shakes her head. "No."

I jump up.

"Katie, you're barely dressed."

I wrap the long coat more tightly around me and walk up to the door. "What do you want?" I say.

"I have to talk to you two."

"It's..." I turn to Maddie. "What time is it?"

"Four thirty."

"It's four thirty," I say.

"Ms. Hawthorne, I need to talk to you now. It's very important. Even at this time. I must talk to you as High Priestess."

"At four thirty?"

"Yes. You probably won't sleep anyway."

As I open the door, Maddie pushes against it to stop him from coming in.

The former High Wizard is dressed in a blue-and-white checkered button-down, black slacks, spectacles, and loafers. He looks like a college professor, not the ringleader of a satanic cult. He nods as he walks in. I'm wondering if any of our neighbors saw him. Professors don't visit dormitories often—like never. Certainly not at four thirty in the morning. I clutch my coat a lot tighter, remembering he's a total pervert. Also because I'm still shivering. But I'm not scared of him. I remember the shield spell that I cast on him.

"I'll be brief," he says. I shut the door behind him. All we have is the dim light of the lamp. He faces me and says, "Ms. Hawthorne, I need your help. All of us are in trouble. The whole circle. And, as proof, I will tell you that I saw you tonight. I saw you in my dreams. We were at the hilltop reliving Enora's and Bryce's initiation. I saw you standing by my wife. And I know you weren't there a few years ago. You were there because of a spell. It happened in your sleep too. Tonight. Right?"

"I wasn't sleeping. I was wide awake on Hilltop Bluff."

He furrows his brow and looks at me as if that's impossible. Then he looks down at my naked legs. I don't like that. I snap, "What do you want?"

"Panthera entered my dreams," he explains. "Her hunt has begun. I knew this would happen. My hope was that my wife's efforts to make peace would stop her lust for revenge. My wife and I were able to keep her under control while Alondra lived, but now that she has passed, Panthera is free to torment us again."

"Alondra made peace with her before she died."

He shakes his head. "Enora is an evil witch." He leans against the wall and shakes his head. "Wicked. A twisted woman. She tormented me for months. She has great power and is well versed in witchcraft. She probably knows more of the arts than I do, maybe even more than Alondra. Not only that, but her energy is similar to yours. The combination is powerful. Her greatest talent is to work dreams. We need the witches in our coven to fight her."

He runs his hand along his goatee. Then he sits in our wooden desk chair. It sickens me to think that Professor Reardon is sitting in my bedroom on my chair.

I look at Maddie. Her pretty blue robe. Then I look down at my naked legs again. It reminds me of what this creep really is.

"Just get out," I snap, shaking my head. "I can't help you."

He furrows his brow. I admit, my anger seems random, but remembering his perversions disgusts me. He puts his hand up. "Wait. I need your help. You've proven your powers. I can help you channel it. I can cast a spell with you. You're stronger than Panthera, but you don't know how to use the craft. I can show you the craft through ceremony. I can—"

"Like you showed Bryce? No. I don't blame Enora. For all the sick—"

"She wants us to fight. She wants to break me. And to break the circle. She showed you everything tonight to align with you. She wants you to help her destroy me. That's why she had us share the vision." Reardon finally looks at Maddie. "I need you. Both of you. We can join the coven and fight her." He turns back to me, looking stern again. "If not, she won't stop. She'll slowly wear you down. I know. She did it to me for months until Alondra helped shield me from her. Now I'm asking you to help me."

"You came to me in a trance too. I had to cast a spell to ward you off."

He shook his head. "I dreamt that. That was her again, Ms.

Hawthorne. She brought me to you in my sleep. She's trying to get you to hate me."

I already hate you.

"Why should we help you?" Maddie asks.

"She would never think I'd approach you. But I know we can only defeat her together. She means to break the circle. Joining together is our only hope to fight her. If we can't, she'll finish me, then she'll go after your boyfriend and then the rest of you. I warn you. She was once a part of our coven. Alondra had to expel her."

"Like she expelled you," Maddie says.

He nods impatiently. "Look ..." He stands up and focuses his eyes on me. "I heard about your vision at the party. Do you think I conjured *that*, Cadence? Isn't that proof enough?"

"Then why did Alondra make amends to her?" I ask.

"My wife was kind to a fault. She told me many times over the past year that her biggest wish was to befriend everyone she had slighted before she died...even you, Ms. Cadence Hawthorne."

I look away from his gaze. I hate him so much.

I walk over to the window and open the drapes, just like Maddie did earlier. Outside is my ghost witch. Immobile. More like a dark statue. Somehow, I knew she'd be standing across the street, facing me. I just knew it.

"Please leave," I say with my back to him. "But...I'll think about it. For my friends. Honestly, I don't like either of you."

"You don't have much time, Windstorm," he says. I hear the door open. "Come to my home when you two come to your senses. We will hold a ceremonial rite of protection. Our shield spell. But be quick. If you don't, none of us will be sleeping anymore. Goodnight, witches."

The door shuts behind me.

I hear whimpering. I whirl around, and it's my best friend with her head in her hands, crying on my bed. I run over and crouch beside her. I'm still filthy, but she doesn't seem to care. She falls into my arms.

"What's the matter, Maddie?"

"I'm scared, Cadence."

"I thought you thought I was crazy?"

"No, Katie," she says, shaking her head between tears. "I'm scared because I know now you're *not* crazy."

21

THE LOVERS

It's Tuesday morning and Reardon was absolutely right—neither Maddie nor I can sleep. Maybe his threat was just enough to keep us up the rest of the night. At least we don't have bad dreams.

So the two of us decide to go to our art history study group, being taught by you-know-who. It's the only way I can think of how to make up with Bryce. Well, I can't very well call him. Can I? That would be weird, right? I don't know. I'm so ashamed of what I did.

We arrive early, take two seats in the front—that's Maddie's idea—and wait for Bryce to arrive. There are only four desks at the front and three are taken, so I sit in the front and Maddie sits right behind me. It's cold and smells wet in the classroom from the rain outside.

I don't know why I want to see him teaching. It's a weird way to apologize. But I do want to see him. Besides, Maddie thinks it's a good idea to talk to him about Reardon. But we haven't been to Bryce's class in weeks. So I feel odd and a little nervous about the whole thing. But I suppose I have Maddie pulling up the rear behind me for support. My best friend's always there for me. I don't know, the whole thing is fucked up. It's screwy. But I don't know what else to do. I think I want to see him again. But then again…

"You look good," Maddie says, tapping my shoulder with a smile.

"So?"

"You look good. That helps."

Helps what?

I do look good. I cleaned myself up. I'm not wearing anything spectacular, just a light blue sweater and pants, but I took the time to apply some makeup and fix my hair in a pony-tail. And I'm not wearing black makeup today. I'm even wearing red lipstick. I went with the normal-girl look because I want to feel normal. Like a normal college junior.

The three people sitting near me in the front row are looking me over too, but not in a nice way. These girls remind me of those snoots in the coffeehouse. They're talking about me. I'm not dressed like a witch, so it's not that. Maybe they heard gossip about me coming home in the dead of night, naked, in my best friend's arms?

Half the room fills up, which is impressive being that it's a study group. Bryce might not be as exciting as the professors, but he always gives away the most important stuff to know for the final exam.

Maddie taps my shoulder. I cock my head back, and she's pointing to the door, grimacing. Bryce walks in with his short hair soaking wet. He has a habit of not bringing an umbrella. He lugs his heavy brown bag up to the desk and looks out at the twenty or so of us. He has bags under his eyes. His gaze falls on me for a second, and his expression becomes hard to describe —like he was looking forward to seeing me, but also dreading it. He runs his hand through his short hair and sighs. Then he pulls out his computer and textbook, acting like he didn't see me.

"Open your textbook to page one hundred and thirty," he says. "If you don't have it, just log on to the website. I've highlighted what we're covering this morning. Surrealism." He presses a few buttons on his keyboard. "I was going to talk about Salvador Dalí first, perhaps the most famous surrealist artist, but this morning…" He looks right at me. "Suddenly I feel inspired." He puts a painting on the screen of a couple with white shrouds over their heads, embracing and kissing. "This one is from René Magritte. Magritte is my favorite surrealist. Actually, Dalí and Magritte met each other in 1929. They were contemporaries.

"What does this painting mean to you? It could mean that the couple is anyone you know who's in love. Perhaps your own wife or husband, girlfriend or boyfriend. Or the white clothes could represent shrouds. The death of love." He glances at me. "But this is a history class. I'll leave your artistic interpretation to you." He pauses and looks down at his computer.

Maddie taps my shoulder. I look back, and she's got a big smile on her face. She thinks he's being funny.

"The surrealists came out of the Dada movement. Know about the Dada movement for your exam. The Dada movement strove to break down all the rules in society following the horrors of World War I. A famous example is the urinal by Marcel Duchamp. It's literally a urinal signed by the artist." A picture of a urinal comes up on the screen, and students laugh. "You all know how silly modern art can be. This is one of the earliest examples.

"Out of the chaos of the Dada movement came surrealism. Remember, this period was a time of great turmoil. We had the 'war to end all wars,' World War I. Estimations vary from twenty to eighty million deaths in the world. Some of the deaths, of course, can be attributed to the Spanish Flu epidemic of 1918. Then there was the Great Depression, starting in 1929, followed closely by World War II. Obviously, World War I was not the 'war to end all wars.'

"World War II introduced us to Nazi gas chambers and fears of complete domination by the new racist-fascist world order of the Third Reich. And, of course, the H-bomb. Nuclear fission. I postulate that all these horrible things made society ripe for escapism, to transport people away from the world's troubles. In film, the fantasy *The Wizard of Oz*, in 1939, is another great example of this. Many of you are history majors. Knock yourselves out citing examples like this in your final essay." He pauses for a moment, types something on his keyboard, and looks back at the screen. "Here's my absolute favorite."

On the screen behind him is a painting of a nude woman, blue at the level of her chest and skin-colored below. "This is Magritte again. This is called *Black Magic*. I love how Magritte blends the woman's profile into the surrounding clouds and nearby rocks. This is one of my all-time favorite paintings. Magritte is mixing her body into nature. It's magnificent. Many different adaptations of this were painted during World War II. This one, the greatest in my opinion, was painted in 1945. Obviously, Magritte was trying to deflect the stresses of war."

He stops for a moment. Then he rubs his chin, walks pensively around the desk, leans back, and looks at us. His eyes fall on me and he says, "Why do you think he called it *Black Magic*?"

No one answers.

"Cadence?" he asks, infernally looking right at me.

"She didn't raise her hand," Maddie snaps behind me.

"I just want to know her thoughts, Maddie," he says with a shrug. A few girls snicker behind us. I think by now it's a foregone conclusion that he and I are dating—or were dating. Everyone knows the three of us know each other, and there's plenty of gossip about our weird goth cult. But, as I told you, I don't like it when he picks on me in class, and he knows it. So does Maddie. We've told him a thousand times.

"It's a lovely painting of a naked girl's body," I reply with as much smugness as I can muster.

The class laughs. Bryce, who's trying to act cool, blushes a little.

"But the title's interesting, isn't it? I did some research." He jumps up, paces a little, and walks behind the desk again. Then he looks down at his computer screen. "Magritte never explained why he called it *Black Magic*. It almost makes you wonder if he had knowledge of the occult. For those of you in last year's metaphysical history class with Dr. Johansen, you might recall that the occult deals with how nature affects the human condition. Certainly, this painting broaches this subject. The woman is blending in with nature, and practitioners of the occult, particularly witchcraft, worship nature. This is why I adore this painting so much—not just because the model is naked"—the class laughs again—"but because Magritte has blended his model into nature. The lower half of her body is flesh-toned and part of the rock. The upper torso is a part of the clouds. This also hints at the dichotomy of our very existence, doesn't it? Some parts being of the earth, our animalistic primal nature, others being a part of the heavens. It is the dichotomy of the human condition. I love this one."

I raise my hand.

"Yes, Cadence?"

"I think I prefer the painting of the couple kissing behind white shrouds." I challenge him with the bitchiest look I can muster. If everyone weren't looking at me, I would have stuck my tongue out at him.

The class laughs again.

"You can fancy whatever painting you want. This is a history class." *Yes, I know. So why don't you stop making it a talk about US?* "*Black Magic* became a theme for Magritte in the mid-

1940s," he continues, "in the same year as the Battle of the Bulge, the last German offensive. And, of course, the same year as the dropping of the bomb on Hiroshima and Nagasaki. Once again, I suggest that Magritte was taking us away from the horrors of his time. And by showing the dichotomy of the heavenly and the earthly, I believe he made the figure in the painting more human. Fallible in a way." He checks his computer screen again. "Well, there I go interpreting again. Know the dates of the Battle of the Bulge and the bombs dropped on Imperial Japan. Delve into the details, like how many soldiers, tanks, and bombers were used in the last German offensive. When the atomic bombs were dropped. Etcetera. These two events were critical in ending World War II. Magritte provided us a refreshing respite during this terror."

I do like the painting *Black Magic*. And I like *The Lovers*. I even like Dalí's stuff. Bryce and I have similar taste in art, you know. I even fancy Dalí's weird mustache, because I like weird stuff too. But I kind of think that my boyfriend is extrapolating his feelings into the artwork. And I don't like how he was looking at me while talking about *Black Magic*. Like I represent the half-earth, half-heavens girl to him.

I jot down the dates and yawn. Then I zone out for the rest of the class. This is a bad idea because, unlike the last time I came to Bryce's class, I haven't gone to lecture this week, so I haven't seen the paintings he's showing on the screen.

Class ends.

Maddie and I join the line to talk to Bryce as the classroom empties.

"Are we supposed to be *The Lovers*?" I quip when it's my turn to talk. Maddie and I were the last people in line, so I don't think he'll mind my bluntness.

"So we're talking, Cadence?" He shoves his computer back into his bag. "That was a really strange night last night."

"She saw Enora," Maddie says.

"I know," he says with a slight smile at Maddie. He throws the bag over his shoulder. Then he says, "I know you were having a hard time, Katie. But running from my house naked—did it make you feel any better? Because I thought it was reckless and stupid."

Then he looks at Maddie, probably wondering why she hasn't left us alone. Maddie's holding my hand. This is my best friend's opportunity to get to the point. But instead, she's defending me. "She's having a real hard time, Bryce. We all are."

"You two," he says, looking down at Maddie's hand. "You're inseparable." He leans against the desk. The classroom has emptied out. Then he looks at Maddie. "Can you give us a second alone?"

"As long as you tell him," Maddie says, looking at me.

I nod.

Maddie's gone. Now it's just me and my "boyfriend."

It's pouring outside. I have an umbrella in my backpack. I walk over to my chair, pull it out, and hand it to him. That's my unspoken attempt to sort of apologize. It's weird, but sometimes I just can't be direct when I'm upset.

"I told you everything, Cadence." He stares down at my umbrella in his hands. "I've never lied to you. Enora was an old flame, but it's over. I'm sorry you saw what you saw—both times. But you hurt me." He looks into my eyes. "I loved you, Cadence. But I can't love someone who doesn't trust me."

It's silent except for the rain. Bryce looks out, still holding my umbrella.

"I need some time," I say.

He furrows his brow. "It didn't seem like you needed time last night."

"I was under a trance. I don't know what came over me. I'm sorry."

He nods.

"I just need time to think. On Halloween...Halloween, that night, I do think you were under Enora's spell. But I'm not sure that—"

"Okay, Cadence." He walks to the door.

"Wait."

He stops and turns.

"Reardon came to my dorm last night. He saw me watching you and the circle in my vision. Enora had him reliving the past in his dreams. It was Enora. Just like it was Enora who flipped me into a trance. He thinks Enora is conjuring spells to hurt us. She threatened us last night in my vision. Reardon thinks she's going to do worse in our dreams if we don't do something."

"She is. She's messing with us, Katie. And she's done it before. I told you she's a wicked, evil witch."

"Then I need your help. That's why I came here this morning."

"That's why you came here this morning?" he repeats, finally permitting a smile.

"Well..." I bite my lip. "I'm also a little rusty on studying. You know, I didn't go to lecture this week."

"I won't tell Professor Riker."

"Maddie and I talked things over. In order for the circle to be complete, we need you. You. You know the last thing I want to do is hold a Witch Sabbath, but after last night and Halloween, I believe Reardon. I know Enora is casting spells to hurt me. To...hurt us. I'm scared for us. Reardon can preside, but he's still technically expelled by Alondra. We need you there."

"You didn't let me preside over Alondra's funeral."

"I know. God, I'm sorry, okay? How many times do I have to tell you that?"

"How many times do I have to tell you?" he asks, and he takes a deep breath. "I've apologized about my past. I don't want to go over it anymore. When are you going to just forgive me?"

And that reminds me of Alondra. It was so hard for me to accept her apology. Only in the final moments, when she touched my hand, did she hear me accept her apology. I felt she heard it. I just know she did. Now Bryce is asking the same thing.

But the things they did. Is it forgivable? Alondra asked that too.

"I accept your apology, Cadence," he says formally. But he looks a little angry.

"Oh, Bryce," I say, tearing up. But we don't embrace. And I'm thinking of last night. I wanted so desperately to hold him. It wasn't just a trance. Or lust. I wanted desperately to be near him again. And that makes me choke up even more. I force my words. "Just meet us this Friday. Mira's already preparing. We're going to see if we can invoke a shield spell. The same one Alondra cast to protect Reardon. He's the last old fart I'd ever want to protect, but if it will protect our sisters, I'll do it. I'll meet with our coven this last time."

"I don't like this." He shakes his head. "I don't trust Reardon anymore either." But he takes a deep breath. He walks a little closer. In the past he would have gathered me in his arms, but he's still hurt. I suppose I could grab him... but I already tried that last night. I'm so conflicted.

"If you do this," he says, "you can bet Panthera will fight. Are you ready for that, Katie? She'll use her powers again. If she can get you to channel your power with the High Wizard, she could turn it against us. Then there's Reardon himself. You'll empower him too. This is so risky."

"I don't think she'd ever expect me to try to help Reardon. I can't believe I want to do it myself. But she's got to be stopped. I know she's messing with us, Bryce. I don't think Reardon is. And it's for a shield spell."

"All right. Name the time."

"Friday, of course. At ten."

He looks down at the umbrella in his hands, shakes his head, and hands it back to me, but I don't take it.

"We'll walk together," I say.

"Are you sure?" he asks.

"Yes." I nod. "Friends?"

"Always, Katie."

22

TACO TUESDAY

Taco Tuesday is my absolute favorite meal at the dining commons. It's like you can mix just the perfect amount of shredded beef, cheese, lettuce, and salsa with either their crunchy shells or tortillas. I don't know. I mean, it's not *that* amazing, but I look forward to it every week. I always fix up a couple of tacos with a couple of cookies. They usually bake fresh cookies on the same day. You'd think they'd spread out their cuisine and leave the really good stuff for Meatloaf Monday but, apparently, they want Taco Tuesday to be perfect.

So I'm sitting with Maddie at a table, in these blood-orange plastic chairs, watching cartoons on the TV screen on the wall and waiting for Mira. And since when have I ever waited for Mira? She doesn't even go to the dining commons anymore, being that she's living in an apartment off-campus her senior year. So she'll have to pay. But Maddie and I invited her.

Now I'm throwing some extra shredded cheese on my taco.

It's really busy. The semester is coming to an end, and finals will be here soon. Christmas will be here soon too, but you'd never guess it at Hawthorne. There's no celebrating Christmas at Hawthorne U. From what I heard, the college felt that celebrating Christmas would be prejudicial to all the other holi-days. This is why Halloween is so big.

Anyway, I'm enjoying my stuffed soft taco when Maddie, who hasn't touched her food, says, "How are you and Bryce doing?"

"Good, I guess." I shrug.

"That bad, huh?"

"I don't know. I told you after class we walked through campus, but I used my umbrella more to keep us dry than to keep us together, you know?"

"He likes you."

"He said he loves me, but it's just distant right now."

There's a stupid cartoon on with a cat. It's like a take on Tom and Jerry. There are so many cartoons like that about cats. Of course, half the students are staring at their phones anyway. I think the TV show is really old, like from the '90s.

"The two of you will come along." Maddie finally picks up her taco. She picked a hard shell this time, and it crunches as she eats. She's in such a sour mood that it looks like the crunching bothers her.

"What about you and Rock?"

"I told you it was over, Katie. You know that."

"Too bad," I say with a shrug.

"He's an asshole. Not like Bryce." Then she looks at the shadow cast on our white plastic dining table.

"Hey, guys." Mira waves.

"I paid for you already," Maddie says with a smile, standing up and giving Mira a hug. "Did they tell you up front?"

"No. But it doesn't break my bank."

"Fucking fuckers." Maddie hits the table.

"It's okay."

Everyone in the room is staring at Mira. She's wearing a really long black dress that's trailing from her back. She's got on the same black lipstick and mascara we're wearing tonight, but it's thicker. Mira takes one of two open chairs. Then she looks at me and smiles lasciviously. "Hi, Windstorm," she says with a wink.

"Hi, Mira."

"Shall we get down to business?" Maddie asks.

"If we must." Mira tries to make herself more comfortable in the plastic chair.

"You should get some tacos," I say. "They're to die for."

"I already ate," Mira says. "So, what did that jerk tell you?"

I put my taco down, wipe my face, and nod. "He says the circle's in trouble. He says we need to perform magic to shield the coven from Panthera."

"More like shield her from him. Alondra protected him. Panthera hates Reardon more than anyone. I don't like either of them."

"Bryce told me that. But—"

"How are you and Bryce?" Mira asks, renewing her grin. She's leaning back in the chair with her head on her hand, staring at me. I look around the room again. Some of the eyes have left us, but I still feel like we're being watched. Because of Mira. The funny thing about Mira, with her large glistening nose ring and red-and-black demon tattoos along her neck, is that she doesn't really care.

"Fine," I say. "So what do we do?"

"You two still copulating? I told him that sex weakens magic."

"Shut up. That's none of your business."

She laughs. "Don't you love it how Cadence gets flustered, Maddie, when I tease her about sex? She gets so worked up." Her black-lace-gloved hand touches my hand. "Sorry, you're still a Bo-Peep at heart. No longer a Bo-Peep, no offense, but just a Bo-Peep at heart. It's really cute."

"My sex life is none of your business."

"Aha."

"Can you prepare a shield spell with Reardon or not?" asks Maddie.

"Of course I can," Mira says, turning stern. "But why would you want one? The things he did to our circle. He deserves anything coming to him from Panthera. Let her torment him. And as for the rest of us, I'm not sure she cares. I think she might just leave us alone." But then she looks at me pensively for a moment and wags a finger. "But maybe not you and Bryce. You and Bryce... Cadence, Bryce was Reardon's *special* assistant. Perhaps he's not safe either. Maybe she's not just trying to make you jealous. Maybe she's tormenting him."

More like tormenting me.

"Did he ..." How can I say this? My stomach turns. I've never asked Mira this. "Did he partake in the sex ceremonies with Reardon?"

Mira laughs. I don't think it's very funny. "He had his way with Enora in ceremonies, Katie. That made him powerful in the circle's eyes. But that was their initiation. Bryce didn't screw other girls in the circle—as far as I know. He helped arrange things for the High Wizard, though. So did I. He even helped him with—" She looks really uncomfortable for the first time. "Me." Then Mira falls quiet. She narrows her eyes and looks angrily at the table. "Are Windstorm and Bryce still having romantic problems? I told her—"

"I said it's none of your business," I interrupt.

Mira laughs again. "You just asked me if he had sex with other women in our ceremonial rites." Mira looks up at the TV cartoon. She rolls her eyes and shakes her head. Then she looks back at me. "I told you the tarot cards showed a disturbance in love. I told you it would probably be you and him."

"What do we need to prepare?" Maddie asks impatiently.

"She doesn't want to know," Mira says, pointing a thumb at me.

"Tell us," I say. "That's why you're here."

"No, that's not why I'm here," Mira snaps, wrinkling her nose angrily at me. "I'm here because your friend invited me."

And that's when a familiar voice says, "Hi." I've heard this voice all my life but, here and now, I just can't place it. So when I see a tall guy with long light-brown hair thrown to the side, wearing a T-shirt and jeans, I'm dumbfounded. It's Damien, my kid brother.

"Hi, sis," he says with the same smile he used to give me when he wore Mom's frosting on his lips and cheeks. It's cute. But under the current circumstances, it's not. I'm in complete shock. He nearly loses his smile, probably because I don't jump into his arms. The absolute last thing I want is for him to be a part of our special witch meeting.

"Why are you here?" I ask rudely. That seems to confuse him even more.

Maddie gets up and shakes his hand. "Hi, Damien."

"Hey, Madison." He puts an arm around her. Then he looks at Mira, who is looking at Maddie, waiting to be introduced.

"This is our friend Mira," Maddie says.

"Charmed," Mira replies, shaking his hand. When Mira does her famous wicked grin, it's too much. I jump up, take Damie's arm, and pull him from our table.

"It's hard right now," I say, dragging him away, "'cause finals are coming up and everything. And, you know, Alondra and all."

He gives me a hug. I think he's shocked I still haven't hugged him.

"Don't worry, sis, I'm here with Harvey and some friends. I just wanted to say hi. Harvey's probably coming here next year. Isn't that great? You know, Katie, that Harvey's like my best friend. It's going to be so much fun. And being that it will be your senior year, you can show a measly little freshman around town. Right?"

"Sure, Damie."

We're near the table and I'm, like, physically pulling him away, but he's resisting. Mira and Maddie are all smiles, and that's upsetting me more.

"Wait a second," I say. "Did you say *coming here*?" *No way. Nuh-uh.* "No!"

Damien steps back. It's like I struck him in the face. You have to understand that I love my brother to death, but I can't stand the idea of him coming to school here.

"I thought you'd be excited," he says, furrowing his brow. He looks bewildered. But then he recovers his usual kid-brother energy and says, "Harvey's premed too, you know... Katie, I just wanted to say hi. Forget it. I can see you're busy. I'll see you 'round later. I'm going back home tonight."

"Okay, fine. Hi," I say derisively. And that seems really mean.

"It's sure good to see you again, Damie," Maddie hollers from our table, being a bitch.

"Nice meeting you, Mira," he says.

"You too," Mira says with a wink.

Damien leaves.

I sit down and stare at my tall brother as he walks back to a table full of boys. He glances back, still looking confused. I feel really awful for being so mean. I really love him. I feel like he should be joining us or something. But if he knew the weird stuff we were talking about, he would probably be happy to stay away.

When I turn back and see Maddie staring at him, I hit the table. "Cut it out!"

"What?" Maddie asks.

"What do we need to do, Mira!" I snap. "Stop beating around the bush and just say it."

"What a nice brother," Maddie says.

"Shut up, Maddie," I say.

"Just saying." Maddie shrugs. "I was a lonely child. I think you're pretty lucky, Cadence, to have a brother like that."

"What do we need to do to prepare, Mira?" I ask for like the fifth time.

"Windstorm," Mira says.

"Yes, what do we need?"

"No." Mira shakes her head. "We need Windstorm. Windstorm is what we need, Cadence. *You* have to prepare Windstorm. You haven't let us hold a true Sabbath for months—with the exception of the time you let Panthera cast her spell in Alondra's backyard. You haven't let us perform sacrifices, which"—she narrows her eyes and shakes her head at my taco—"would excuse you for eating meat. You don't abstain from sex outside ceremonies." She infuriatingly chuckles. "All that weakens a witch. No doubt you hold the strongest magic in the coven, but your lack of belief, your disregard for Selene, for our circle, even for your lover's power, might lead us to peril." Mira pauses and looks around the room. She frowns. "So...are you two witches or are you losers like all these stupid kids enjoying cartoons and tacos?"

"I like tacos," I say.

"Serves my point." Mira opens her hands in an irritating gesture of mockery.

"But what do we do?" Maddie asks. "What do we need for the ceremony? Just tell us."

"I've prepared things at Alondra's house. The stones have been placed around the logs, our unused cloaks remain on the wall, and I do not foresee any clouds to upset our ceremony." Mira glances at me with a grin. "Unless Katie plays with the weather. We have to cast a spell around us. We can use the normal circle with our stones, but we need to amplify our power. Specifically, we will need to name the witch that threatens us: Panthera. Reardon will have to be present but, of course, he's been banished—and I don't think, Katie, you're about to reinstate him. So your boyfriend Bryce will preside as our High Wizard. I hope you're not fighting so much that Bryce is refusing to come. Are you?"

"No, he'll be there."

"Then it's all set. Everyone just come to our Sabbath on Friday."

"Do we have to hurt Enora?" I ask.

"How sweet." But Mira looks down in thought, as if I just asked her about a difficult scientific theorem. "She will fight back. She's not one to back down. When she sees what we're casting, she will want to shatter our magic shell. She might get very aggressive." Mira's auburn eyes stare into mine. "You'll have to be ready. You are our High Priestess. She's already fought and tested you. She now knows your weaknesses. But she's also likely to be afraid of you. No one doubts your power. You're going to have to be ready for a tough fight."

I don't want to fight. Especially with magic. I hate witchcraft. I don't mind being a witch and feeling one with nature, but I hate spells.

"Cadence doesn't know how to conjure spells like you do," my best friend interjects. "Do you plan on running the incantation?"

"No, Bill will."

"No." My eyes open wide and I shake my head. "No way."

"You're kidding," says Maddie.

"He's cast out," Mira explains, raising her hand, "but he's the only one who can recast the same protective spell Alondra used. He knows the spell. I can help, but we'll need his grimoire. We could cast a different spell, but we know this one worked. As long as we conjure a protection spell and name the excluded party, Panthera, Reardon should stay in line."

"I trust him even less than I trust Enora," I say.

"Yeah, but without Reardon's help, you won't be able to shield us from Enora with the same spell Alondra cast. Again,

Bill will come as our guest, not the head warlock of our coven. That's why we need Bryce there."

"So that's it?" asks Maddie. "We all meet and just cast the old shield spell?"

"Aha," says Mira.

"No nudity," I warn. "And no drugs."

"You're no fun," Mira says with a grin.

"Alcohol's all right, Katie?" asks Maddie with a grimace.

"Nothing, guys. You promise?"

Mira shrugs but nods. Maddie nods too.

I finally bite into my taco. Somehow it seems to have lost its taste. Maybe it's the butterflies swarming in my stomach. I'm so scared. This is why I never go to meetings with the witches in my circle anymore. I love them, but I don't want to face magic.

"Don't worry, it's gonna be fun." Mira touches my arm with a wink.

23

THE BLACK SABBATH

The three days from our meeting with our Sabbath planner in the dining commons to Friday were painful, sleepless nights. Almost every couple of hours, Maddie woke me up, asking if I was sleeping. She was scared too. Not only were we worried about today, but we were afraid Enora was going to attack us in our dreams.

Now we're together in Alondra's backyard, and there's relief in that. All my friends grab their black cloaks from the wall. We're somber. Few laugh or even talk, which is not normal for my friends, but not only are they anxious, but coming to her house reminds them of Alondra's passing. We haven't gathered since the funeral.

Bryce is here. He grabs his cloak next to me, nodding coldly. That bothers me too. It makes me wonder if we will ever be close again.

I see Reardon. He takes his cloak off the metal hook just like the rest of us. His bald head reflects the patio lights. He even smiles at me, the weirdo. I don't smile back. I just wish he weren't here.

Mira has already arranged all the white plastic chairs

around a low simmering flame. It's dark out without a moon and a little cloudy, and the flame is so low that we can barely see the yard, aside from three lights on a backyard overhang. When the fire rises and we're more accustomed to the night, we'll shut the unnatural lights off.

It's cold, but it's not raining or snowing. Mira was right about that, as usual. That's one of her quirky powers—forecasting weather. I've got on a sweater and two shirts under the cloak, but it's not warm enough to stop me from shaking a little —unless I'm shivering from nervousness.

As we make our way to the large white stones and chairs, the ceremony has kind of already started. Even walking together makes me feel like we're worshipping. Some of us carry lit candles by our sides, and others carry incense in their palms. Mira is walking in front of us, carrying an old book with a crescent moon on the cover. She's chanting something in gibberish in front of me. Usually it's funny, but somehow tonight it's not. It's creepy.

All of us except Reardon sit down on the white plastic chairs, which have been arranged around the fire. Reardon stands and faces us, with his bald head glistening in the red light from the flames behind him. The fire is about three feet high, and it's difficult to see the girls behind him. Maddie and Frida are sitting beside me. I've lost Bryce. Mira hands Reardon his small grimoire before sitting down a few chairs to my right.

"Close your eyes, girls," Reardon says. "I am honored to have been asked by Windstorm to perform this shield spell with the Hawthorne coven one last time. A disturbance has entered our circle since the passing of my wife. We are here to stop it." Sounds sensible enough. I just want him to get it over with. "By shadow and darkness, we focus. Hold hands." He closes his eyes. I don't. Just as in the past, this bald figure with a pointed beard, wearing a black witch cloak with flames behind him, looks like the very manifestation of Satan. He opens his eyes and starts reading from his small wizard book. "All hail the dark lord. Come to us. We beckon you. We stand before you. We call on your names, prince of darkness. Mephistopheles. Beelzebub. Lucifer. Baphomet. We are safe within your arms inside this sacred circle. The white stones defend us against all who attempt to penetrate the circle. Neither scourge, nor dagger, nor sword shall pass. *Lux tenebris*."

We all say "*lux tenebris*." And the magic has begun. Because the words come from my lips, but my mouth is not fully under my control.

"Sacrifice yourself in meditation and allow atman to flow, girls. With virginity cometh my seed, sacred semen, to enter your very being. My offering." Here we go. I'm squirming. And I feel Maddie's hand tighten. She knows I'm super uncomfortable.

"*Lux alba*," Mira says meekly, not at all like her normal self.

"Bring me the mandragora, disciple."

I didn't see it prepared. Bryce walks between Maddie and Hope, carrying a heavy barrel. He sets it next to Reardon. Then he lifts the lid and stands beside the High Wizard, placing his hands behind his back, and closes his eyes. In my trance, it takes me a moment to register what's going on. This is mandrake, or mandragora. Mandrake is a drug. A powerful hallucinogen. And I forbade all drugs for tonight's meeting.

"Wait. No." Everyone opens their eyes and awakens from their trance. "We had an agreement. I said no drugs."

"You asked Raven and me to protect the circle," the High Wizard says. "The only way is with potions. This is what Falconsong used when she protected us. If you want protection for the whole circle, there's no other way. I can't cast this spell without it."

"No drugs," I repeat.

"There can't be a shield spell, then. You must consent."

Am I to stop everything now? Maddie looks at me, knowing

I'm capable of canceling the whole thing, and shakes her head. And certainly, Bryce didn't object. He just brought the barrel over. I'm trapped.

"I don't consent," I say. "I am the circle's leader."

"No doubt you are, Windstorm. But I tell you that the spell is worthless without mandragora. This is the only way. If you permit me, I can sprinkle but a small amount on our sisters."

I look at Bryce. He hesitates, but then he nods somberly. I turn to Maddie, sitting beside me, and she nods too. Then Mira. Mira doesn't move. She's just staring into the fire.

Using mandragora is not that strange to us. In fact, we had countless Sabbath ceremonies with mandrake last year without sacrificing virgins or worshipping the devil. But I don't like it.

"It is clearly written in this grimoire," the High Wizard continues. "In fact, Falconsong herself officiated with it many years ago. Your own initiation involved it. This comes from the ancient rites as far back as Eliphas Levi. It is a secret rite used by Falconsong and the Hawthorne coven and the only way for the magic to fully manifest itself. I assure you"—he addresses everyone in the circle, even the witches behind the flames— "this will shield us from the coven's threat. Once and forever. Do you not want me to do this, witches?"

And this is what everybody wants. Everyone's afraid of Enora. In fact, I was not the only one with visions. Hope, Frida, and Marilyn came to Mira and told her of their own terrible nightmares. The whole coven has been affected by this evil witch. And then I think of Halloween and her casting a spell showing me my boyfriend and nearly tearing our relationship apart. And the eclipse and Panthera's nasty smile.

"Raven?" I ask Mira. "Do we have to use mandrake? Is there no other way?"

Mira looks away from the fire and finally meets my gaze. She is already in a trance. "If he must use such powerful black magic, there is only one other way under Baphomet." She shakes her head and looks fearful. "But you won't consent to that, Katie. I'm absolutely sure. And even he"—she points to the High Wizard—"has never performed it."

"What?"

Mira hesitates.

"Blood," the High Wizard says with a nod. "A disturbance with blood would be enough to throw you all into a trance. Human blood. My wife always chose mandragora. There are other witches practicing under Baphomet who perform human sacrifice. Injury, murder, or even sacrificial abortions."

"Disgusting," I cry.

"It'll be quick, Katie." Maddie squeezes my hand. "Let him use mandrake to protect the group." Maddie looks into my eyes in the flickering light. She nods. "Please. Panthera's hurting us."

I hesitate. I look around the circle.

"Are you all willing to do this?" All of them nod. "Do you all consent to this?" I look at every one of my sisters. They all nod.

I reluctantly give a quick nod to the beast.

"Everyone circle the fire slowly," the High Wizard says with the hint of a smile. I sense triumph in his grin. "I shall stand here and anoint you with the holy magic of mandragora. I will sprinkle it on your skin."

I return to my place and begin walking behind Maddie. Frida, one of my other favorite friends, walks behind me.

"Walk sideways," the High Wizard instructs. "Hold hands as you walk, facing the fire. We weave this shield."

We walk facing the flames with craggy old Bill Reardon waiting for Bryce to hand him the flask beside the fire. Bryce dips the flask in the barrel. Surely, I figure, Bryce is already getting a dose of the drug by scooping his hand in. Mandrake is potent through skin contact. This is the reason witches dance naked around the fire. Naked, the full potential of the drug is felt as it permeates the skin. But as Bryce hands the High Wizard the flask, Reardon takes it a step further. He tilts his head back and empties the entire flask of reddish-brown fluid into his mouth. This is a powerful dose, one that once made me very sick. Indeed, Reardon's eyes become wide, and he looks at us with madness. It's as if he's been given great power.

I'm already ashamed. I should have stopped him. I feel weak. Alondra trusted me with her coven. She handed me responsibility. Now I'm handing it to a pervert to shield us. Why? Why should I trust him? I don't trust him.

Reardon hands the flask back to Bryce, and Bryce refills it. I glance at Bryce as I circle the fire. Judging from his blank stare, he is already getting high off the mandrake too.

As we circle around like schoolchildren, holding hands, Reardon begins sprinkling the liquid on each of us. Each witch, as we slowly pass, gets a few spritzes and then a few more. He sprays it on their faces and, after a few slow circles around the fire, I catch some of the witches licking it off their lips, bobbing their heads up and down, loving the blood-colored liquid. He does not spray me. But some of the liquid meant for the others hits me anyway. How can it not?

"The purification is almost complete," says Reardon with wild eyes. "I can feel the power, witches! We purify our circle once more. We anoint you with our dark magic. *Lux tenebris!*" He starts laughing like a madman. "*Lux tenebris!*" he shouts. "Say it."

"*Lux tenebris!*" the witches repeat, laughing.

"*Lux tenebris!*" Reardon shouts again, as if trying to rile up a crowd.

"*Lux tenebris!*" the witches shout. Frida and Maddie are beside me, yelling the words.

"*Lux tenebris!*"

The witches shout and I feel a warm wind circle around us. It becomes hotter. Purple smoke, like fog, circles the white stones around the fire. It reminds me of the fog I saw during the eclipse. My palms feel wet holding my friends' hands. That's mandragora. Did I get a dose even though the High Wizard avoided sprinkling it on me? Or is it their hands? I look at Maddie, and she's bobbing her head up and down, dancing hysterically. She's very high.

But Maddie's also becoming blurry. My God, the drug *is* affecting me.

"Bring forth dark light," Reardon says. He's reading from the book again with wide-open eyes. "Close thy soul and turn your back on me, and within feel the great presence of Baphomet through the shadows of darkness." He closes his eyes tightly. Many of the witches are closing their eyes too. "Adramelch. Marduk. Proserpine. Beelzebub. Lucifer." He stops for a moment, opens his eyes, and takes a deep breath.

The fire behind him rises like it did the night I lost control. But this time it's not sucking him in. It's like he's using the bonfire. He's still spraying the mandrake on each witch as we circle the flames. And he spills some on me this time by accident.

"*Hoc circulo, Satana.* With your great wisdom, I ask for protection. Bring us protection. *Hoc circulo.*" His words echo through the yard. "*Lucifer Lucifer. Lucifer. Satanas!*"

"*Lucifer!*" the witches in the circle repeat in rapture. "*Lucifer!*"

"And now, as I feel the power of mandragora course through my veins, I invoke the spirit of Selene," the High Wizard shouts. "Hecate, in this protected circle, I shall name the accused who shall be cast out from our Hawthorne circle. They shall remain behind the walls of the Hawthorne coven."

The High Wizard's skin changes to a darker hue. His ears elongate and he grows a tail and horns. As I walk by him, still locked in Frida's and Maddie's hands—now feeling as if my friends' hands are no longer comforting me but chaining my wrists to the circle—he picks up the entire barrel and lifts it above my head.

The circle stops. I look up at the barrel above me and feel frozen. A third of the barrel has to be full of mandrake. I can't move. I'm so sleepy. All the witches are frozen, staring at me with excitement. He pours the remaining fluid in the barrel over my head.

NO! I cry in my soul. And there is lightning and thunder from above. For a moment, the circle's spell is nearly broken. Some awaken and gasp. Maddie looks over in horror. But most of the witches giggle. The sticky red-brown liquid drips down my face and neck after soaking my hair. I feel humiliated, too weak to even move.

Then everyone, even those who objected before, bursts into an uncontrollable laughter, pointing at me in derision and mockery. Even sweet, shy Frida, who is the nicest girl I've ever known, is pointing at me. She removes her cloak, sweater, shirt, and bra. Maddie completely ignores me, staring at the flames. But she, too, removes her cloak and unbuttons her jacket, kicking off her boots. It's not long before they're all laughing, rolling their eyes back, and dancing naked around the flames. They have let go of my hands and are dancing in circles around me as I stand paralyzed, surrounded by purple smoke, before the bonfire.

"Panthera," the High Wizard says. "*Venite foras! Venite foras!*"

I hear another scream. It frightens me. As I use all my strength to blink the warm, sticky liquid out of my eyes, I see the totem from my vision on Hilltop Bluff appear beside the High Wizard. Yet in the back of my mind, I know we're still in Alondra's backyard. Enora is tied to that same horizontal wooden X with a red ribbon circling the totem and forming a pentagram. Enora is struggling with her restraints again, but this time she is not young like she was in my vision, and she is not blindfolded. She glances at me in fear.

Reardon removes a curved dagger from under his cloak. The purple fog circling us alters to crimson.

"How dare you!" Enora hisses to the High Wizard. But her eyes look everywhere in panic.

"I am the High Wizard of the Falconsong coven," says Reardon.

"Windstorm is High Priestess." Enora shakes her head and looks at me desperately. "She can cast you out. Do it, Windstorm. Please! Use your power and stop him. Stop him now! It's your coven."

"*You* are the accused, and *you* shall be cast out," says the High Wizard.

"Let her go!" I yell. But I can't move. And it took every ounce of energy I had left to utter my words. I feel so dizzy. Everything is beginning to sway as if I'm on a boat. I'm so nauseous.

He responds by stabbing her in the chest with the knife as if she were an animal sacrifice. Blood sprays from her torso. Then —I can't believe my eyes—my friends turn, like rabid wild dogs, rush to Enora's bloody body, and lick and suck the blood squirting from her chest and stomach. I am the only one not engaging in this hideous act. Even Maddie and Frida are leaning over and partaking in this sick meal. They're cannibalizing her. Hope and Marilyn have grown fangs. Then I remember that the High Priest spilled mandragora on me. This must be a hallucination.

The High Wizard Reardon turns to Bryce, who still stands beside him. Bryce is staring at the fire.

"Expel Maverick's seed from the circle now, disciple. She aligns herself with Panthera. She has hurt you with evil magic. You heard her objections to our acts against the black witch. The two witches conspire to do the coven harm. No longer is Falconsong here to protect us from these wicked witches. Change Windstorm so that she can never hurt us again."

Bryce nods, in a trance. As the witches continue to feast on Enora, Bryce walks to me. His eyes are glassy and I spontaneously step back.

"I expel you from the coven," Bryce says to me like a zombie.

I cannot form words from my lips to even object.

"Disciple, help turn her," the High Wizard says. "Help her transform. She needs your assistance. Change her. *Muta. Serpentus. Mutatio.* Turn her. Then she can no longer harm you."

"*Fiat voluntas tua.*" Bryce bows his head toward Reardon. Then he turns back to me, glassy-eyed.

"She is cast out," the High Wizard shouts. "Rid our order of the evil witch. Begone. Cast her out and shield us from her harm."

As Bryce turns to me, there is an explosion by the fire. Even in his trance, Bryce turns. A thousand black birds launch into the air, and Enora is no longer on the totem. All the witches of my coven circle around the totem, looking everywhere in confusion as their meal has left them.

Bryce pushes me, with an index finger, outside of the surrounding red smoke. His single finger feels like a hundred people shoving me out of the red fog into the wild grass. I feel so weak. So sick. I stumble. I still cannot utter a word. I try to shake my head or raise my hand to stop him, but it takes all the strength left in me to keep my eyes open. I fall.

Tears flow from my face and Bryce blurs before me. I think he recognizes me for a second, but then he shakes his head as if shaking off poison. Not only is he under the influence of mandrake, he's under the High Wizard's spell. Bryce points a finger at me. "*Proditrix.*" I have no strength. I close my eyes as I hear Bryce speaking these strange foreign words. I close my eyes, hoping that everything around me will stop spinning. "*Proditrix. Muta. Serpentus.*"

I feel cold, freezing cold. Whereas before our ceremonies always warmed me, now I feel frigid. I force my eyes open and see Bryce become larger. He fills my view as I seem to fall under the ground. The colors change as if through a prism. The central bonfire becomes almost too bright, and I avert my eyes. I feel like I'm descending, in an elevator, under the earth.

I finally utter something from my lips. I scream with all my might, but it's inhuman, guttural, low-pitched. It sounds like a drum.

I feel pain in my throat and a tearing sensation in the center of my tongue. I no longer see Bryce's cloak, only a huge blurry red blob with yellow and blue around it. And, even stranger, when I blink my eyes, the color fades into black and white. I move to clutch my neck with my hands, but I don't have hands. Then I try to run, but I don't have feet. I'm bound like Enora was to the pentagram, only I'm not bound by ropes. I'm bound because my arms have been consumed into my body.

My cloak and all my clothes cover my eyes. I wiggle, shake free of them, and make my way along the ground. I'm surprised at how fast I can move. I turn to my side and look back. The fire is blinding my eyes, but I like the heat emanating from it. Yet I fear their feet as they dance around the fire. The witchgrass is taller than my head. I have shrunk, I think?

My ability to think is fading. I'm confused. I can't recall what is happening.

Why am I here? I have to get warm. Somewhere, but not near that fire. No, not the fire. I dread their feet.

I'm so cold. I have to find warmth.

I can't hear well. In the background, there is a low drum-like sound. I quickly wiggle my body away from the flames. But out here, in the night, it is cold. So cold. I need to find shelter.

I smell something. Gamey. It reminds me of barbeque meat, and for a flash I recall the smell of an animal once sacrificed by Alondra in this very yard. But this smell isn't coming from a cooked animal.

I see something in a bush. I change my vision from black and white to a weird blend of yellow, red, and green. I can do that easily. I don't know why. Now I see something clearly in the leaves. It's a towering beast two times taller and fatter than I am. It's so big and soft. I can see its heart racing. And it's shaking. I'm so hungry. Why is it shaking? Why is it hiding when I can so clearly see it? I reach closer and its odor is overwhelming. I stick my tongue out—don't know why—but when I do it smells wonderful. But I don't feel wonderful. My heart races again in a panic because, you see, my tongue is forked and as large as my head.

24

I DECEIVE YOU NO MORE

SOMEWHERE IN THE RECESSES OF MY MIND, THERE IS CADENCE. But that person slips away. Now I am remembering her. I must gather my thoughts before I fade.

I've gone through many sunrises without knowing who or what I am. At times, I just recognize light and the glorious warmth of the sun. I don't want to live like this, so I fight. I must retain my identity. I'm thinking of this, not only for you, but for my very existence. For when it fades, my identity fades, and I go with it.

~

Another day passes and I am awake again. I will try once more.

I'm under a white structure. Rather, I'm under white boards, hiding from the tower sticks. That is what I call these creatures. I have seen many tower sticks walk on their two long branches and make their way across my garden. I don't know what they're looking for, but they have no business being here.

There's one close to me now. The sticks are dangerous, but

they move slowly. I fear they will trample me. They are the only things I fear. Tall and smelly.

One of them is searching the danger road, full of tall blades of grass, crouching and looking around the flowers. What is it doing? I love my flowers and bushes. They aren't theirs! They're mine!

I have had my fill of the large, furry animals under my shelter. They are so easy to catch and drag down here. So easy to eat.

One of the tower sticks approaches. I hear it walking above me now. I am under it, hiding, like the furry animals hide from me. And just as the furry things quake under me, I quake under the tower sticks. They are so tall. But they emit such strange sounds.

Two more approach. One is looking right at me. I laugh.

You're so dumb! Can't you smell me? Can't you see me?

I flick my tongue at it.

Right here. Right here. Don't you see me? Idiot!

They never see me.

It gives me a sense of confidence, you know. So I quickly slither out of my hiding place and let them chase me. It's a daring game, but I'm much faster than they are. I've done this a few times now, and this time I decide to let them have my home for a while. They chase me. One even throws a net. But they're far too stupid. I consider biting one, but that would slow me down, and then I might as well be shaking for good.

∼

I like the morning light because it warms my garden. Sometimes, I'll come out just to feel the warmth when it's not too cold.

∼

I'm alone. When I don't think, I don't care. But right now, I'm thinking. It makes me angry. Why am I angry? I am so alone. I am so mad.

I hunt. I'm not hungry now, but I want to kill. In my rage, I want another creature to suffer. So I wiggle my way around the trees, looking for something to strike dead. I'll kill it and leave it for some other animal to devour. As long as I can make it feel pain like I do.

It's dark—which I love—but cold—which I hate.

There is no friend of mine. I am utterly alone.

I can't cry. I learned that on my first night. Then, I wanted to cry. My greatest wish was the power to cry. What would I cry about? Why would I cry?

I'm caught. I don't know how, but one of the tower sticks snared me. I'm wiggling terribly with my armless torso, trying to escape, but I cannot. I hiss. And I spin wildly. But I cannot bite and get out of this cloth net.

I squeeze through a hole. *Ha!*

"*Hominis, venite foras.* Transform back, Cadence. *Muta.* Find peace within your heart. *Mutatio.* Follow. I free you of this curse. I demand you transform now. *Muta. Hominis. Hominis, venite foras.* Come out, Cadence Hawthorne."

My eyes open. I run, actually I wiggle, shifting my body back and forth very fast across the field. Circling above, I see a black bird chasing me. It must want to eat me. So I scurry as fast as I can to the bushes. But I fear that I cannot escape it like I can the tower sticks. The tower sticks are slow, but this bird is quick.

It must want to eat me. It is my comeuppance for going after the shaking furry things under the bushes. This is my fate. Now it's my turn to be eaten.

I stop by a bush, but I don't go under it. I turn and face my adversary. It swoops down but does not grab me. Instead, in lines of perfect black and white, the black bird stands over me. I don't know why, but I feel as if it has no interest in eating me at all. In fact, I feel as if I recognize this bird.

Words come from its beak. "*Et nos unum sumus*, I deceive you no more. *Et nos unum sumus*."

"*Amica?*" I say. I'm shocked to hear the word from my mouth and to understand it. My word is like a low growl, but it can still be heard. I have said this word before. The bird dips its head down and touches mine softly, and for the first time in such a long time, I do not feel alone.

"*Mutatio*, Cadence," Amica says. "*Mutatio*."

I answer by flipping my forked tongue at it. I am still beside the bush and, although I feel safe with this bird, I am still apprehensive.

I shake my head.

I can swear I see a smile from the black bird's beak. "*Mutatio*."

The bird shakes and crouches along the grass. Already, the bird was twice my size; now it becomes even larger, rising toward the clear sky. It forms into a tower stick. An unclothed one. I look at its face, and it is strangely familiar.

"Change back, Cadence. Now. It's okay. Change."

I shake my head.

The tower person reaches out a hand larger than my head. For a moment, I consider biting it. "*Et nos unum sumus. Hominis, venite foras*," the tower person says. And she repeats it again and again. Her hand remains stretched out. "*Et nos unum sumus. Hominis, venite foras. Et nos unum sumus. Hominis, venite foras.*"

I feel like I'm rising. I feel pain in my throat. I'm shaking. The leaves around me move as I get bigger and bigger. Everything becomes vibrant. Beautiful. I am in a clearing of grass surrounded by trees.

I recognize the woman in front of me. Enora.

I grab her hands and burst into tears. The ability to cry makes me cry more than I've ever cried in my life. My tears are so sad, but being able to shed them makes me so happy.

Enora takes me in her arms.

"I'm sorry," I say, shaking my head in her arms. "I'm so sorry."

But when she gently releases me and those familiar bright blue eyes stare back at me, my old distrust returns. She's smiling, but I feel like I'm being deceived.

"But you were being eaten by my coven," I say, shaking my head.

She laughs. Then she narrows her eyes toward the trees and looks dangerous. "He has the power of illusion. Like a stupid magician. But the feasting of the witches was incomplete. And not real. I believe he had every intention of killing me that night, but he did not know of my power to turn into a bird and transform back." Then she looks down at me in pity. "But you, you don't, you poor thing. He had hoped to fog your brain so you would be trapped as an animal forever. He did not know, as you didn't, that I could turn into a bird at will. And I don't think he predicted that I would help you."

I look down and my naked body is covered with dirt and filth. It's like I rolled in mud. Enora isn't totally clean either, but at least she resembles a woman. I can't even see my skin under all the dust and muck.

Her blue eyes look deeply into my eyes. "You know, Cadence, I didn't do this as a friend. I know you hate me after what I did to you and Bryce. But I need your help. Witch to witch. Coven to coven. Woman to woman. For revenge. I help you, you help me. Understand?"

She reaches down and helps me stand. Standing on two legs is so weird, and I have to lean on her to straighten my body. But when we walk, it's even weirder. I don't know how long I was gone, but walking feels like I am pressing on cushions instead of feet. My legs are so weak.

To my amazement, I realize that I'm still in Alondra's backyard. We pass logs in the center of a wild grassy field. In all my slithering, I wonder if I ever left.

My stomach aches. God knows what's in there. Believe me, I don't want to know.

"It will take you at least a day to recover, Cadence," she says, cocking her head, as we walk.

"Thank you, Amica." She looks at me slyly. "I mean, thanks if you helped me. And...I guess we are kind of friends if you're my bird."

"I am not your friend," Enora says. "And I am not *your* bird. But I'm surprised you remember my transformation. It's rare to remember anything unless you're practiced like me."

I'm blinking as my eyes adjust to the sunlight. It is so bright. And all the colors are so vibrant. I feel good. Wonderful. The warmth outside feels glorious against my skin even though I'm not wearing clothes. Then I notice my bare feet squishing into the leaves. We're walking through mud. Even though the sky is clear, it must have rained. Or snowed? In my other form, I never noticed. It was cold, but it was always cold outside my shelter.

When we make it to the backyard patio and I see all our witch cloaks hung on the wall, I lurch back and start shaking violently. But I'm not shivering from cold.

"What?" Enora asks.

I shake my head, opening my eyes wide as I look toward the house.

"He's not there. The asshole leaves every Sunday morning. I bet you it's not to worship in church. All I know is I've been watching him from the trees for the past week, waiting for the right time to bring you back."

We enter Alondra's house, and the warmth of the living room feels like heaven. It must be cold outside, but I've felt so cold that just being human again warms me. Here, it feels like a warm toasty fire. I'm alive. Not dead. But I shiver.

"Go shower." Enora looks at the hallway. "I'll watch for him. If he dares return, you and I will face him alone, but this time he won't be prepared."

"What if he changes me again?"

"He needs the circle to do that." She looks down at my filth with disgust. "Go shower, Cadence."

I still don't trust her. And I think she knows it. The way she looks at me when she talks.

So, she saved me? So what? And Reardon hates her? And she's Amica? So? Does that make us suddenly friends? Isn't this the same Enora who opened a portal to hell? And who paraded her sex with my boyfriend?

"Now that you're human, you have the human curse of thought," she says as if reading my mind. "Stop thinking, Cadence. Just go take a warm shower."

But I don't mind thinking. In fact, I like it. Even the shivering. I like all of it.

When I turn on the shower in the guest bathroom and close the white curtain, I feel fear again. It's like I expect that creep to throw open the shower curtain, like in *Psycho*, and kill me. And then, even worse, I wonder if Enora is tricking me. Maybe the curtain will fly open to reveal not a psycho killer dressed in drag, but a witch holding a curved dagger. So I wash myself with both eyes open.

The warm water feels soooo good against my skin. And washing off the clumps of dirt and leaves makes me feel as if

I'm washing off scales from reptilian skin. It's like I'm shedding a terrible costume. I run the water down my long dark hair for the longest time. It starts to fog up in the bathroom. Enora's probably pissed it's taking me so long, but I'm glad I'm taking my time to get all the mud off. And there's a *lot* of it.

"Cadence, we have to go," Enora says with a knock.

On the counter is a change of clothes. I didn't see Enora bring it in—I was probably too enthralled with my wondrous warm water. I look at the clothes, and they're a little large. I recognize them. It's a white button-down and black slacks. On the floor are gray tennis shoes. I've seen the clothes before. They're Alondra's.

When I get out of the bathroom, Enora's not there.

"Come upstairs, Cadence," Enora shouts from upstairs. "I want to show you something before we go."

I walk upstairs, and it fills me with dread. I've only been up here a couple of times, and the last time was when Alondra was sick and I called the paramedics.

"Come on," Enora says again.

I turn left to the master bedroom, but Enora's not in there. I enter the hallway again and go into a small room across from the master bedroom. It is a library with books on shelves. But Enora's not here studying books. She's standing by the window, pulling back a white lace curtain, staring outside. She points.

I look down and see a bunch of people walking around the front yard, searching under rocks and bushes. And I recognize them. There's Maddie, Bryce, Mira, and a handful of my other friends in my coven. They don't look like witches. They look like students gathering trash or collecting butterflies in Alondra's garden.

"What are they doing?" I ask.

She chuckles but, when I turn, I am surprised at Enora's expression. She's not amused. She looks angry.

"Idiots," she replies. "They'll be surprised to finally find you."

I turn and look out again. Maddie's in tears as she crouches down, pulling back the only yellow flowers in the garden. All the other bushes are just branches. Bryce is focused too, looking under the wooden deck.

I rush out of the room and run down the stairs.

When I open the door, the fresh smell of the bushes, trees, and grass overwhelms me. It's winter but it might as well be spring. I remember my black-and-white vision when I was my former disgusting self. Color only came in blurry blotches. Here, everything is so brilliant, in all the colors of the rainbow. It is so beautiful. The lilies and roses. The yellow sun as it warms my face. I feel so good. Then my eyes fall on Bryce, who's only a few steps away from me, looking under the patio with a stick. As the wood creaks under my shoes, he looks up. When he recognizes me, he rushes into my arms.

"Oh, God, Katie, I thought I lost you forever!" he says. His voice cracks. He clutches me tightly. "God, never leave me again. Don't ever do that again! Never!" And he draws me even more tightly in his arms and kisses me repeatedly on the face. I would never let go if it weren't for the others. I hear shouts as they run to me. They too embrace me. Mira, Frida, Hope, Helen, and Tammy. They all run into my arms. Last comes Maddie. She's too distraught to say a word. She just stands by the porch looking at me. She starts to cry. I do too.

The strangest thing, as if anything could be stranger than all this, is that they all keep looking at my body. From head to toe. It's like they want to make sure I'm really human again. Then I remember running, or scurrying, from the "tower sticks." They were so tall, like buildings. For me it was just a stupid game, like hide-and-seek. For them, it was desperation to catch me and make me whole again. They must have been looking for me all this time.

Our exuberance is dampened by the opening of the front door. All my friends in my coven step back in fright. I think they fear it's the High Wizard. When they see it's Enora, they look relieved.

In the excitement, I didn't even realize that Enora is now wearing one of our black cloaks. She puts the hood over her head and stands beside me on the deck, looking straight ahead.

"Meet me with your coven on Hilltop Bluff," she says, still facing forward. Then, almost in a whisper, "The very same hilltop where the wizard unveiled my ravishment to you. Meet at midnight on the Witch's Sabbath this week. Both High Priestesses, you and I, Panthera and Windstorm, shall have our vengeance. That is my price for restoring you."

And she proceeds down the walkway, ignoring anyone else who greets her, down the dirt path, and into the forest alone.

25

THE WITCHING HOUR

AND SO WE MEET, MY WHOLE COVEN, BESIDE THE JONATHAN Brewster Taylor Library, at the appointed time set by Enora: the witching hour. Midnight. I'm seriously conflicted because half of me never wants to come near any magic again. But the other half wants to conjure up a serious windstorm, a goddamn tempest, that will bury that old bald-headed creep in the hell where he belongs. He destroyed my dignity. Then he buried my grades. (I'm gonna fail another fall semester at Hawthorne University, by the way. I wonder if that was his contingency plan in case I was changed back to a human. He's a professor, you know).

My friends are pretty intense too. They're all gathered under a dim floodlight, silently changing into black hooded cloaks behind a trash dumpster. I welcome my cloak because it's cold outside. Gilda brought the clothes all the way from Savannah because you-know-who isn't about to lend our cloaks from Alondra's backyard. How Gilda got enough of them for all of us is beyond me. Well, she's highly resourceful. Anyway, it's good that it's late and we're hidden beside the building because, even though it's after midnight, there are still students walking to the library to study. The school keeps the library open during the wee hours of the morning for finals. Of course, that reminds me of how I'm going to fail again.

I straighten my cloak and throw my hood over my hair. Bryce takes my hand. "Are you sure you're up to this, Katie? Maybe we can meet another time?"

"Yeah, babe?" Maddie asks. She's beside me too. "Are you? After everything that happened?"

"Especially after what happened," I reply. "Let's just say that if I have the chance to throw the dick in the fire this time, I will."

"Hell yeah," Mira says behind me.

"Hey, Mira," Maddie says. "What's the plan?"

"Yoozh. Gather around a pyre, dance, and let Windstorm throw the dickhead in the fire." She chuckles and winks at me. "Didya bring your Book of Shadows?"

"Yeah. Why does she want it?"

Mira shrugs.

"I'm not here to hurt him, Katie," Frida says in her thick Brazilian accent. "I...I want him to just leave us alone."

"Me too," says Helen.

"Yeah," echoes Tammy. "What is she planning up there?"

"Don't know," I reply with a sigh. "But he tricked us." I look at Bryce and nod. "Yeah, I'm ready. I agree with Enora. We have to do something."

"Enora tricked us too, Cadence," Bryce says uncertainly, forcing a smile. "Nearly broke us apart. I don't trust her either."

I just nod.

"Let's go," I say to all of them with as much confidence I can muster.

Tucked under my right arm is my old book *Broomstick*, my Book of Shadows, and Bryce is holding my left hand as we wind our way down into the thick dark woods. The rest of my friends trail behind. When I look back at them, their eyes are fixed forward under the moonlight, ready for a fight.

We wind our way through more dirt paths under the trees, soon nearing the sound of my beloved waterfall. Then I smell smoke and see red flickering flames. The red fog looks like it's over the hill on Hilltop Bluff. That slows me down for a moment, because it reminds me of the vision Enora gave me.

"You okay?" Bryce asks me. He can sense my hesitation, I think.

I just nod. We head up the grassy hill.

When we make it up to the summit, Enora is the only one there. She's sitting cross-legged, in a black lace dress, with a tall bonfire burning behind her, in the center of the grass field. Her black-gloved hands are folded over her lap, and her face is covered with thick witch makeup. None of this is surprising. What is surprising is what's behind her—another wooden totem between her and the fire. It's the same totem that was in my vision and the same one that materialized in Alondra's backyard before I was transformed into a snake. A burgundy velvet cloth is wrapped in a circle over the large wooden beams, forming a pentagram. Fortunately, there's no one bound to it this time.

"Yatu, Windstorm," Enora says pleasantly. "Happy Yule."

Happy Yule? Who cares about Yule right now?

Yule is the Witch's Christmas. Shows how much I'm paying attention to time. Of course, Christmas falls near finals, which reminds me yet again of how I'm going to fail my exams.

"Sit, Hawthorne coven," Enora says. "Let us gather around the warm fire, witches, and celebrate the upcoming sacred night of darkness."

All of my coven sit on their knees or cross-legged on the grass, but only after they look at me. They wait for my permission. Enora sits beside Mira and Bryce. I sit on the grass opposite her, beside Maddie and Frida.

"Raven, can you say some blessed words to our witches about the change of seasons?" Enora asks Mira.

"We're here to celebrate Yule?" I interject, glancing at the pentagram behind her.

I mean...really?

"What do you mean?" Enora asks. "Revenge or not, Cadence, we're still witches. Don't you want to celebrate our Winter Solstice? I want to." Then she turns to Mira. "Can you recite some of the words of the turn of seasons? Do you remember some of them?"

"Yes," Mira says.

Mira's hesitant, and for her to be hesitant about anything is really something. I think she's spooked by the pentagram too. Not that she's never seen it. She's accustomed to practicing ceremonies, but she's probably wondering why this is happening *now*.

"Yule is a special time when energy has left our world," Mira begins. "Like fire, it extinguishes only to be relit once more in the turning of the wheel." She casts a stray glance at the pentagram. "Yule. A powerful turn of seasons. The world changes from wetness and ice to warmth again. Just as Ceres mourns the loss of her daughter Proserpine and waits for her return above in Ostara, so does warmth become reborn. Remember with joy, fellow witches, that even under your cold feet, the warmth of the earth remains. All things pass. But together, in the comfort of our touch, may we never thirst."

"Yes," Enora says, closing her eyes and nodding. "Yes. Blessed be your words. So well said, Raven. I knew it would be from you. Indeed, shall we hold hands, witches?"

I catch Enora looking at me with that same determination I saw in my friends when we walked across campus to the bluff. She's in for a fight too. I just know it. But I don't trust her.

Enora closes her eyes again and looks down. "*Sacrificium*

consecratum." She quietly says the words repeatedly like a chant. Mira repeats it too.

"Wait a minute," I say. They open their eyes. "What are you planning, Enora? After everything that's happened, you can't expect us to blindly follow you. I mean, I owe you for changing me back, but with everything we've been through, you need to tell us your plan."

"I know what you've been through more than anyone here, Cadence. Of course I'm not here just to celebrate the solstice. I'm here to hurt the devil who hurt you. Who hurt me. But you need to be patient."

"How are you going to do it?" Bryce asks.

"With patience," Enora replies with a fake smile. Then she turns to me with a more genuine smile. "Did you bring your book?"

"Yes."

"Bring it to me. We should chant using your book. I will use it to summon him."

"Tell us the plan first," I insist.

I agree with Bryce. What's going on? I recognize her words. That is the same incantation we used to sacrifice animals that we would eat during gatherings. But why now? There's no animal here. There's just that infernal pentagram Enora forced me to see in my vision.

"The book." Enora gestures to me. "Bring it to me and I'll show you."

Bryce shakes his head. "Your plan."

For a moment, Enora loses her smiles and looks dangerous. "I intend to use the power of your circle to sacrifice the High Wizard. We will summon him, bind him, and prevent him from ever fucking with you or the Hawthorne coven again. The fool thought he could get rid of Cadence and me. He knows our power, and he wanted to expel us—for good. Now I will help you get rid of him instead. Is that simple enough, Bryce?"

"But why the pentagram?" Bryce points to the wooden totem.

"We're witches," she says to him with a laugh. "That's our symbol. My sisters helped me put up the decoration for Yule. Why does it disturb you?"

"It's inverted with two points projecting up. That's not the symbol for witches, it's the symbol for Satan."

"It never stopped you before."

"I have told my coven never to practice under Baphomet again," I say.

"Are we fighting?" she asks all of us. "This is exactly what your demon wizard wants. He wants us to fight, to keep the circle broken. Just as he wanted to imprison Cadence in the body of a snake." But none of my witches seems to be on her side. They keep looking at me, and that seems to make Enora more upset. "Come on. How can a pentagram disturb *him*? Bryce of all people? He consummated our love using one before your coven."

"Maybe we should go," I say, getting up. "Look, I owe you, Enora, but I don't feel like you're being straight with us. My coven's been through so much already. We don't worship the devil anymore."

"Wait," Enora insists. "Sit. Please." She takes a deep breath and raises her hand. "Sit. You used to worship the devil, but I'm not asking for that. I simply need the symbol to stop your High Wizard. You all brought this upon yourselves when he tricked you into protecting him." She addresses all of us. "Please, sit." She laughs. "Come on. We're all witches under Selene."

But Bryce and I are still standing. So is Maddie. And Mira. And Tammy. And a few other witches are getting up too.

"Katie, bring me your book," Enora says. "Give it to me so I can summon him and stop him from disturbing you. That's the plan. The book will help summon Alondra's husband here. I can't reach him through your protective spell without it."

I look at Mira and she hesitantly nods. Bryce folds his arms and shakes his head, refusing to sit down.

"Bring me your book, Katie," Enora says.

"Is this why she wants it?" I ask Mira.

"Yes." Mira nods. "I think so. It's Alondra's Book of Shadows too. A Book of Shadows is representative of a witch's inner being. Her soul. We've used these books to evoke witches who have passed on before. She can probably use it to bring forth Reardon."

"Yes, I can. So can we get on with it?" Enora asks, lifting her eyebrows. "Or would you prefer to fight? May I remind you all that he turned Cadence into a snake? I changed her back." She looks right into my eyes. "Remember?"

My friends look to me again. I answer by walking over to Enora. She's still sitting cross-legged in front of the bonfire, looking up at me.

"Here, get it over with," I say, handing her my book, "so we can go home. We want to be free from harm, and I owe you for making me human. But...I don't want to be a part of all this." I look at the fire and the pentagram with disgust. "I just want to go to school. Away from magic and hexes. Okay?"

Enora nods with her infamous smugness. She takes my book and jumps up. Then her black-gloved fingers glide over the frayed old cover and open it beside the fire. It's like she's using the light of the bonfire to help her read it.

I walk beside Bryce and hold his hand. His palm is wet and his hand is shaking.

Enora throws her hand up without turning to us. "Sit down. Please, witches." She cocks her head toward me. "You've logged everything. *Broomstick*, huh? It's become a bit of a witch's almanac, hasn't it? A diary. You even wrote about this year's Halloween party and me and Bryce. Sweet. And here is last year's party at the Billington House."

"It's my Book of Shadows.".

"But not the beginning," she says, shaking her head and raising a finger. "Alondra jotted down her experiences too."

Everyone's watching her read my book. Why? She has so much charisma. She is a natural leader. Unlike me. How does she do that?

"This is your past too, Bryce," Enora says. He's sitting near her again. "Don't you want it to be over?"

He furrows his brow. Before he can answer, she turns her back to us once more, facing the fire. She closes the book, presses it against her forehead, and quickly bows three times. Then she says, "In this time of renewal, I sacrifice the past. As the book turns to ash, let it burn the sins of the Hawthorne coven." And then she tosses my book into the flames. She throws it so casually, as if she's simply adding more wood to the fire.

Everyone leaps up. There's so much noise and pandemonium that I can barely hear my own screams. Then lightning strikes from above. Then thunder. That's my rage.

Enora looks up at the sky with a grimace. A shiver runs down my spine when she glances at me, her eyes flickering pearly white.

Bryce and I run to the fire. She threw it dead center in the flames, and it ignited by some sort of magic. I can't even make out the border of the cover anymore. I reach in, but Bryce snatches my hand so I don't get burned. The book is already unsalvageable.

Mira answers my rage by walking up to Enora and decking her in the face. The violence is so strong that it throws Enora to the ground.

"That was her book!" Mira yells. "How dare you. No one has the right to burn a witch's book."

"How could you do that?" Bryce adds. "You had no right to destroy Katie's book!"

"Are you all stupid?" Enora shakes her head. "Reardon's

shielded from me otherwise. The book must be burned so that the coven's sins can burn. Like the solstice, the wheel must turn."

"Windstorm is our High Priestess, not you!" snaps Mira. I've never seen Mira so mad. "You had no right!" Then she turns to me, and I get the feeling she's about to spit something nasty at me too.

"It's my past too!" Enora snaps. She's still on the ground. We're all crowding her, hating her. "All of you are guilty if you accept it. Don't you see, burning it represents the wish that it never was. I cleansed you. Now you all need to calm the hell down and—"

"Yatu!" cries a young voice from down the hillside. "Yatu!" cries another.

We all turn. Two bright torches are making their way up the hillside.

"Yatu!"

"Ah, they're here." Enora rubs her cheek. She's lying on her side. "Watch the change now, witches. Yatu, Manthis! Yatu, Adder!"

As they arrive, there are more gasps. It's Enora's two witches from her coven, Beatrix and Cordelia. They're pulling a man by thick ropes. The man is blindfolded in red burgundy velvet cloth, like the one used on the pentagram. He's dressed in a brown Capuchin robe. He's bald with a goatee. Professor William Reardon. The High Wizard. He can't speak. His mouth is covered in gray duct tape.

We panic. This is not a vision. None of us has ever seen anything like this before. No one has partaken in mandrake. They literally kidnapped a professor.

"My God, Enora, what have you done!" cries Bryce.

Enora answers him by jumping up and brandishing a long curved dagger from inside her dress. Bryce steps back. Enora smiles at us playfully. We all back up.

Beatrix and Cordelia pass us, pulling their prisoner to the fire. Reardon's head is jerking all over the place. Enora walks over and tears the duct tape from his mouth.

"Help!" Reardon shouts. He's still blindfolded, turning his head all around. "Help! My God! Please!"

"What?" Enora asks, bursting into laughter. "Something the matter?"

"Let me go! How dare you! Take off this blindfold now!"

"What? No one can hear you. Because nobody cares! Go on. Shout! Do it. I want you to try, devil." Enora runs the dagger along Reardon's neck. "Cry to the heavens! Yell to your god in hell. No one will help you. What did you think? You thought you could humiliate me again? Then turn the leader of your coven into a snake? And nothing would happen to you? Scream until you don't have a voice! Come on, warlock, let me hear your impotent cries. To the High Priestess. To all your witches. None of them care!"

But I care. I can't believe my eyes.

"Let him go, Enora!" I yell. But my shout is one of many. I don't even know if she hears me. She runs her tongue along his beard and cheek. Then she laughs heartily and stabs him in the arm.

A few of my witches rush to her, but she raises the bloody knife back to his throat. "Uh, uh, uh. Step back, Hawthorne witches! Return to your seats and watch the spectacle, or I'll slice his throat and then you'll be to blame."

Beatrix and Cordelia laugh. Then Beatrix, the blond teenager, kneels before Enora. Enora looks down at her, still holding the blade to Reardon's neck. Beatrix touches Enora's free hand and bows her head. Enora nods. Beatrix leans down near Reardon's arm, still on her knees, and sucks the flowing blood from his wound.

"*Sacrificium consecratum,*" Enora says in Reardon's ear. Her two witches repeat the words. "*Sacrificium consecratum. Sacrificium consecratum.*"

Enora stabs his other arm. This time it's Cordelia who licks the blood dripping down to his fingers.

"Black witch!" cries the High Wizard. "Step back! I warn you!"

"Get away from him," I cry.

Enora laughs harder.

"Stop!" I yell. I look to my friends. "Stop her!" I shout again. I feel so helpless. I feel like I did when witnessing the past under Enora's spell. Most of my witches are in too much shock to lift a finger. But we can't let her keep hurting him.

"There's no magic here, Cadence." Enora turns her head back toward me with those creepy white eyes. "That's what you wanted, isn't it? You asked to just go back to school, away from spells and hexes. Right? See, I can't cast a spell because you stupidly shielded him from my magic. So I have to do it the old-fashioned way. Blame yourself. Either way, believe me, I shall have my sacrifice this Winter Solstice."

She yanks off Reardon's blindfold. His eyes are bulging. He sees me and pleads, "She's going to kill me!" Then he sees Bryce. "Please, disciple! Help untie me. Stop her!"

Meanwhile Enora's two witches are repeating the mantra, licking, sucking, and biting at his wounds. Enora draws a little blood from his neck and runs the dagger along her tongue. Then she thrusts the knife into his stomach.

I'm horrified. Sick. I'm remembering Enora being stabbed, but that stabbing was an illusion under mandrake. This is real.

Mira rushes to Enora. But, yet again, Enora brings the knife to Reardon's neck, and Mira backs up. "Uh, uh, uh, Raven," she says mockingly. "Why you? This man turned your leader into a snake. And the things he did to you and me. You actually want to save him?"

"Let him go," Mira says.

"We didn't want to hurt him!" I shout. I'm only about a foot away from her, reaching out to her. "We just wanted him to stop hurting us."

"Step back, fools," Enora warns me. She's still holding him with the blade near his throat. "Step back. There is no other way for him to stop hurting you."

Then she smiles widely, joining her two witches again as they continue their chant and lick his bloody arms:

Sacrificium consecratum. Sacrificium consecratum. Sacrificium consecratum.

I look at Bryce. He seems helpless. All my witches do. Every time we rush them, Enora threatens to slice Reardon's throat with her dagger.

Reardon's in too much pain now to object. He's crouching near the ground, hanging by the ropes. "Help me," he groans quietly.

I feel so sick. The hilltop is spinning. I close my eyes for a moment, but my dizziness remains. This can't be happening. This is not a trance. Enora has literally kidnapped a professor from our school and is torturing him in front of our eyes. I can't stand him, but I hate her too. She's right, this isn't magic. It's far worse.

I rush Enora. I have every intention of tackling her, whether she stabs him or me. I don't see any other way. Cordelia stops me. She's bigger than I am. She grabs me and throws me to the ground.

"Why don't you try a little magic?" Enora taunts me, laughing. She's terrifying, with pearl-white eyes. "Now I shall sacrifice him like he sacrificed me." Then, as if she's too impatient, she shrieks, "I sacrifice you, Satanas! Beast. Lucifer. Baphomet. Come take this warlock, Satan from hell, and drag him to your pits! Bring him down to the depths he so covets! *Sacrificium consecratum!*"

Enora runs the blade across his neck. Reardon falls lifeless, still held by the rope like a puppet, hanging a foot from the ground. Cordelia releases me, but it's too late.

Everyone's quiet. Stunned. The only sound is from Beatrix as she gets up and unties the ropes from the totem, releasing his body. Reardon's limp body slams onto the ground.

Enora laughs, walking in circles, twirling her bloody dagger. She seems drunk with her kill, as if she really did take mandrake.

I charge Enora again, but Bryce snatches my arm, trying to protect me.

"How could you do that?" I shout.

"We trusted you," Bryce yells.

Enora looks at Bryce and me and then stares, with her pearly-white eyes, at his hand holding my arm. She loses her smile.

"Traitor," she says. "Of course, you would complain and take his side. You betrayed me too, Bryce. So, you see, this season shall not only turn with Bill Reardon's death. No. You wanted to know my plan? You. *You* are my plan. You and that devil who now lies dead. Any High Wizard of your coven needs to be cleansed. And as you, Bryce Wallace, are now the Hawthorne coven's High Wizard again, in order to cleanse all the coven's past sins, I will sacrifice you too."

"Stay away from him!" I warn.

Enora laughs. "You have no magic, Katie. You let me burn your book. That's like inviting a vampire through your front door. You let me in, and I stripped you of your powers. All of you shall witness my sacrifice. But then I will let your broken circle go home in peace."

She takes off her left glove and pushes her palm right up to Bryce's nose. I see a red pentagram painted on her hand, like that girl in the Billington House on Halloween.

"Sleep," she says to Bryce. "*Prohibe.*"

Bryce falls to the ground like a stone.

"What are you doing!" I cry.

Then she lifts her left palm before me too. "*Prohibe*," she says, almost in a whisper.

I fall. I feel numb. So weak. I have no control over my arms or legs. I can only move my eyes. I see Enora face Mira and Maddie, who are beside me. "*Prohibe*." She repeats the incantation to every witch of my coven. We all fall frozen before her.

Enora looks at her two witches over Reardon's dead body and snaps, "Manthis! Adder! Leave him. It is time. Take little Katie's concubine and strap him to the pentagram. We might not have been able to burn Reardon in sacrifice, but we can burn Bryce."

I can't say anything because my lips won't move. I'm trying. I'm desperately moving my face, but I can't say a thing.

I'm facing the fire. I'm lying on my side, totally helpless. I watch Beatrix and Cordelia drag Bryce's limp body over to the pentagram. Enora looks at me and walks over. Then she kneels in front of me with those creepy white eyes.

"As they prepare, I shall explain, Katie," Enora says. "This is a blood sacrifice, High Priestess..." Her goons have stripped Bryce, who is still paralyzed, and they turn his naked body upside down on the wooden planks, laying him on the pentagram. "A witch's magic derives from emotion. You saw that when you cast your famous bonfire spell. But unlike me, you failed to kill the devil. It was anger that fed your power. Rage. What I do tonight comes from blood. Human blood. That provides just as much punch as mandrake. In fact, more. That, mixed with my burning your book, makes you too weak to object. What amazes me"—she turns and points to Mira, who is lying frozen and immobile—"is that Raven didn't warn you. She should have known.

"What I suggest is you just lie back and relax. Just watch. It will only take me a moment to burn your sinful boyfriend alive. And when I'm done, you can gather his ashes in an urn, along with your book, and go home and study. See? I never really wanted him back. I just messed with you two to hurt him. Understand? I didn't mean to hurt you. I just wanted him to feel pain. Like the pain he made me feel... Why I'm your friend Amica, right?" Then she roars with laughter, twirling the dagger in her hand, thinking she's being so funny. "Right, *Windstorm*?"

I'm panicking, doing everything I can to say an incantation. To say anything. To do something! But she's right. Normally, with so much rage and anxiety, I could send a whole tempest down onto the bluff. But I can't cast a thing. I can't even move.

That's when I see black boots and a witch's cloak pass by my immobile head. I see Beatrix, Cordelia, and Panthera hanging over Bryce, so I figure it can't be one of them. Maybe it's one of my witch friends? But then I see that this witch is transparent. I can see Bryce and the fire through her cloak. No. This is not a witch, it's my ghost. And for the first time, the ghost turns her face toward me. I'd recognize those bright jade eyes anywhere. Alondra.

The ghost stops over Bill Reardon's dead body. Neither Panthera nor her henchwomen even notice her. Panthera—that bitch—is running her bloody curved blade along Bryce's naked chest. I'm screaming inside.

"*Sacrificium consecratum.*" Enora kneels beside Bryce's face and nods. She runs her hand along his cheek. "I loved you once. I think it was that night when you used me in the ceremony that you destroyed my love. And now you can feel the way I felt that night." Enora watches her witches struggling to tie his wrist on the other side. "Hurry up!" Enora snaps. "Then bring me the torches. Let's light this up so his fucking girlfriend can go study."

I'm screaming in my brain, but I can't say a word. Can the ghost hear me? And can Alondra's ghost even help me?

Alondra kneels before her husband, still staring at his dead body. Enora turns back to me with her stupid grimace, probably to gloat more, and finally notices my ghost. She looks at Alondra and quickly looks back at me. She steps back and trips on a stone. Her witches, still having difficulty tying the ropes, are oblivious, but when Beatrix follows her master's gaze, she screams in fright.

"Why do you disturb my rest, Panthera?" Alondra's ghost asks. Her voice is so calm.

Enora can't say a word. Her face pales, and her eyes change from white to blue. She starts shaking.

"I approached you in friendship, pupil," Alondra's ghost says. "We finally made our peace. Why do this to my husband? Why are you doing this to his disciple?"

"You're not real." Enora looks at me and points. "You're from her."

Alondra turns to me once more. It is eerie how real her facial features appear. She smiles. "And you torment my students. This is how you repay our friendship? Release them from your spell."

"This said by a ghost?" Enora laughs nervously.

Alondra loses her smile. "*Resurrectio*," she says, facing me and twirling the fingers of one hand. She utters the spell as if it's a bother for her.

I'm free. I can move. I don't know what's more shocking—the fact that Alondra's ghost just helped me or that her ghost can cast a spell. Like I care at the moment.

I sprint to Bryce, shoving the witches away from him. They're still in too much shock at seeing Alondra to resist me. Bryce is still paralyzed, but I see him follow me with his eyes.

"Why did you kill my husband?" Alondra asks.

It's taking me forever to untie the ropes. It drives me crazy.

"And now you attack my coven?"

Enora shouts at Beatrix and Cordelia. "Why are you letting

her untie him! She's tricking you! This ghost is her magic. It isn't real!"

But they can't stop staring. Alondra walks right up to Enora, who slashes her with her curved dagger. The knife passes through Alondra. Then Alondra grabs Enora's wrist and violently shakes the dagger from her hand. Enora stares wide-eyed at her wrist, in Alondra's grip. "Impossible!" Enora says.

"You summoned me," Alondra says, shaking her head. "Your blood sacrifice ends now."

"I didn't summon you."

"You burned my book."

And with that, Alondra throws Enora to the ground. Then Alondra crouches down, once again grabbing Enora's wrist, and drags her across the grass. The whole time Enora's hollering in surprise and terror, twisting and turning, trying to break free. Beatrix and Cordelia run to help their master.

My coven starts getting up. They appear drugged. I loosen the last rope on Bryce's wrist and throw my arms around him.

"Oh, Bryce."

"I'm...okay...Katie."

Enora isn't. She's screaming.

Mira and Maddie rush over to help us. Then Mira grabs my shoulder and turns me toward Enora.

Alondra's spirit is dragging Enora to a boulder at the highest point on the bluff. It's that same boulder where I once stood petting a wild deer while talking to my dad. The steepest, most treacherous drop from Hilltop Bluff.

"She's going to throw me off the cliff!" shrieks Enora. "God, Cadence, send her away! I freed you. You owe me!"

"Let her go, Alondra." I approach. I can't believe I'm addressing a ghost.

"Revenge for revenge, Cadence," Enora cries. "Life for a life. Save me. Save me and I won't hurt Bryce. I promise. Just rid me of this vision, sister. Stop it, Cadence. Stop it before she throws me over!"

"Leave her, Alondra," I repeat.

"No." Alondra shakes her head.

I can't believe this. Whereas before I was yelling at Enora to release Reardon, now I'm yelling at Alondra to let go of Enora. I'm trying to protect the people I hate. Why? But I don't want Enora to fall and die. I walk past Reardon's dead body. I didn't want him to die either.

This is so like Alondra. She saved Bryce, but now she's going to kill Enora? I loved Alondra when she was alive. She would do anything for me. But that included evil. And she was evil, because she let her husband and the coven do all those terrible things to my boyfriend and my best friend. Things I could never forgive. I love and hate her so much!

When I realize Alondra won't listen to me, I follow them onto the boulder. Her two witches, Beatrix and Cordelia, are reaching out, but they don't follow me. They're too afraid of the height. This rock overlooks a hundred-foot drop, and there's nothing to hold on to on either side. When I petted my deer, I was never crazy enough to venture this far. My knees are shaking as I crouch down and approach the two of them at the edge. I'm less than a foot away from death on all three sides.

"I ..." I sputter beside them. "I demand that you let her go, Alondra!"

"She burned your book, killed my husband, and tried to kill Bryce," the ghost says, holding Enora over the ledge. It's so eerie how calm Alondra is as Enora fights desperately to break out of her grasp. "Why don't you want her to fall?"

"Why would I want you to kill her? I want your protection, not another murder. You're as bad as she is."

Alondra turns from me and moves Enora closer to the ledge.

"You said you gave me Abigail's magic once!" I cry desperately. "By both her and Escoba's power, I demand that you leave her alone. I command you as the High Priestess of the Hawthorne coven."

"Then where's my book, Cadence?"

I can't believe this.

All the witches are now near the edge of the bluff. I'm closest. Alondra is standing upright now, holding Enora effortlessly with one hand. All it would take is just a small push to throw her off the cliff. I creep closer to Enora on my knees and grab her leg. I can see pitch darkness on three sides of me. I'm so close to the edge that I feel I'm balancing on one side. I even wonder if the weight of Enora and me alone could cause the rock to break and send us hurdling down the bluff. My friends are yelling for me to come back.

"Take my hand." I reach for Enora. "Come on."

Enora kneels down and reaches.

Alondra squints down at me. Then she yanks Enora's body upright, holding her right over the drop. I think Enora's too terrified to say anything.

"Why don't you want this, Cadence?" Alondra asks.

"I am Windstorm!" I say. Lightning strikes with a roar of thunder. I feel magic returning to me. The lightning and thunder are from me. A gust forms, blowing my hair to one side and swaying the trees far below. This is *my* gust. "Go away! Leave her alone!"

But Alondra turns her back once more, looking ready to drop Enora.

"I don't forgive you!" I yell at Alondra's ghost. "Okay? This is why. You're as evil as she is. You want her to die? God, I will never forgive you, Alondra! Just go away! I will never forgive you for what you did!"

Alondra stares back at me for a moment. Her face is so vivid with her bright green eyes. She's here. Somehow. And she actually looks hurt. She shakes her head, but then she nods. She finally starts to fade. As she disappears, she says, "All right, Cadence. Forgive *her*, then."

Nothing is left to hold Enora. She teeters on the edge, but I'm close enough to fall to my knees, scoop up her waist and legs, and pull her to safety just in time. Then I feel my friends grabbing for my feet and ankles. I'm holding on to Enora with as much strength as I can as my witches pull us from behind. We make it to the center of the boulder. Then, slowly, we're dragged further from the ledge.

Enora stares down into the abyss on both sides of us when we're finally safe. The wind stops blowing. It becomes very quiet.

"Get out!" I shout at her. She jumps. "Leave! Take your witches and go. You killed him. How could you do that? You're a murderer!"

Cordelia and Beatrix help Enora up. It is so nauseating how the two witches' lips and cheeks are stained with blood. Enora turns to me. She stares as if trying to think of words to say. It reminds me of when she watched me during the eclipse. It's like I'm such a mystery to her. But this time, it's not only confusion that I see in her bright blue eyes; it's fear.

"Get out!" I repeat. "Stay away from us."

Bryce and Maddie help me up. Then all my witches stand behind me. They have that determined look again, as if it's a standoff between our two covens.

Most of Enora's power is gone. She's no longer drunk on a trance. She's seems almost somber.

She finally flashes an infernal smile at me. She just mutters, "*Et nos unum sumus, amica.*"

Then she turns and walks with her witches to the bonfire and collects three torches.

"What about him?" Cordelia says to Enora, pointing down at Reardon's dead body.

Enora dips her fiery torch onto his body and waves her

other arm in the air. "*Lux.*" Her words stoke the fire, and his body bursts into flames. Then she turns to the pentagram, throws her torch on it, and says yet again, "*Lux.*" Now there are three bonfires burning in the night.

"Never come anywhere near Hawthorne again," I repeat.

She nods with her back turned to me. Then the three of them make their way down the grassy hill as if nothing happened. We watch them, not wanting to drop our guard, as their torches move down the hillside and onto the trails in the wilderness below.

When I finally lose sight of them, I turn to Bryce. He takes me in his arms. All my friends hug me together. Some of them cry. Others just stand holding one another. We're in shock. No one can believe what just happened.

When things are calmer, quieter, Maddie touches my shoulder and points to the conflagration. The flames surrounding the pentagram and Reardon's body are brighter than the bonfire. Apparently, the wicked witch still had a little bit of magic left in her after all.

"What about Enora, Katie? Should we report her to campus security?"

It seems like such a weird suggestion. A very normal weird suggestion. But even if we do, what the hell are we going to tell them? I nod anyway.

"And of Reardon? Should we call the cops?"

"It's too late for that, Maddie," I say with disgust. "Much too late."

26

CANDLES

Maddie and Mira are standing in the foyer of Alondra's house wearing long black dresses and black goth makeup. Bryce and I just walked through the front door and saw them next to Uncle Hanley near the stairway. My friends look like witches. Bryce and I don't. I'm wearing a sweater and jeans. It's fairly warm outside today, even though it's December. And anyway, witch clothes are the last thing I want to wear at the moment. Of course Uncle Hanley has on his suspenders, a white cap, and his huge smile.

"Hey, guys!" says Maddie. "Wait till you hear what Uncle Hanley's got to say."

"You guys can come here anytime you want," Uncle Hanley says with a nod. Then he tips his cap to me. "Especially a Hawthorne. And if you'll agree to care for the place, why, it's yours. See, I've got the farm, but I don't want to sell this place. It's been in the family for generations. And, well, Madison told me you guys love to hold parties in the back. So why not? If you guys agree to care for the house, you can come here to stay. I think Alondra would have wanted it that way. I'll give you the keys."

"Seriously?" asks Bryce.

"Yeah."

"How do you like that, Katie?" Maddie asks with a wink.

"Thanks, Mr. Hanley," I say.

He surprises me by hugging me. "Call me Uncle Hanley, Cadence. And don't mention it. I know how much Alondra liked you."

"We were planning on throwing a barbeque out back next Friday, Uncle Hanley," says Mira with a sly grin.

"Suit yourself. Just tidy up when you're done. I saw you out in the garden in the morning, a couple weeks ago. If you guys keep working the garden like that, I'd be eternally grateful." And he walks to the door.

"You're leaving already?" I ask.

"Yep. Got to go back home and arrange the rest of the estate." He looks down in thought for a moment, holding the door. "You know, it's a common thing for a husband or wife to die right after their loved one, but I didn't expect this from Bill. He was so healthy. It's so damn peculiar, him being struck on that hill. I mean what're the chances? Lightning? The authorities said the energy to do what happened to his body had to come from a bolt of lightning, and there was some lightning that evening. But come to think of it, there was a fire that night, like the fires he and Alondra used to light in the backyard. A bonfire right next to his body. I don't know. I'm thinking the damn fool probably was doing some unorthodox shit by the fire again, excuse my language."

We look at each other, but no one says a thing.

I don't think Uncle Hanley cares what really happened, but he's such a sweet man that he removes his cap for a moment, out of respect for Bill Reardon, and shakes his head with a sigh.

"Well, goodbye," he says.

Mira and Maddie walk beside him to the door. I'm surprised because the plan was for the two of them to join us.

"You guys leaving too?" I ask.

"We'll leave you lovebirds alone," says Maddie chuckling. "Anyway, I've got a final tomorrow and we have to study."

She had to say *that*. I bite my lip.

Finals. *Shit.* Bryce reads my mind. He squeezes my hand more tightly and nods as if to say, *It's all right*, but it's not all right. I'm certainly going to fail this semester again like last year. Bryce said it's okay because I was "sick." He said I can make up for it and that, as he's my TA and "close friend," he can vouch for me. Still, he can't very well tell the provost I was a snake. Daddy's going to kill me.

Before I can explain my anxiety, my two friends are out the door.

"Come on," Bryce says, tugging my hand.

We walk down the hall to the guest room. It's a familiar room that I used to sleep in from time to time last year. It's a simple room with a mahogany dresser, a white canopy over a large single bed, a draped window, and a small nightstand.

I pick up two candles from their candleholders on the dresser. They're yellow memorial candles. One is from last year, for my mom. I left it here. The other is for Alondra. Mira left it here. Now Bryce is holding both of them.

I pick up the lighter on the dresser. Then I light the candles. I gaze into his eyes. The flickering light is reflecting in his to-die-for baby blues. "So, what are you going to say, Bryce?"

"Do you really think she was evil, Cadence?" Bryce asks. The question surprises me.

"Who? Enora?"

"No," he says, shaking his head. "Alondra."

He looks like the question is of such great importance. But knowing him as well as I do, I kind of think he's referring to himself.

"Oh, Bryce." I run my hand over his short hair. "I don't think anyone is pure evil. Alondra said that herself. I think there's evil in all of us. But we should be judged by our love. Who we love. What we love. And not just in the past, but in our future, you know... Don't you think? Right?"

"I love you, Cadence."

I touch my lips to his and then, after we've kissed for a few seconds, I say, "I love you more, lover. Now... what are you gonna say?"

"You go first," he says and hands me a candle. "Talk to your mom."

"Okay." I take a deep breath and close my eyes. "But you know I hate this stuff." I really do. I'm so bad at it. It's like how I can never think of the right thing to say on a card. I can write a whole essay, but I can never think of a few words. But I try.

"Mom, I love you so much and miss you more than you can imagine. I miss...your smile. Your voice. I miss going to see you and Dad and seeing you stand by the window, just watching me until you can't see my car anymore. I miss talking to you about all my troubles. And how, well, everything about me was so important to you. I...miss you... And, well, so much more.

"I'm with Bryce now, Mom. I wish you could see him. He's such a wonderful man, and I'm so lucky to have fallen in love with him... We both hope that wherever you are, you're happy and at peace."

Simple, right?

"Your turn," I say, opening my eyes with a thin smile.

He leans down and kisses me on the lips again. I guess it's romantic with just the candlelight. But I push him away. "Cut it out," I say with a laugh. "Just say something."

"Couldn't resist," he says with a shrug. He clears his throat and closes his eyes with a smile still on his face. But his smile fades. "Alondra, I...I can't believe you're gone. You know, Katie here always says you were like a mother to her, but you were my mother, Gilda's mother, Mira's mother, Maddie's, everyone's mother in the circle. The whole group was under your bright white light. You were so wise. The coven hopes you are in peace now. That you have crossed into the Summerland. We love you and will miss you so very much. Goodbye, Falconsong."

A tear falls from his eye and he brushes it back. I nod as he hands me the two lit candles, and I put them in their candle-holders on the dresser.

"Thanks, Katie," he says.

"Oh, Bryce, I should have let you say all that at Alondra's ceremony," I say, feeling really guilty. "That was so stupid and selfish. It was so wrong."

"I wasn't thanking you for that. I meant, thanks for mentioning me to your mom."

And that is soooo sweet. I turn and look deeply into his eyes again. We touch hands. Our fingers entwine.

"I love you, Bryce. But I'm done with the past. Let's just move on. Together. Okay? You know, have a 'normal' rest of the year."

He grasps me in his arms and we kiss. "Let's go home, baby," Bryce says, running his hand through my long hair.

I nod.

Before we walk to the door, I turn once more to snuff out the candles. I wave my hand because I can't resist just a little magic but, before I do, I gasp. Bryce pulls back and lets go of my hand.

"What is it?" he asks.

Sitting on the nightstand by the bed is my book *Broomstick*. I point at it.

"Spooky," he says, but he's not trying to be funny. His eyes are wide open.

"I hate her, Bryce. She's such a witch."

I wave my hand and will both candles to blow out.

THE END

EXCERPT FROM BOOK III

THE FOLLOWING EXCERPT IS FROM "CHAPTER 1 - ADDER" IN THE HAWTHORNE WITCH, BOOK 3 OF THE HAWTHORNE UNIVERSITY WITCH SERIES BY A.L. HAWKE

I'm worried. One reason is real dumb. I've prepared for this service all week, and even though these are my closest friends, I hate talking in front of people. I should never have become their leader. But there's a far greater reason for my troubles. A witch showed up at my doorstep last night and ruined what was supposed to be a romantic evening with my boyfriend, Bryce. As all my friends hug each other, with their hoods back, revealing smiling faces by flickering firelight, they're oblivious to my uninvited guest, hiding somewhere behind me in Alondra's dark nineteenth-century home.

Outside, I enjoy the smell of the burning embers of our bonfire as everyone sits in the circle of white plastic chairs. The crescent moon and stars shine brightly in the center of Alondra's backyard and I still can't get over how lovely the night sky is away from the city. The stars are so vivid and bright. You can even make out the river of light across the Milky Way.

After everyone sits, all smiles, we hold hands. My best friend, Maddie, sits on my left and the love of my life, Bryce, is on my right. I clear my throat and prepare to recite the words I rehearsed.

"Yatu," I say.

"Yatu," they all repeat with a nod. Yatu means "hello."

"We celebrate Lammas. Lammas recognizes hard times ahead. It is a turn of the season, like all holidays on the wheel. This afternoon was hot. Soon it will turn cold. Lammas is the first harvest. Mabon comes next, and finally, my favorite, Samhain." I face two new recruits across from me and smile. "Samhain is Halloween."

The newbies look nervous and out of place. I mean, they're the only ones not wearing black cloaks and thick witchy makeup.

I pause and gather my thoughts. It's quiet. The crickets chirp more loudly. The fire crackles.

"Lammas is a special harvest, as it represents the time when Apollo radiates his energy down upon Gaia, growing our first grain. As such, we celebrate the reaping by partaking in bread. And as we share the grain, we consume the Earth. Gaia is a part of you. You consume the Earth, and as you pass into the Summerland, you shed her. So as you partake, I ask that you reflect, deep inside, about your place among Earth and..." I raise my arms and feel the sleeves of my black cloak slide below my wrists. "The moon and the stars. One soul. Atman. Blessed be my coven under the gods Gaia, Selene, and Astraeus."

"Atman," says Bryce, nodding and closing his eyes with a smile.

"Atman," says everyone else.

"Blackbird, please hand me the bread."

Blackbird is the mystic name for my best friend, Maddie. Maddie jumps up and walks over to a white linen cloth behind us on the grass, where there's a chalice and a loaf of bread. She seems so happy. Everyone is. We're all loving the festival and seeing each other again.

"It's buttermilk bread, Katie," Frida explains in her beautiful Brazilian accent, reaching over and touching my hand. She's next to Bryce. I can't wait to taste it; she always bakes the most amazing stuff. "And I brought pomegranate wine."

Maddie hands me the loaf. I tear off a piece and lay it on my lap. It smells fresh and sweet. I hand the loaf to Bryce, on my right. Bryce nods to me, breaks off a piece, and passes the rest to the witch beside him.

"Happy Lammas," I say with a big smile.

They all burst forth with "Happy Lammas!"

Then my friends jump up, saying the words over and over in greetings to one another. Hope hugs Mandy, and Helen leans down and kisses Maddie on the cheek. Tammy leans over and lays a white flower wreath around my neck. As I'm still technically officiating, I'm seated in the middle. I sit quietly, readjusting the sleeves of my cloak, just enjoying the warm, clear starry night in the company of my best friends.

"May you never thirst," Maddie says on my left.

May you never thirst.

Usually those words make me happy, but tonight I'm a little sad. I first heard the saying from my friend and mentor, Alondra, the owner of this house, who passed away last year. These words have many meanings, but to me, the most personal is love. A wish that the togetherness between me and my twelve closest friends, who are in this circle, will never dry up. That's sweet...but bitter. See, this is my last year at Hawthorne University, and my friends are leaving. Every event, starting with this one, takes me closer to the end.

"May you never thirst," I echo, feeling the bitterness. I try to hide my thoughts.

Hope, the only one still standing, walks behind me and grabs a fancy-looking gold chalice from the white lace cloth behind me. (Shh, don't tell anybody, but the cup's a brass trinket I bought with Maddie in Atlanta.) Hope hands it to me, and I hold the cup with both hands, drinking some of the tart pomegranate wine.

"Umm. This is really good, Frida."

"Thanks, Katie." We laugh.

I wait for Bryce to pass the cup to all the other witches in the circle. When everyone has sipped, I nod to Maddie.

"Thanks, Windstorm," Maddie says. "Hey, guys, have a nice summer? I want everybody to meet our two new recruits, Josie and Debra. They're considering joining us. Can you believe it? Crazy, right? Try not to scare them. They're terrified."

"We're not!" cries Josie.

"Yatu, Josie," says Bryce. "Debra."

"Yeah," Maddie continues with a chuckle. "Josie likes hiking. Not your enjoying-the-fresh-air type of hiking but mountain climbing. Like risking her life hiking in the mountains at Zion State Park. She's also a physics major, and that marks the first witch we've ever had in our coven that's a scientist. What is the world coming to, right, Katie?" I just nod. "And—my best of friends—Debra is a local girl, living close to Flintwood. I knew Debra in high school, guys. She's quiet but has more of a love for magic than anyone I know—except maybe Mira. In fact, she was practicing witchcraft even before I joined. She's also real scared."

"Yatu, Debra," says Tammy, who is sitting close to them. Tammy's a super-sweet bald black girl. "Relax, girls. The only one to be afraid of is Cadence over there."

"Stop," I say.

We laugh some more. It's fun. This is the part I love about our coven, just turning to friends and talking, you know.

"Thank you, Madison," I say. "Welcome, girls. This is just an introduction. If you're still interested, let us know and we can initiate you."

"Thank you, Windstorm," says Josie. Then Debra nods.

"Thank you for introducing them to the group, Madison."

"Don't mention it, Cadence Hawthorne." There's more laughter.

"Let us eat," I say. "And as we eat, be thankful for the food that the gods have gifted us."

And that's it for the ceremony, thank God. Like I said, I don't like talking in front of people. Alondra made me their leader last year, but I never asked to be.

"Are we going to make puppets tonight, Cadence?" asks Frida innocently.

"I've gathered the cornhusks in the kitchen," replies Maddie. "The newbies have already made some. If you guys want, later tonight we can do it with popcorn."

"And I brought beer," says my boyfriend.

"Hey, Bryce, how was last night at the house all alone with Cadence?" Tammy asks. But we weren't alone, and Bryce loses his smile.

"It was fun," he says after swallowing some bread. "We just got back from Atlanta, where Katie introduced me to her dad and brother."

"Oooh," says Tammy with a big smile. "Getting serious, guys."

"They're as amazing as she is," says Bryce, hugging me.

"Ah," I say, leaning into his arms.

Everyone's happy. But, you know, the minute I talk about the visitor, things will sour.

I glance back at Alondra's house. I left her in the bedroom upstairs, where a floor-to-ceiling window looks out into the backyard. But it's dark inside. Well, I don't want to do what I did last year. Last year I opened my mouth at our reunion gathering, and it was a total downer. But Bryce keeps looking at me. I'm guessing he expects me to say something. As Tammy talks about a date she had with a pilot in Savannah, Bryce grabs me by the arm and leans close to my ear. "You want me to tell them?" I shake my head. I think Maddie overhears, but she's busy stuffing her face with bread.

We go around the circle, and everyone talks about their summer, enjoying the freshly baked bread.

"Did you guys hear about Greg and me?" Frida asks, showing off a big diamond on her finger.

"Congratulations," I say. "I'm so happy for you. Maddie said he's cute."

"Duh," Maddie says. "Look at Frida."

"He asked me in Hawaii, Katie," Frida explains. "I'd just been having fun in the sand, and I was lying on a towel when I felt a hand on my belly. I tipped my shades and my Greg was on his knee." She laughs again. "He's so romantic. I said I dreamt once that I'd be asked for my hand in marriage on the beach. Greg had planned the whole Hawaii thing just for that moment, I think. He's wonderful."

"Cute," shy Helen says. Frida nods.

"Greg is really cute," Maddie says with a nod. "Wait till you guys meet him. But then why wouldn't such a swell guy be hanging with Frida?"

"I can't wait to introduce you," Frida says.

We talk about clothes. Then shopping. It's times like these that I feel like Bryce is left out. He's the only boy in our group. But that's tradition. One male High Wizard and twelve witches always make up a coven.

"I went with Don to Europe, guys," Tammy says. She's just as boisterous as Maddie. "England. The traditional home of witches, you know. Mother Shifton's Cave in Yorkshire and the Petrifying Well. It was cool. You know, maybe it was Mother Shifton's famous ugliness that made everybody think that we witches are ugly." We laugh and she tells us about all these petrified teddy bears and hats.

I feel more at ease. As my friends keep yapping, I glance over at the tall, thin trees in the shadows of Alondra's yard.

The trees surround Alondra's backyard field. I love the woods.

I've wandered alone there many times. It's so peaceful. If you venture down the hill from here, along some dirt paths, you'll be at my college. Hawthorne University is surrounded by trees too. And looking over the trees, if you gaze far enough, you can see the nearby mountains. But everything else is shadowed by the woods.

I have an urge to leave and wander right now. Besides the sound of crackling wood and my friends' laughter, there's a calmness in the air. The crickets are still chirping. Air brushes gently against my cheek. A squirrel darts up a tree trunk, running away from a deer whose hooves are crunching leaves. The deer looks right at me, but I know she can't see me. The deer is standing near a ditch, in a clearing in the forest, about a fifteen-minute walk from the backyard. I know because I've walked along the path many times before.

Then I feel something in my chest. Magic. I feel myself slipping into a trance, and that puts me on edge. It's bad because usually when I've slipped into a trance unknowingly, it's been for protection, with a spell.

Someone shrieks. Tammy stops midsentence with her mouth wide open. There's another gasp. Then another. Everyone is looking at the house behind me. I turn.

Beatrix—you know, the unwanted guest I still haven't told anyone about—walks slowly from the back porch to our bonfire. She's wearing the same brown leather jacket, jeans, and shirt she wore last night, with her long blond hair flowing around her pale face. But her makeup isn't running down her face from crying like it was last night. She's an uneasy young girl, only seventeen. And she's close enough for my friends to recognize her. How could they forget her? Last year she helped murder a professor and tried to hurt Bryce.

Maybe I should have told them?

Everyone except Bryce and the two new recruits jumps from their chair. The newbies have no idea who she is. My friends do. They remember her licking and sucking the blood off our murdered professor's arms last year.

"Yatu," Beatrix says with a shy wave.

No one's "Yatu-ing" anyone.

Bryce gets up and tries to shush everyone, but they're in a panic. I remain seated, but I turn my chair toward her and the house. I wait for everyone to calm the hell down. When they're quiet enough—

"Guys, I invited her," I say. "And if you all knew what she's going through, you would too."

That makes them go nuts again.

"Everyone, quiet!" shouts Bryce. "Let Katie explain."

"I didn't come for your service," Beatrix says to them. Then she looks down at me. "I'm here to warn you. Adder is coming. She'll be here any minute. She's coming for me, so...I have to go." But she pauses, looking very unsure about it. "I don't want any trouble for you. Thanks for everything, Cadence. All of you are so lucky to have Windstorm as your High Priestess. Remember what I told you about Raven. Adder's not only coming for me, she's coming for you. All of you. Don't trust her. She only wishes bad things for you."

"Go back to the house, Beatrix." I finally rise from my chair. "I won't let her touch you."

"You can't do that," Bryce says to me. "You need to let her go."

I stare at my boyfriend, dumbfounded. You have to understand that this is Bryce. Nice Bryce, the nicest guy in the world.

"She told us Enora has it in for us, Bryce," I say. "We're in danger whatever we do. Why wouldn't you want to protect her? Enora will kill her if I let her go."

"What's going on?" asks Josie.

"They're forbidden to come anywhere near us," Mandy

says to the new recruit, pointing with hatred at Beatrix. "Everyone from the Abaddon coven has no right to step foot in Hawthorne. That was your own order last Christmas, Katie."

"Her life is threatened."

"So?" Mandy replies. "Ours is too if you let her in the circle."

The recruits look scared again, but now they have good reason to be. For them, this was just another visitor to our holiday festival. An excuse to meet new friends to help them make corn dollies.

"Maddie, please take Josie and Debra into the house," I say. Maddie nods and quickly corrals the two girls in her arms and rushes them back to the house.

I turn to Mandy, a witch with long blond hair who's in a perpetually bad mood. Well, she doesn't like me, anyway—especially as the coven's leader. She and Natasha have never accepted me. "I'm not letting her in our circle," I say.

"You're involving us if you let her stay," Mandy replies. "Weren't you here when Reardon was killed? Or what about Bryce? Weren't you there when she tied up your boyfriend? Tried to burn him alive?"

"Of course I was!"

The two recruits look back as they walk to the house. They heard that.

And now Beatrix is walking away. It looks like she's heading into the woods.

"Wait, Beatrix."

"Let her go!" Mandy snaps.

"If you heard what Enora asked her to do, you'd protect her too."

"What? What's so bad that you're willing to risk our lives for her?"

Beatrix stops. She begged me not to tell anyone. She made

me swear. She turns and looks right into my eyes, reminding me.

"She was asked to have ceremonial sex with a stranger."

"So? They're a black witch cult."

"That's not all."

"No, Cadence!" Beatrix runs back, shaking her head desperately. "No!"

"She was to have sex until bearing a child," I continue. "Then in six months, the fetus was to be removed through ceremonial abortion and—"

"Cadence! You swore!" Beatrix violently shakes her head.

"They planned to drink her baby's blood."

"*I told you not to tell them!*" Beatrix is right up in my face, practically spitting on me. "*I told you!* How could you tell them? How could you do that!"

Everyone turns quiet. Some sit back down in the white chairs and stare at the fire.

"Why'd you tell them!" Beatrix shouts again in my face. "Why? You swore, Cadence! How could you do that!"

"They have to know why I'm protecting you."

"I don't need your protection!"

I laugh. Yeah, I actually laugh in the poor girl's face because, honestly, right now I hate her. I spent all night talking her down from killing herself when she threatened to slice her wrists in front of Bryce and me. I've lost all patience, and now she's destroyed our holiday. She's exhausting me. I don't want to protect her. I wish she had never come here.

"She's not a part of our circle," I explain to my friends, "but that doesn't mean she doesn't have a right to stay at Alondra's house. Alondra would have wanted us to help her."

"Keeping her here is the same thing," Mandy says quietly, shaking her head. But she doesn't seem to be in the mood to fight with me anymore. She doesn't say another word.

Beatrix turns to the house hesitantly, looking like she's going to leave again. It's too late. She screams instead.

Another witch, carrying a torch, is slowly walking toward us from the side of the house. Her cloak is similar to ours, but it's scarlet. Under the fire, I recognize a face completely covered in black tattoos. Cordelia. Her mystic name is Adder. Last year, Cordelia and Beatrix were Enora's henchwomen—her favorite witches. Yeah, Cordelia tried to kill my boyfriend too.

TO BE CONTINUED IN BOOK III OF THE HAWTHORNE UNIVERSITY WITCH SERIES

ALSO BY A.L. HAWKE

PARANORMAL ROMANCE

- THE HAWTHORNE UNIVERSITY WITCH SERIES I-III
- THE HAWTHORNE UNIVERSITY WITCH SERIES 4-6
- THE HAWTHORNE UNIVERSITY WITCH HOLIDAY COLLECTION
- SHADES
- PHANTOM MASQUERADE
- HAUNTING JOY

- MY EVIL EYE
- THE GUARDIAN
- NECTAR OF AMBROSIA
- CORA

FANTASY: THE AZURE SERIES

- HARMONIA
- CORA: RISE OF THE FALLEN GODDESS
- AZURE BLUE
- CORAL RED
- PRINCESS SOJOURN

SCIENCE FICTION

- CANDY SAVANT SERIES

Books available at https://alhawke.com/books

PARTING WORDS

What did you think of *Windstorm*? By placing a book review, you can inform others of your thoughts and help spread the word about my book.

Want more? Periodically I like to send news regarding current or new projects. If you'd like to be privy, I encourage you to sign up to my email newsletter. Your information will remain private and you can cancel any time.

Sign up at www.alhawke.com or scan the following QR code:

ACKNOWLEDGMENTS

I want to thank my beta readers George B. and Rob C. You two have been providing me invaluable story advice for years and this one was no different. And to my line editor, Stephanie Ward, and proofreader, Eliza Dee. Stephanie Ward did her usual amazing job at fixing inconsistencies and making *Windstorm* a smoother read. Eliza Dee, yet again, went far beyond a proofread adding further suggestions to make this a better novel. Finally, Regina Wamba touched my work with her art brush, once again providing a face to my writing. Thank you all!

ABOUT THE AUTHOR

A.L. Hawke lives in Southern California torching the midnight candle over lovers against a backdrop of machines, nymphs, magic, spice and mayhem. With a medical science background, the author specializes in paranormal romance, urban fantasy, and science fiction.

Visit A.L. Hawke at www.alhawke.com

Email: contact@alhawke.com